DEADLY

SIXTEEN

DUANE WURST

ISBN-0-9883947-3-1
ISBN-978-0-9883947-3-5

Text and cover design by Duane Wurst, Berne Studio
Cover images © Duane Wurst

Printed in the United States of America

ACKNOWLEDGMENTS

When it comes to writing a novel, it is the creative process that I enjoy. Writing is very similar to painting a picture. I love that I can paint hundreds of pictures with words that together tell an entire story. My characters, setting, and plot are painted with words, instead of oils. Still, the novel is my painting

I wish to dedicate this novel to my wife, Sharon. She has been my wife and friend for over thirty years. I know there are times when she would rather I wasn't spending my time at the computer writing, but then she sits at the kitchen table, and reads the next chapter, telling me to get back to work.

I also thank M. Teresa Calkins, a friend and fellow member of my writer's group. Her comments helped me catch grammar errors, and those obvious errors that only an editor would see. Thank you for helping to make this novel better. A special thank you also goes to Kathy Nichols, RN. Kathy checked my E.R. scenes to make sure I wasn't too far from reality.

The Huron Area Writers Group listened and advised me. They have been there when I needed a shoulder to cry on, or the incentive to keep going.

Because this novel covers the 300 year history of Detroit, I had to do research. The library and internet made this process easier, and I was able to transport myself into the streets of the past and present day Detroit. There are many novels and web sites dedicated to history and the preservation of all that we consider a part of our heritage. At the end of this novel I have listed many sources that I studied. It was not my intention to write a detailed history of Detroit. I wanted the history to be a part of my story, not my story. But when dealing with a great city like Detroit, it is important to come as close to reality as possible. If I missed a few dates or names, remember, this novel is fiction.

Thank you and enjoy the adventure.

CHAPTER 1

Tianna was in a deep sleep. The dream she was having would not be remembered. As a young Indian girl, she was sitting with her grandfather, Eluwilussit. He was a wise and holy man, the spiritual leader and medicine man of her Huron Indian tribe. Her grandfather was teaching her the ways of a medicine man.

"Child," Eluwilussit said, "when you reach your sixteenth year, you must be very careful. The spirit leaders told me you have magical powers. Only the spirit leaders can have such powers. You, my granddaughter, will walk with the spirits and be a leader. You will guide others into the spirit world. But you must have a pure heart. You must never let your emotions lead your actions. Your mind, Arianna, must be your guide into the spirit world. Not your heart. Arianna, heed my warning. Never let your emotions and desires overrule your mind."

Arianna said she understood. She held her grandfather's hand, and together they walked with the spirits. The dream lingered and then faded. Tianna stirred and fell back into a deep sleep.

As the clock approached six in the morning, Tianna was only half awake. She knew it was time to wake up and get ready for school, but another dream still played in her mind. She rolled over and fell back to sleep, hoping to finish the dream and see if Eddie, her current fixation, would ask her out or just walk by without noticing her again.

Her dream continued like a YouTube video. As he approached, she felt him looking into her eyes. He smiled that big-toothed smile.

Oh my God, he will stop. Yes, he will ask me to the party.

Eddie stopped in front of her and placed both hands on her shoulder. Leaning close to her, his eyes sparkling with potential adventure and romance, he said, "Get up, Tianna. I have to go to work, and you have to get to school."

Damn, she thought, realizing it was her mother calling. "Do you want breakfast? Or are you still on that diet?"

As Tianna walked out of her upstairs room, toward the small bathroom, she replied, "I'll have toast and peanut butter. And I haven't been dieting for the last month."

"Good, you're skinny enough, honey."

Tianna let the water run over her mocha skin, her mind wandering back to Eddie. He's in her English class, but the most they have said to each other was hello. She knows he is interested in her because Amber, her best friend in the entire world, told her he keeps asking about her. As the water grew cold, she jumped out of the shower and grabbed a large oversized towel. After drying off, she wrapped a smaller towel around her head to help dry her long black hair.

Tianna's morning routine was quick and easy. She didn't like to spend a lot of time using makeup. It helps that she has a perfect complexion, and she inherited the straight black hair from her father's side of the family. He was a mixture of American Indian, French and African-American. Tianna's hair and lighter complexion made her look more Indian than Black. Living on the East Side of Detroit, some students teased her for not being black, but she knows who she is and doesn't let the teasing bother her.

Combing her hair out, she remembered that today is Friday. Tomorrow will be her sixteenth birthday, and she's positive she will get a new iPhone for her birthday. She knows this because of the number of hints she has made to her mom and grandfather. They have to know the new phone is the only gift she wants this year. Her old phone has a cracked screen, is over two years old, and as her friends would say, "Is God awful *gross*."

It only took a few minutes to jump into her blue slacks and white shirt. It was the school uniform, and no matter how she tried, it was impossible to make the work. At least she could wear pants instead of the mid-length skirt. Tianna was not a skirt type of girl. Shorts or jeans is her preferred uniform, but she loved attending King High School, and would wear anything required.

Well, almost anything, she thought.

Running down the stairs, Tianna yelled, "Mom, can I go to Amber's after school? I'll be back by dinnertime."

"Yes. But I won't be home until after six. Could you and your grandfather make dinner tonight? Or do you want me to bring something home?" her mother asked.

"You know the answer to that one, Mom," she said. "Either pizza or Chinese would be great."

Tianna entered the large family kitchen where her mother stood at the counter packing lunch for the two of them. Her grandfather, Clarence Gulliver, a gray-haired elderly man, sat at the table drinking a huge mug of coffee. Tianna walked over to him and kissed the side of his face.

"Good morning, Grandpa," she said.

"Morning, birthday girl. So, when do you turn that magical sixteen?" he asked with a twinkle in his dark black eyes.

"You know when, Grandpa. Tomorrow morning at six o'clock. At least that's the time you always tell me you first laid your eyes on me."

"I remember that day like it was yesterday," he said.

Tianna sat down as her mom, Thelma, placed a dish of buttered toast and orange slices on the table for her. Tianna took a bite of toast and said, "Mom, I hope I didn't cause you too much labor pain sixteen years ago."

"Dear, if that is the only pain you cause me, I will be a blessed woman. Keep doing well in school and get yourself into a good college. That will make all my labor pains vanish."

"Your mom is right," her grandfather said. "An education is important, but then I'm sure you know."

The doorbell rang, and Tianna ran toward the front room.

"It's Amber. We're walking to school together," she said as she opened the door to greet her friend.

Amber was about five feet tall and a little chubby. Her hair was full and frizzy. When she smiled, her entire face beamed.

"You ready to walk?" she asked Tianna.

"Come on in, I have to finish breakfast and get my backpack," Tianna said, leading Amber into the family kitchen.

"Hi, Mrs. Gulliver and Grandpa Gulliver. Are you ready for Tianna's big day?" Amber asked.

"We sure are. Remember, Amber, be here at noon tomorrow for the little party we have planned. It's nothing big, just a few people," said Thelma.

"We invited Usher and Jennifer Hudson, but they were too busy to attend," laughed Grandpa.

"Now I'm disappointed, Grandpa. I told my friends they would be here," Tianna said as she lifted her backpack over her shoulder. "Well, we have to go. It takes a good half hour to get to school."

"I could drop you off," offered Thelma.

"No, Mom. It's not too cold today, and it doesn't look like rain, so we'll enjoy the walk. It's excellent exercise, and you don't have to go out of your way," she said. "Oh, don't forget to pick up my new iPhone today."

"Phone? What phone?" Grandpa said with a boisterous laugh.

* * *

As Tianna and Amber ran down the steps of the old house on Charlevoix Street, Grandpa Gulliver stood at the door and watched as the two teens bounded down the sidewalk. He had a strange feeling that something bad would happen today, but he did not understand why. It felt like the day his son, Joe, died in Iraq. That deep, empty feeling that lives in the pit of your stomach warns evil is coming.

"Thelma, I will say a special prayer today, and I hope you do too," he said.

"Why? Is someone in need of a prayer?"

"I don't know. I have a bad feeling," he said.

Amber and Tianna have been best friends since before kindergarten. Only two houses separate them, and when they were toddlers, they would watch and talk to each other from the backyards of their homes. Tianna's mom noticed their conversations and decided they should meet. She walked with Tianna down the sidewalk and rang the doorbell of the Thornson's brick home. A slender woman opened the door and laughed.

"Lord, you must be the little girl from down the street. My Amber keeps asking me to go get you to come here for a tea party," she said.

Amber and Tianna ran toward each other and hugged and then they then ran into the Thornson's home and played.

"My name is Thelma Gulliver, and that's my daughter, Tianna."

"Come on in, dear. I'm Alice Thornson. My husband, Lester, is at work. He's a police officer, you know."

"Yes, I saw him in a uniform, but I wasn't sure if he was a police officer or a security guard. It makes the community feel safer knowing he's here, though," Thelma said.

"And the older man living in your house, is that your husband?" Alice asked, trying not to appear inquisitive.

"God, no! He's my father-in-law. My husband died thirteen years ago in Iraq. His dad lived alone, and he asked us to share his home. He's such a great person. He retired from Wayne State University, where he was a history professor for thirty years. Smart and kind. An impressive combination in a man."

The two girls and their mothers have been best friends since that day. Now, Tianna and Amber attend King High School, one of Detroit's newer and larger high schools. They plan their class schedules around each other, taking as many together as possible. In a large school like King, it helps to have close friends you can count on.

Their relationship in school is symbiotic. Amber is fun and adventurous compared with Tianna's calm disposition. Tianna, though, is beautiful. Because of her light skin, guys keep trying to hit on her. Amber meets more guys as they keep asking her about Tianna, and she helps Tianna decide which guys are for real, and who is just out for a good time.

Amber laughed as the two teens walked past their former elementary school. The school stands a block from their homes and looks the same today as it did on their first day of kindergarten.

"Remember Ricky Clawson?" Amber asked, glancing at the colorful outdoor play equipment behind the school.

"Yes, he was a sweetheart back then, wasn't he?"

"Sure was, but do you remember how bad he wanted you to be his girlfriend, even though he was ten and you were only seven. Tianna, he wanted you so bad, and the things he did to impress you were hysterical. Like how he would give you stuff he stole from the market down the street. And the silly rap songs he made up, telling you how beautiful you were. Lord, that boy was crazy in love. You said, *Ricky would be OK if he were taller and not an old guy.*"

Tianna thought for a moment and then said, "Ricky was small and older. I thought he was in our grade, and when I heard he was in the sixth grade, I couldn't believe it, because he was shorter than I. But when we got to high school, everything changed. He got taller, smarter, and sexier. I had a crush on him until he graduated from school."

Tianna looked off into the distance and thought. Then she whispered, "I hope he doesn't follow in his dad's footsteps. I heard he's in jail for killing a woman in the 'burbs. He tried to *'jack* her truck for drug money, and she wouldn't let him have it. So, he shot her. A real idiot."

Amber whispered back, "I heard his older brother raped a girl in high school and disappeared to keep from going to jail. They say he's a gang member now, hiding from the law."

Deadly Sixteen

The girls continued down their street to McDougall, and then they turned south, passing abandoned houses and businesses. Amber commented on a few pleasant homes she wouldn't mind living in when she grew up. They agreed there are more empty lots today, overgrown with weeds and trees, than there were the last time they walked to school. Just a few weeks ago.

"Grandpa says this used to be a prosperous part of Detroit a hundred years ago. It's hard to imagine a genuine community ever being here. Today, it resembles a war zone," said Tianna. "But you can tell it was fancy by the looks of the old business buildings and churches. I bet it could have been a nice place to live at one time."

"Too bad they let it go to hell," Amber added.

"Yes, too bad."

The two girls loved walking this route. It took about twenty-five minutes and led them through the Elmwood Cemetery, a beautiful tree lined sidewalk winding along the edge of the graveyard. The route is a peaceful world in an enchanted forest. One needs to be careful of gang members and homeless bums lurking behind the shrubs, and you also have to share the path with the ghosts of those buried in the cemetery!

"We should study the gravestones to see who they buried here. Grandpa says there are former governors, senators and famous Detroit people buried in over eighty-six acres of graves, and I know I've seen a lot of dates from the late seventeen-hundreds," Tianna said.

Tianna listened to her grandfather's stories about Detroit and Michigan history. Ever since she was a little girl, he would set her down and tell tall tales of early life in Detroit. She loved the stories and once considered going to college to become a historian. Unfortunately, there are few opportunities for making money in that field. She would have to become a teacher, and that is one profession she doesn't want.

The girls stopped halfway through the cemetery to rest on a park bench. They listened to the birds, small animals, and the hum of distant cars.

"This is nice," said Tianna. "Oh, Amber, I had a dream about Eddie last night."

"You did? You know that's an omen."

"About what?"

"An omen he will talk to you today about going to the party. I keep telling him to get some balls and talk to you. I think he figures you're too good for him," Amber laughed. "He should know you better."

"That's not nice, Amber."

"Tianna, you need to lighten up. Everything is always so serious with you. After all these years being my friend, you should know when I'm pulling your leg," Amber said, with a note of seriousness.

"Sorry, I'm just feeling a little emotional today. My birthday is tomorrow, and I have the rest of my life facing me. It can be daunting," Tianna said.

"Well, lighten up. You want to enjoy your future, not fear it. Besides, my birthday is next month, and you don't see me getting all uptight."

"True. But I feel like I have been through all of this before. Just like now, sitting here. I almost feel like I remember being here a long time ago."

"You were. Two weeks ago when we walked to school. And a week before that. We come here all the time, Tianna. What do you expect?"

"Not like that. I mean, it feels like years ago. In another life."

Amber stood up and grabbed Tianna's arm. "Let's go; you've been in this cemetery too long. One of those ghosts is trying to take control of your soul. Come on, let's get out of here."

"OK. I'm coming. But I get those feelings. Don't you sometimes feel you've been here before?"

"NO. But even if I did, I wouldn't be telling anyone. They might think I took drugs or something," chided Amber.

DEADLY SIXTEEN
* * *

Tianna and Amber continued along the pond road through the park-like valley. They stopped at an ancient bridge overlooking Bloody Creek.

"Did you know there was a battle between the British and Chief Pontiac here?" asked Tianna.

"Yes. You tell me about it every time we see this bridge," laughed Amber. "It's an interesting story, though." She looked down at the stream and asked, "Wasn't the creek named Bloody because it turned red from the blood of the British and Indians killed here?"

"That's what Grandpa said. Pontiac must have been quite the Indian chief. He won that battle, but ended up losing the war," said Tianna.

"Isn't that the way it goes? You stand up for your rights... win a few battles, but still get shut down. Black, red, brown, or white. Seems like if we come from the wrong side of town, we get screwed."

"Yes. But I plan on making something of this life. I'm proud of who I am, and I will be someone important," insisted Tianna.

"Good! And remember me when you're rich and famous. I might need a job, you know."

"Always. You'll always be a part of my life."

The two girls hugged and continued on toward school. They could hear the sounds of students as they approached King High School. The usual mass of black students crossed Lafayette Street heading toward the school entrance. Amber looked across the lot and saw a group of boys arguing about something.

"Looks like a fight's going down over there," she said to Tianna, pointing at several gang members.

"There's always something going on with those hoods. We better use the main entrance. Don't watch them; it might give them a reason to bother us."

"I won't. Trust me, I don't want to get messed up with any of those guys. Today, or ever."

As the girls turned onto the sidewalk leading to the school doors, Amber heard two loud bangs. She turned toward Tianna, and in slow motion watched as the back of Tianna's head exploded. Blood rushed out as bone fragments and brain matter flew into Amber's face. She screamed and fell to the ground, holding her best friend in her arms.

"Tianna............ Oh my God," Amber screamed. "Someone, please help us!"

At first, everyone tried to duck for cover, but when they saw that the shooting was over, they watched Tianna as she lay bleeding on the cold gray sidewalk. Forming a circle of students, they took out their cell phones and filmed the action. Two senior girls actually laughed and pointed at Amber as she tried to stop Tianna's wound from bleeding out.

Amber screamed at them, "Damn it, call 911! Don't just stand there, help us."

One girl said, "Why? Your friend is as good as dead. Look at her; half of her head is on the sidewalk. She's as dead as my dad, and all the other guys who get shot every day around here."

Through the crowd, an older muscular man pushed the girls aside. It was Mr. Ewald, Amber and Tianna's English teacher.

"Don't worry, Amber. I've called 911; they'll be here soon."

Mr. Ewald spent two years in Iraq as a medic before becoming a teacher, and his training came rushing back. It was as if he were on the streets of Baghdad again, helping soldiers hit by an exploding device along the road.

He rummaged through his and Tianna's backpacks and grabbed a plastic bag, a towel and a T-shirt. He placed the plastic on the head wound and then wrapped the towel around Tianna's head to stem the bleeding.

Two of the school's security guards moved the throng of students back to make room for the ambulance, if it arrives.

Henry, a thin black guard dressed in a dark blue uniform, yelled at the students, "Get back, there's nothing more for you to see here. You students need to get into the school. Now!"

The students moved back, but none of them headed toward the school entrance. Even though most of them had witnessed violence, it fascinated them and they couldn't stop staring at Tianna and Amber.

Kneeling down to help, the security guard said, "Mr. Ewald, is she alive?"

"There's a faint heartbeat, but her breathing is shallow, and she's bleeding from the head wound. Any idea when the ambulance will get here?"

"I'll call," he said. "Charlie, this is Harry, chief security guard at King High School. When the hell is that ambulance getting here? We've got two young girls in trouble here. One probably won't make it."

As he was talking, he heard an ambulance and police cars growing closer.

Amber, in a state of shock, sat on the sidewalk facing Tianna. Harry took her arm and asked her to stand up. When she stood, he realized that someone had also shot her in the arm. It appeared to be a flesh wound, but she was bleeding.

"Oh, my God. Child, your arm is bleeding, too," he said.

Amber looked at her wound and continued to cry. The guard put his arm around her for comfort as he directed the ambulance to the scene.

"You'll be OK," he said. There were tears in his eyes as he looked down at the lifeless body of Tianna. "I'm sure your friend will be fine too," he added, knowing it was a lie.

The ambulance backed up to where Tianna lay on the sidewalk. The driver, Steven, jumped out and opened the back door of the ambulance. Two paramedics, Jason and Carol, jumped out of the back with a gurney. In doing a quick assessment of Tianna's condition, Jason spoke with the Detroit Receiving Hospital trauma center. Meanwhile, Steven took a pulse reading and placed a mask over the girl's face and squeezed in oxygen through an Ambu bag. Tianna's breathing was so shallow that the medic feared losing her. "We have to intubate her with a breathing tube now!" insisted Steven.

Jason prepared her for intubation while he checked her pulse and breathing. As soon as he inserted the tube, her respiration improved. Then, Jason kept talking to the doctors at Detroit Receiving Hospital, giving them a rundown of the injuries and condition of the victims. It was obvious to Mr. Ewald and the medics that Tianna was near death. The medics continued to pump air into Tianna's lungs as they prepared to rush her to the trauma center.

After assessing Amber's wound, the female medic, Carol, wrapped her arm and tried to console her. Amber screamed when she saw her father, Officer Lester Thornson, run up to the scene. She tried to run toward him, but the female medic and the security guard stopped her.

"Amber, what happened? I got the call that there had been a shooting here. What happened?" As he looked down at the girl on the sidewalk, he realized it was Tianna.

Mr. Ewald turned to the police detective and said, "Mr. Thornson, I'm Carson Ewald, a teacher here at King. Someone shot Amber and Tianna. I was behind them on the sidewalk, walking from the parking lot to the school, and I saw it happen. I called 911 and ran here to help."

"You're the girls' English teacher, aren't you?"

Carol interrupted, "Detective, we're taking the girls to Detroit Receiving. Please have a family member meet us there as soon as possible."

"Thank you," Lester said. "Amber, Mom will meet you at the hospital. Honey, we love you, and everything will be OK," he said, kissing her forehead.

The paramedics lifted Tianna's gurney into the back of the ambulance. Because Amber would not leave her side, she sat in the same ambulance next to the medic. With a slam of the back door, the ambulance siren wailed as it sped off.

Several police officers stepped up to Mr. Thornson.

Jim Lee, a heavy set Asian Detective put his hand on Detective Thornson's shoulder.

"Are you going to be OK with leading this investigation? I'm sure headquarters would understand, as it's your daughter and her friend."

"I'll be fine, Jim. Begin interviewing these students and check their phone cameras for anything useful. I have to call my wife. Then I'll interview Mr. Ewald. He was the first responder."

"You heard him, boys, let's move. Get these teens in the building and set up interview stations," Detective Lee ordered as he walked toward the high school entrance. "Officer Brown, get two men and search the perimeter. See if we can find out who did this."

"Excuse me, Carson, but I have to make this call," Detective Thomson said as he took out his cell phone and hit dial.

"Honey, get down to Detroit Receiving. Amber and Tianna were involved in a shooting at the school. Honey, slow down... don't panic. Amber is OK, but it looks bad for Tianna. Call her mother and grand-father. They have to get to the emergency room."

Tears filled the detective's eyes. "I don't think she'll make it. It was a head wound, and it's terrible."

CHAPTER 2

With its siren blaring and lights flashing, the ambulance made a sharp turn west on E. Lafayette Street. Amber was sitting with Carol, the female medic. In the center of the ambulance, lay Tianna on a stretcher.

"She's stable for now, but her breathing is shallow. Steven, how much time 'till we get there?" he asked as the ambulance slowed for the St. Aubin Street intersection and slid through the red light.

"We're coming up to Chrysler Drive and I-375. Should be less than five minutes. Will she make it?"

"We'll get her there alive, but I don't know if she'll make it," Jason said as he started a saline IV solution and checked Tianna's blood pressure, pulse and oxygen level.

Carol could see that Amber was listening to their conversation, and she cried again.

"Honey, we're doing everything we can for your friend," Carol tried to calm Amber. "I take it the two of you are close friends?"

"Yes, best friends since before kindergarten," Amber said, wiping the tears from her eyes. "Who would do something like this? It's not fair. Tianna was just walking to school."

"I know there's a lot of stuff going on that's not fair. Trust me, Honey. I've seen more of this crap than anyone should see," Carol said as she wrapped Amber in a blanket and hugged her.

"I'm sorry your arm hurts. It's not a real severe wound, but you will need several stitches," Carol said.

The ambulance sped down the expressway and turned onto the Mack Avenue exit, ran the red light and headed west to St. Antoine

18

Street.

"We're there," yelled the driver as he turned into the emergency entrance and pulled up to the double doors.

As soon as the ambulance stopped, the back doors flew open and two attendants took Tianna out. Amber stepped down, guided by Carol. They rushed through the emergency room doors and saw Tianna being circled by a group of doctors and nurses.

Amber lost sight of her friend and panicked.

"Where are they taking Tianna?" she asked Carol.

Carol helped Amber onto a gurney and told her, "Don't worry, she's in expert hands now."

Two emergency room nurses took Amber through the wide doors of the trauma center. As usual, the center was busy. Amber watched as groups of doctors and nurses sped around, pushing gurneys into stations so they could help patients.

"What's your name, sweetheart?" asked the young nurse.

"Amber."

The nurse removed the bandage wrap covering her wound and said, "This may hurt, but I have to see how bad this wound is."

Amber hadn't thought about her arm. She was more concerned with Tianna's injuries than with her own. When the nurse pulled the gauze bandage off, she cried a little. There was a sharp pain that ran down her arm. She looked down and could see her bloodstained white blouse.

"Is it bad?" she asked.

"It looks like the paramedics did a good job. This will sting," she said as she bathed the wound with an antiseptic. Another nurse was checking Amber's vital signs. She showed the triage doctor her readings.

"Everything looks good, Amber," the doctor said. "I have to stitch this up, but first, I will give you a shot for pain. This will also help you relax. You've been through a traumatic event, and your heart is racing."

Amber nodded, but remained upset because she could not see Tianna. "Where is my friend? I need to make sure she's OK. Please let me see her."

The shot did its job as the nurse and doctor helped Amber lay back on the gurney. Amber felt as if she were floating, and didn't hear the nurse say, "You'll see your friend soon. Don't worry."

Amber couldn't see Tianna because as soon as she arrived at Detroit Receiving, she disappeared into a triage room with an entire emergency crew doing everything they could to save her. The lead E.R. doctor, Dr. Raj Patel, barked orders to his staff.

Dr. Patel had seen many shooting victims in Detroit, but when it's someone so young, his heart aches. He has a daughter who is almost Tianna's age, and couldn't imagine something this tragic happening to her. This morning, he will treat Tianna as if she were his daughter lying on the gurney.

"There are two gunshot wounds to the head," he noted. "Make sure the on-call neurosurgeon knows that he's needed, stat. As soon as we stabilize her, we need to get her into surgery and do what we can to repair the damage. I'm sure there's internal bleeding, unfrequently there is a bullet lodged in her brain."

"Let's get a CAT scan," he instructed.

* * *

Amber and Tianna's mothers, Alice Thornson and Thelma Gulliver, arrived within seconds of each other. They met in the emergency parking lot and rushed down the street to the entrance. Neither took the time to talk, running as fast as they could through the automatic doors and into the reception room.

"I'm Alice Thornson, and this is Thelma Gulliver. Our daughters, Tianna and Amber, were brought in from King High School," Alice said while trying to catch her breath.

The young receptionist checked her computer and said, "Yes,

please take a seat and someone will be with you soon."

"No! Where is my daughter? I want to be with her, NOW!" insisted Thelma.

"I'm sorry, ladies, the girls are being taken care of, but you cannot be in the trauma room."

"Damn. I want to talk to someone. Who is your supervisor? I want to see my daughter. God, don't you know she needs me?" cried Thelma through tears.

Both women were crying as they hugged each other for comfort. A nurse tried to comfort them. She directed them to a chair in the waiting area and asked if they wanted coffee or water to drink.

"No! We want to see our daughters," responded Thelma. She turned to her friend and asked, "Did Lester say what happened, or how bad their injuries are?"

Alice didn't want to tell Thelma that he feared Tianna might not survive the shooting. "No, just that Tianna suffered a head wound. But they got to her quickly and, thank God, she's here. This is a good emergency room, Thelma. They'll take care of her."

Tianna's grandfather, Clarence, rushed into the emergency room. Before he could reach the front desk, Thelma yelled to him, "Dad, we're here."

"Have you seen them? Are they OK?" he asked as he reached his daughter-in-law. Panic was in his eyes, and his weak heart was racing.

"No, they won't let me see her."

"Want me to talk to them?"

Before she could respond to Clarence, a nurse approached her and asked, "Are you Alice Thornson?"

"I am," responded Alice.

"Please come with me; you can see your daughter now. She is fine, but we would like to keep her for a while. We had to sedate her because of the mental trauma she has suffered," the nurse said, leading Alice away.

Thelma watched as her friend went down the hall toward the trauma room. "Dad, did you hear anything about what happened?"

"No, just what Alice told me. We both need to calm down, Thelma. It won't help anyone if we get worked up and make ourselves sick. When they have news for us, they'll call us like they did Alice," Clarence said. He didn't want to show how worried he was, and deep down he feared the worst. Having gone through the loss of his parents, his wife of 40 years, their first child Matt, and then his son, Joe ... he knew Tianna was in God's hands. There was nothing they could do except pray.

* * *

Dr. Patel didn't expect Dr. Edmond Kohl to walk into the trauma room. Dr. Kohl is the best neurosurgeon in Southeast Michigan. He has surgical privileges at several hospitals, including Ann Arbor, and his practice is very select. Having him here made Raj both happy and anxious.

"It's my understanding you need a neurosurgeon. I was in the hospital doing my rounds when I received the call because the on-staff neurosurgeons are in surgery. Could you give me the details of the situation?" requested Dr. Kohl.

Dr. Patel went over Tianna's case, showing him the CAT scan, and vital readings. "There is still a bullet here, in her cerebellum. As you can see, there is also minor damage to the medulla."

"I take it she can't breathe without a ventilator? What about her heart?"

"Her heartbeat is irregular and weak, so we have her on life support."

"Someone told me her sixteenth birthday is tomorrow," said Dr. Kohl. "I want her to be around to celebrate, if not tomorrow, eventually."

Dr. Patel smiled. "Yes, we all do. Our surgical staff will prepare the patient for surgery. They are an excellent team and can assist you."

"Yes. One of my assistants was with me today, and I have requested that another surgeon come in, but they can help until he arrives."

"Understood, sir. Thank you."

Dr. Patel gave instructions to prepare for the surgery. They were so lucky to have Dr. Kohl on hand. The on-staff neurosurgeons are excellent, but Dr. Kohl's skills as a surgeon are what Tianna needs to survive.

A triage nurse approached Dr. Patel and said, "The patient's mother and grandfather are in the waiting room. They're eager to learn about their daughter's condition."

A pained look overcame the Doctors. Dr. Kohl told him to speak with the family.

Dr. Patel said, "Yes, Diane. I will be out in a minute."

After the attendant took Tianna, along with the machines keeping her alive, to surgery, Dr. Patel walked through the triage room's door, into the waiting room. He asked the receptionist to point out Tianna's family and then approached them.

"I'm Dr. Raj Patel. I worked on Tianna. Come with me so we can speak for a moment," he said as he guided Thelma and Clarence to a small private area near the receptionist station.

As he was walking, Clarence asked, "It there any good news for us? God, please say yes."

"Tianna is alive, but she has had major brain damage and is in a serious, life-threatening condition. She suffered two wounds, both to the head. At this moment, the best neurosurgeon in Southeast Michigan, Dr. Kohl, is preparing for her surgery. If anyone can repair the damage, it is he."

Thelma grabbed an arm of the chair to steady herself. She said, "Be honest, Dr. Patel, what can we expect?"

"Your daughter is a fighter, and I want her to celebrate her birthday tomorrow, but I cannot promise you she will. I pray Dr. Kohl will save her life, but there was damage to the area of her brain that controls her breathing, heartbeat and autonomic functions. Even if she survives, she may be on life-support for the rest of her life."

"Oh God. No," cried Thelma, as Clarence put his arm around her.

"Thelma, we need to pray. God will help us," he said. "I will call Rev. James to spread the word."

Dr. Patel put his hand on Thelma's shoulder. "Yes, I know prayer can help. I have seen its power, and I know miracles can happen."

"How long will the surgery take?" asked Clarence.

"It will be several hours. The receptionist will keep you informed. You can wait in the surgery waiting room on the third floor." Dr. Patel turned to the receptionist and asked that she find a map showing the directions. "I have other patients in the E.R., so I have to go now."

Thelma and Clarence took a few minutes to collect themselves. As they stepped out of the cubical, they met Alice.

"How is she?" Alice asked.

Clarence took her hand and said, "Not good, but with God's help she might make it. She's going into surgery now, and we're on our way to the third floor waiting room. Do you want to join us?"

"I will later. I have to get back to Amber. She's resting; they are concerned about mental trauma, so they gave her something to let her sleep. I'm not sure how long she will be here, but she's doing well."

"We're so happy for you. Now we need to get Tianna on the road to recovery," said Clarence.

The three walked down a long hallway toward the elevators. As they walked, Alice dialed her husband, Detective Lester Thornson.

CHAPTER 3

With over sixteen years of experience as a Detroit police officer, Detective Thornson has seen all kinds of inhumanity inflicted on the residents of his city. They say police officers must harden their feelings to avoid falling victim to the job, and many of Lester's fellow officers have destroyed themselves and their families because they took the job home. Detective Lester Thornson is an exception because he can separate his personal feelings from the job. Except today. His two worlds have collided in a big way.

Detective Thornson and the school administration agreed to take the school off lock-down mode. As he and his partner began investigating the shooting, Detective Thornson struggled with the reality that his daughter and her best friend were the victims. He was sure of his ability to handle this investigation, even under these difficult circumstances.

When his personal cell phone rang, he reached into his pocket, hoping for good news.

His wife, Alice, said, "Lester, Amber will be fine. It was an upper arm flesh wound, but they want to keep her in the hospital for observation. The doctors felt the trauma of seeing Tianna's injury may be too much for her, so they gave her a mild sedative."

"And will Tianna be OK?" Lester asked, almost not wanting to hear the answer.

"She's in surgery now. I will wait with Thelma and Clarence until we get word. From what I've heard, it doesn't sound good," Alice said with a heavy sigh. "Have you found the shooter yet?"

"No, but now that I know Amber is OK, I'll be able to concentrate better. We're interviewing the kids who witnessed the shooting, and I'm downloading all their video. It's sick how everyone records accidents and street fights these days, but it may be a blessing this time."

"Well, call me before you head home tonight. I'm not sure when I'll be home."

"OK. I love you, Alice. I'm so glad for Amber, and I'll pray for Tianna. Bye, Honey," Lester said as he ended the call.

Detective Thornson looked over the parking lot and sidewalk at King High School's entrance, where a bullet had struck the girls. He had watched a few of the downloaded video recordings and wanted to check the angles to see where the shooter could have been hiding. He also needed to get his mind cleared and some fresh air.

Jason Arborsen, the lead crime scene investigator, approached the detective when he saw him finish his phone call. "Sir, I will have my preliminary report this afternoon. I'm sorry about your daughter. Have you gotten any word about how the girls are?"

"My daughter will be fine, but the other girl, Tianna, is in critical condition."

"Too bad. This is such a nice school, but it seems like there is just so much violence anymore. It's always something," muttered Jason as he returned to his work on his computer tablet.

"Jason, do you have any idea yet where the shooter would have been standing?" Detective Thornson asked.

"The group of gang members was standing at the edge of the sidewalk over there," he said, pointing south of the school entrance. "And the girls were standing north of them. About two hundred feet, by my calculation. If the shooter aimed at the boys, then he was somewhere over there."

The area that Jason pointed to included parking lots, East Lafayette Blvd., and Elmwood Cemetery. It was a large area that needed searching

"I have two men covering the area. If they find anything, you will be the first to know, Sir," said Jason.

"Thank you. We need a break in this case. The mayor and police chief are both urging me to wrap this up as soon as possible. They like calling it gang related, but I'm not sure it was."

As Detective Thornson turned to go into the school entrance, he saw the group of news reporters gathered at the far end of the parking lot. They were being kept away from the scene, but he could see that the assistant police chief was talking to them. *Hope he doesn't make any stupid statements*, Lester thought. *Oh well, at least he's taking the heat instead of me.*

A little over a year ago, Detective Thornson became embroiled in a case at King High School involving a coach getting mugged in the parking lot. The coach shot at the two former students. During that one, Lester had to speak with the media several times. He didn't enjoy the experience one bit, even though it is now part of his job. Any time he could push that job to someone upstairs, he was happy.

With its long history, King High School has seen its share of problems. The school began as Eastern High School in 1901 at the intersection of Mack Avenue and East Grand Boulevard. Eastern High School moved in 1967 to 3200 East Lafayette Boulevard, bordering historic Elmwood Cemetery, and its name changed to Martin Luther King. Today, after tearing down the old school, the new school is modern, with over 1400 students.

Detective Thornson turned and walked back into the school. He and Detective Lee arranged for a room near the entrance for interviewing student witnesses. Mr. Ewald, the English teacher who helped save Tianna's life, stayed at the scene with Detective Lee. Together, the two had identified twenty students that saw the shooting. Of these, ten students had taken photographs and video. The school also uses video surveillance cameras, and copies of all applicable video are available to the team. It was a daunting task for the small homicide team, but by working smart, the detectives hoped they could find the shooter.

Detective Lee and two patrolmen divided the work among themselves while the school security officers helped to identify students and keep order. They had to compile all the data collected, including witness statements, photographs and video collected from the students' cameras. The five gang members were fighting near the school entrance during the shooting. The security officers had them sit in the hallway, and Lee was interviewing them individually in the small conference room.

Detective Thornson approached Mr. Ewald and put his hand on his shoulder. "I got word that Amber will be fine, but Tianna's still in a serious condition."

"I'm surprised she's still alive. In Iraq, I saw a lot of guys with head wounds, but none like Tianna. Whoever shot her had to be aiming. I'm sure of that."

"Well, from what you said, the shots came from behind you. I have men looking in the parking lot for any evidence left behind," said Detective Thornson.

"Do you think it was gang related?" asked Mr. Ewald. "It doesn't seem right. The guys who were fighting are members of a small gang here at school. They call themselves something like *The Kingsmen*, but most of them aren't criminals, and they are active in other school functions. Only one boy has a criminal record. His name is Jerry, the tallest one. He could be on the basketball team, but he's never been eligible. His grades were just too low."

"The mayor and chief of police are on my case to get this solved. It's been only two hours of investigating, and they expect us to have it solved by now. They suggested we call it gang related. You know, it makes it simple to just blame the gangs for everything," the detective complained.

* * *

When Detective Thornson saw his partner, Detective Lee, come out of the interview room with one of the gang members, he approached him and asked, "Jim, did you talk to a gang member named Jerry yet?"

"No, but the other guys said he's sort of the leader. You want to talk to him?"

"We can both question him. Mr. Ewald says he has a record. I checked, and last year they charged him with assault, and petty theft two years ago. The court dropped the assault charge because the kid he hit was just as guilty as Jerry was. They were fighting over a girl," added Detective Thornson.

The two men walked over to Jerry and asked him to stand and follow Detective Lee to the interview room. The rest of the gang members returned to their classes, but they could face charges if more evidence shows up. This comment made them very nervous, and one boy looked as if he would cry.

"But we didn't do anything wrong," the boy insisted. "We were just fooling around before school."

"Then you'll be fine. But I have a girl who might die because someone was shooting at you guys, and missed, or they were sending a message," said Detective Thornson. He was trying to make the boys realize how serious the situation was, and he had succeeded.

Detective Thornson followed Jerry and Detective Lee into the small interview room, which was just off the main office. The room used for various meetings had a large table, and at least eight chairs. Detective Lee sat opposite Jerry while Detective Thornson stood at the end of the table.

Detective Lee spoke first. "I know about your criminal record, and the other guys say you're the leader of this gang. Is that true?"

"What's it to you? We didn't do nothing wrong."

"Who shot the gun that hit those two girls?" asked Lee

"What gun? We don't have no guns," said Jerry.

"Kid, if you don't come up with some believable answers, we will have to take you downtown. We need to know if someone might have wanted to shoot your gang members. Now, is there another gang that is causing you trouble?"

"You can't take me downtown. I didn't do nothing wrong," insisted Jerry. "And we get along with all the other gangs. They like us, 'cause we're the Kingsmen, and they all love us."

Jerry laughed, but when Detective Thornson slammed his notebook down in front of him, Jerry stopped.

"Jerry, my daughter was one girl who they shot, and her best friend is dying at this moment. I have to put someone behind bars or my boss will have my ass. Now, it would be easy to say it was one of your enemies who shot the gun. The press would believe that story. *Another Gang Related Killing*. That would be the headline, and we can make you an accessory to murder, because it's your activity that caused the shooting. That would make everyone happy, and the case would be closed."

"But we didn't do anything," insisted Jerry.

"Who cares? We need to blame someone," Detective Thornson chided. "Now, if you tell us what you know, I might be convinced to look for someone else to put in jail."

"I can't afford another charge against me, but I'm not sure what you want. I heard the shot. It looked like it came from the cemetery area. The only one who's angry with us is Kyle White. We kicked him out of our group because he wanted us to join that stupid singing club. Man, we can't sing."

"Did you see who the shooter was?" asked Detective Lee.

"No! I heard the gunshot, and it sounded like it was from a distance. I've heard a lot of gunshots before in my neighborhood. I'm telling the truth. We were just arguing about Kyle. Two guys are friends of that rat, and they want him back. I told them I'd leave the gang if he's back."

The two detectives whispered to each other, and then Detective Thornson told Jerry to stand up. "Son, if you're lying, I will hunt you down and make sure you spend a long time in jail. But for now, you can go. Jerry, why don't you get your grades up and try out for the basketball team this winter? Word around here is that you could be a skilled player if you would only try. I suggest you make something of yourself."

"Sure, anything you say," Jerry said as he bolted out the door, and down the hallway.

* * *

Detectives Thornson and Lee had been on the scene all morning and completed interviewing the students and teachers who saw the shooting. Two officers continued the review and download of video and photographs taken by the students while school security officers downloaded the school surveillance video.

As Thornson and Lee sat reviewing the interview notes, Harry Davis, one of the security guards, approached them.

"Detective Thornson, you need to look at this surveillance video."

Harry showed the detectives the iPad he was holding and started the video. It was a scene of the parking lot with students and teachers parking and getting out of their cars. Parents were dropping students off at the curb and then driving off.

"What's so special about this?" asked Detective Lee. "Looks like a normal day at school."

"Just watch."

A large black sedan appeared in a parking space, and the driver's side tinted window lowered. A man holding binoculars looked toward the school as a mass of people, including Mr. Ewald, ran toward the school.

"This must have been the moment that the girls were shot," said Detective Thornson.

"Yes, but look at the car. It vanishes as quickly as it appeared.

From nowhere… like magic," insisted Harry.

"There must have been a glitch in the video. Cars don't vanish," commented Detective Lee.

"But I want to know who that was and why he was watching the shooting," interrupted Detective Thornson. "Do we have any other video with that car? We need a plate number so we can trace it."

"There were no errors on the video," Harry continued. "I checked it several times myself. That car appeared like magic and vanished the same way. Poof!"

Detective Thornson laughed. "Harry, check the other videos and see if you can catch that car's plate number."

Speaking to the officers and staff gathered around him, the detective added, "Let's collect our things and get out of the school's way. We can go over this material at headquarters after lunch. Nancy, work with Harry and the other security guards to make sure we have all the security video. You can bring it when you leave. Let's move it people, we have other crimes to solve today."

Detective Thornson thanked the school administration for their help and started out the doors. Stepping outside, he faced two reporters barricaded in the parking lot behind the police line, but as the police team cleared the area, the reporters rushed up to the detectives with questions.

"Do you have the shooter in custody?" asked a newspaper reporter.

Detective Thornson stopped and told the reporters, "The Detroit Police Department will make a statement at headquarters later today. I have no statement to make."

"Sir, I understand your daughter was one victim? Do you feel you should work on this investigation? Isn't it a conflict of interest?" another reporter yelled.

"No comment," Detective Thornson replied.

A television reporter with a camera approached. "Detective Thornson, the Assistant Police Chief suggested that this shooting was gang related. Is that true?"

"No comment."

"We hear one girl is dying. Is that your daughter?" another reported asked.

"No" was the only reply that the detective made. He then walked past the reporters toward his vehicle. As he and Detective Lee got into the police car, his cell phone rang. He could see it was Jason, the crime scene investigator, calling.

"Sir, we found something across the street. You need to look."

"Where are you?"

"We're across East Lafayette Blvd., in Elmwood Cemetery," said Jason.

"I'll be right there."

As Detective Thornson headed toward the parking lot exit, he could see the Crime Scene Investigators at the edge of the cemetery. He checked for the best way to reach them, and crossed the back parking lot, turning north onto McDougall Street. The entrance to the cemetery was on his right. None of the news reporters had noticed where he went, but he was sure they would find out.

After winding through the cemetery for a few hundred yards, he reached the location, and the two detectives got out of their vehicles.

There were three crime scene investigators taking photographs and mapping out the area. "What do we have, Jason?" asked Detective Jim Lee.

"A weapon. It looks like it's the gun used, but we won't know until we check the bullet. We found one bullet at the scene, and they told me that one was still in the victim's head."

The detectives walked toward the fence and saw the Remington M40 rifle. The long rifle was in excellent condition for an older model. It was laying in the grass under a small tree. Detective Thornson squatted down and observed that there was a clear view of the school entrance.

"Looks like the shooter dropped it as soon as he or she made the shots. It's a long distance, but this is a sniper rifle used during the Vietnam War."

Jason agreed and said his men would check for prints and have the gun checked to make sure it was the weapon used to shoot the girls.

"Well, it looks like we might have gotten the break we need," said Lester. "Good work, Jason. We owe you guys."

The men shook hands, and the detectives walked back to their car. Lester asked Jim to drive so he could call his wife and check on Amber and Tianna. As they exited the cemetery, Jim asked if Lester wanted to stop for lunch, head back to headquarters, or go to the hospital.

"I have to stop at the hospital and see my little girl. You're welcome to come in with me, but I know you don't do hospitals well."

"True. I would love to see her, but you better drop me off at Headquarters."

"No, you can drop me off at the hospital, and take the car back to Headquarters," insisted Lester.

"Fine, that should save us some time, but are you coming back to the station?" asked Jim.

"I'll be in touch, but I should make it back in a few hours after I see how Amber and Tianna are doing. My wife can drop me off at the station," he said. There was a long silence as both men thought about the day's events.

The silence continued as they approached the hospital. The car stopped at a traffic light, and Jim turned to Lester and said, "It's not right, but there's nothing we can do about it, is there? We see this crap every day; we just don't want to see it in our own neighborhoods. Especially in our own families. I'll pray for Tianna, and I'm sure all of Detroit is praying for her today."

"Oh shit! Tianna's birthday is tomorrow, and I got tickets for a concert downtown. It's a surprise for Tianna and Amber. Now I need to call and get them exchanged. Damn! This is all wrong."

Lester picked up his cell phone and dialed his wife. It was something he dreaded doing. Deep inside, he had a feeling Tianna didn't make it. "Hi, Honey. I'm on my way to the hospital. What's the news about Tianna and Amber?"

Detective Lee could only hear one side of the conversation, but he could tell that Tianna was still alive, but in a very critical condition. As he pulled up to Detroit Receiving, Lester directed him to the entrance that his wife had told him to use. She was at the door, waiting for him.

CHAPTER 4

Detective Lee watched as his partner entered the hospital. He could see Lester's wife, Alice, gave him a big hug, and then they disappeared. Jim Lee thought for a moment about why he avoids hospitals and doctors. His phobia started after he lost his parents in a horrific auto accident and he spent two months alone in the hospital. Upon release, he was a seventeen-year-old boy forced to face the reality of being an orphan with no family. He spent a lonely year in foster care and then enlisted in the Navy. Jim still has issues with relationships, except those involving his job.

Lester and Alice walked to the elevators and went up three floors to the surgical waiting room. As they walked through the hallway, Alice told him how Amber was doing and asked about the investigation.

"According to headquarters and the Mayor's office, we are ready to declare this shooting a gang argument that went wrong. The only problem is they don't understand what the case is even about. They want it wrapped up, and they love to blame the gangs, and brag about how effective their new policies are at stopping them," said Lester.

"It wasn't gang related, I take it?" asked Alice.

"I'm not sure, but all the evidence shows that there is more to this case than someone shooting at a bunch of boys who belong to a small gang. These guys spend their mornings arguing over whether they should be in sports, choir, or just hang out in the streets. As far as I can tell, they aren't into drugs. We have no evidence of their selling or using."

"If it wasn't gang related, then why would someone be shooting at our girls?" asked Alice.

"That's the magical question."

When the two reached the waiting room, they hugged again and kissed. "I'm so glad that Amber will be OK," whispered Lester.

"Me too. Me too."

Tianna's mother and grandfather, Thelma and Clarence Gulliver, were sitting in the waiting room. Thelma had been crying, but she was now staring at the doors leading out to the operating rooms.

Clarence saw Amber's parents first. He stood and started toward them.

"Ihappy Amber will be OK," he said.

"Oh, Clarence, have you heard anything yet?" asked Alice.

"No. It's been three hours and nothing. You would think someone would tell us what's going on, wouldn't you?" he asked.

"Yes, but they won't," Lester said. "At least not until the doctors complete their evolution. The nurses can't say anything without the doctor's approval."

Alice walked over to Thelma and sat next to her. Thelma turned, saw her friend and cried again.

"Oh, Thelma. I'm so sorry. I've been praying all morning. God will help. I know He will."

"Lester," Thelma said through her tears, "have you caught the bastard who did this to my baby?"

"Working on it, Thelma. We're working on it."

The four sat for a few minutes to let Thelma regain herself. Clarence and Lester discussed the case and the problems Lester was having with the Mayor's office, which was trying to dictate how he should manage the case.

Clarence said, "It wasn't any better when I was young. Gangs aren't new, and mayors always want simple answers and fast results."

"Yes, Clarence. It's just that it's not always the gangs' fault, and I hate jumping to conclusions. It makes it harder to see the truth."

Detective Thornson's cell phone vibrated, and he took it out to see who was calling. "I have to take this, Clarence," he said as he walked into the hallway.

"Thornson here, what do you have?"

It was the investigator, Jason Arborsen.

"We're running the gun through ballistics and found something interesting. According to the serial number on the gun, it was used during the 1967 riots," said Jason. "We also found one bullet at today's scene along with two spent shells, and we're confident it was the gun used to shoot your daughter and her friend. We're also checking for prints."

Detective Thornson asked, "Can you trace the gun since the 1967 shooting?"

"We haven't gotten that far, but you might be interested in knowing the case involved the death of a fifteen-year-old black girl, Amanda Carson, who was just about to turn sixteen. In fact, she died the day before her birthday, just like Tianna. Talk about a crazy coincidence."

"I guess. Just find out where the gun has been since 1967. Were there any prints?"

"Two smudged ones. They might be old, though. It looks like the shooter wore gloves. The prints were likely from handling the gun before the shooting."

"Well, thanks for the update," added the Detective.

Lester thought for a moment about the gun and the 1967 shooting. Was it more than a coincidence? Could it be the same shooter? If it were, he would be an old man now. And why would anyone want to shoot someone because they were turning sixteen?

"Lester, come here," called Alice.

Lester turned and returned to the waiting room, where three doctors now stood. They looked awkward and were not happy to be there.

"Are you the Tianna Gulliver's mother?" they asked Alice.

"No, I am Tianna's mother, Thelma Gulliver. Is my daughter going to be OK?"

"Let me explain her condition, said the oldest doctor. I'm Dr. Edmond Kohl. They called me in to help with the case because I'm a neurosurgeon and your daughter suffered a head wound. We removed the bullet and did as much as we could to repair the damage. One damaged area of her brain regulates her breathing and heartbeat. I'm sorry, but I have to tell you your daughter is dying."

Thelma's knees gave way, and she collapsed. Lester guided her to a seat, and Alice tried to comfort her.

"God, no. Please, not my baby. I want to see her."

"You can after we talk about her treatment," the thin blond doctor said.

"Treatment? You said she was dying," questioned Clarence.

The blond doctor smiled. "I am sorry. My name is Dr. Jerome Carter. I work at the Ann Arbor Nanotechnology Research Department. I am here at the request of Dr. Kohl. When he saw the injury your daughter had, he asked that I get here ASAP. We are developing a technique to use nanobots to treat neuron damage. It is not approved for human testing yet, but we are sure it could help."

Cutting off the exuberant Dr. Carter, Dr. Kohl injected, "Please, let's go to the conference room. Mrs. Gulliver, we have a lot to discuss."

"Is there a chance my daughter could survive this?" asked Thelma.

"We need to discuss that, and Tianna's present condition."

"Then let's get going," Clarence said.

Alice asked Thelma if she wanted them with her and without pause she replied, "Yes, I want both you and Lester to be with me. I consider you part of my family."

The doctors let the group to a small room with a table and several chairs. It was near the surgical waiting room. After they were all seated, Dr. Kohl pulled several pictures from his file.

"As this diagram shows, the area damaged by the gunshot manages many motor functions, including breathing and heartbeat. Tianna is alive now only because we have her on machines that are assisting these functions, but she is paralyzed from the neck down. I have done everything I could to repair the damage. But yes, your daughter is dying. Even with the life support, her organs will stop working, and she will die within a week."

"That's why Dr. Kohl called me in," said Dr. Carter. "Our experiments with nanobots have great promise."

"I've heard of them," said Thelma, "but what exactly are they?"

"They are microscopic robot-like nanoparticles that can deliver treatments on the cellular level. The ones we want to use would place stem cells at the ends of the damaged neurons. Neurons may regenerate over time, and under the right conditions, but we don't have time. We need to speed up the regeneration in order to repair the damage in your daughter's hippocampus brain region," said Dr. Carter. "The longer the damage goes uncorrected, the more likely your daughter will die."

Clarence leaned closer to the Doctor and said, "You said these are experimental. Are you asking that my granddaughter be a lab rat for your experiments?"

"Yes, in a way we are. We can only get permission to treat your daughter with this experimental technique because of her life-threatening condition. I know it will help her, and I will bet my career on it," insisted Dr. Carter.

Dr. Kohl interrupted, "Dr. Carter is passionate about this treatment, and he can get a little carried away. We can't guarantee that Tianna will respond to this treatment. It is, however, the only treatment with the potential to save her life."

"Thelma," said Alice, "I don't want to tell you what to do, but God led us to this treatment. Why else would he send these doctors?"

"When would we know if it works?" she asked.

"Within two days."

"Where will you do the procedure?"

"Either in Ann Arbor or here," said Dr. Carter.

"Could we do it at Children's Hospital here in Detroit?"

The two doctors discussed this idea for a few moments and then turned to Alice. "Yes. Does this mean you want us to use this experimental treatment on Tianna?" asked Dr. Kohl.

With a sigh of relief at deciding, Thelma said, "Yes. I want to give Tianna the chance to survive, and I want to see her... NOW!"

Filled with excitement, Dr. Carter said he would get the ball rolling. He thanked everyone, shook their hands, hugged Thelma and hurried toward the door. Before leaving, he turned and said, "Mrs. Gulliver, I'll do everything in my power to make sure your daughter walks out of Children's Hospital under her own power."

* * *

Dr. Kohl turned to Thelma and said, "Come with me and I'll let you see your daughter."

"Can I come too?" asked Clarence.

"Yes, but only one person can see her at a time."

"Clarence, you go in after Thelma," suggested Alice. "We have to get back to Amber. I would hate to have her wake up without my being there. We'll be back as soon as possible."

Clarence followed Dr. Kohl down the hall and into the waiting room of the Neurology I.C.U., and Alice and Lester walked toward the elevators.

Dr. Kohl turned to Clarence and said, "You will have to stay here until Thelma comes out. Remember, the limit is five minutes. Tianna is in an induced coma, and she will not be aware of your presence. Thelma, I would prefer that you not try to hug or touch Tianna. Her life support is delicate, and we can't afford any accidents."

"I want to touch my daughter's hand," insisted Thelma. "She will know I'm there."

"I understand, and that will be fine."

An I.C.U. nurse entered the hallway, and Dr. Kohl gave her instructions to take Thelma in to see her daughter.

"I have to get back and help with preparations for Tianna's transfer to Children's Hospital. It will be a challenge, but we will have her moved by the end of the day."

Thelma followed the nurse down the hall and into the small I.C.U. cubicle. She gasped when she entered Tianna's room. Bandages covered her head, and a mask made it hard to see her face. There were tubes and wires coming from her body connected to a multitude of machines and monitors.

With tears in her eyes, Thelma took Tianna's hand and said, "Honey, I'm here. Everything will be OK."

Thelma pulled up a small chair and sat down next to her daughter. She had decided that no one would make her leave. *My place is here with my daughter*, she thought.

"Nurse, you can tell my father-in-law that he can come in now," she said to the nurse, who was recording readings into a portable computer cart.

"I'm sorry, but only one person may be in with the patient," she said.

"No, I'm not leaving my daughter's side until she recovers," Thelma insisted. "If you want me to leave, carry me out!"

The nurse walked to the nurses' station and relayed Thelma's message. When Dr. Kohl said he would allow her to stay.

In a few minutes, both Thelma and Clarence were at Tianna's side. Together, they held her hand and prayed. The nurses performed their duties in silence. Tears streamed down their faces as they listened to the two pleading for God's help.

* * *

Lester and Alice made their way down to the emergency room and into the small private room where Amber had been sleeping. When they entered the room, Amber sat up and put her arms out.

"Mom, Dad.... did you talk to Tianna? Is she going to be OK?"

Both Lester and Alice put their arms around their daughter. Alice said, "Yes, she is alive. They will move her to Children's Hospital, down the road. They want to try an experimental procedure using nanobots. Amber, she might not make it. I'm sorry, honey, but Tianna's injuries are very severe."

Perplexed at how calm Amber was, Lester asked, "Tell me how you're doing, Amber? They told me how upset you were when you got to the E.R."

"Well, my arm hurts, but I'm fine," she said with her usual bubbly grin.

"But they said you couldn't stop crying. Are you sure you're OK now?"

"Yes. While I was sleeping, Tianna came into my room and said I shouldn't worry. She said she would be fine," Amber said with a smile. "Dad, I know she will be OK."

An E.R. nurse entered the room and told Alice and Lester that they could take Amber home as soon as he signed the discharge paperwork. Lester followed the nurse to the nurses' desk. As he left, Alice's phone buzzed. There was a message from Tianna's grandfather, Clarence. He said the staff would transport Tianna in an hour.

Dr. Patel was at the nurses' station. When he saw who Lester was, he said, "Your daughter is doing well. When I first saw her, she was hysterical, but when she woke up this afternoon, she appeared almost happy. I suggest you watch her because she may repress her feelings. Also, the nurse will give you instructions for the care of her wound, and a prescription for some pain medication. The bullet went through her upper arm and grazed the bone. It will be painful, but should heal fast."

Lester thanked him and then added, "I wish Tianna were as lucky as our daughter."

"She is in excellent hands. Dr. Kohl is one of the finest neurosurgeons in the nation, and the nanotechnology team from Ann Arbor is on the cutting edge of neurological medicine. Let's pray they can work miracles."

Followed by a nurse, Lester returned to his wife and daughter. The nurse gave Alice instructions for Amber's care. The doctor prescribed pain medication, antibiotics, and a mild dose of Valium.

"Keep Amber's wound dry and clean. If there is any swelling, use an ice pack and elevate her arm. Should she develop a fever, call the number listed for instructions. Dr. Patel wants you to schedule an appointment to have the stitches removed in one week. Just call the number listed here."

The nurse gave Alice the paperwork and then continued, "I'm sorry about your friend, Amber. We will all be praying for her."

Amber smiled. "Thank you, but I know she will recover. It's almost her birthday, and she has a lot to look forward to. That's what she told me."

Not sure how to take Amber's words, the nurse smiled and said, "Yes, dear. I'm sure she did."

As the Thornson family walked toward the emergency room exit, Amber asked, "Can I visit Tianna now?"

"Honey, I think we should wait until she is in her room at Children's Hospital," responded Alice. "Clarence sent a message that Tianna would move in an hour. It will be crazy up there until she is at Children's."

"OK, but I want to see her real soon. I have things to tell her."

"We will. We will," said Lester.

"Alice, I'll get the car. Which lot did you park in?" asked Lester.

"It's just outside the emergency room. I'm not sure if I parked in a legal spot. I was in such a hurry I didn't pay attention to where I parked."

"Well, give me the keys, and if you got a parking ticket, I'm sure I can get it fixed for you."

"Thanks, dear, but I don't want you doing anything illegal for me."

Lester walked ahead and found the car. There was no ticket on it even though she parked in a spot reserved for a doctor. He pulled the car around to the emergency room and helped his wife and daughter with the doors. It was a quiet drive home, as they each thought about Tianna, and what she faced. Amber continued to exude happiness. Her response to the situation made both her mom and dad uneasy. It didn't feel right, and they worried she was not facing the truth.

CHAPTER 5

The nurse informed Thelma that she would have to stand back while they prepared Tianna for the move to Children's Hospital. Portable devices would replace the machines that were monitoring and keeping her alive. This process was one they had performed before, but we must take the utmost care, because any mistake could threaten her life.

"If you get in our way, it could be dangerous for your daughter," she said.

"I understand," Thelma said as she walked out of Tianna's cubical and back to the waiting room where Clarence was sipping coffee and reading the latest Time magazine.

"Is there a problem, Thelma?" he asked.

"No. They are getting Tianna ready to move to Children's. I hope I didn't make a mistake in asking to have her moved. It seems like such a big job."

"Trust me; your instincts are right. As she recovers, the atmosphere there will be so much better," Clarence said.

"That's why I wanted her there. I remember when her cousin Emily had surgery a few years ago, and Tianna just loved the way her hospital room looked. She kept asking me to change her bedroom to look like a hospital."

"You sound like you're in a much better mood. Do you think the procedure will work?" asked Clarence.

"I don't know why, but after being with Tianna, I feel better, and I get a strong feeling she will be fine."

"I get the same feeling. She's a strong girl, Thelma. And I know God has plans for her. Big plans."

Dr. Kohl walked into the waiting room and sat next to Thelma. He was smiling, which made her feel better about the visit.

"You have a wonderful daughter. The nurses all say they will miss her, and she's only been here one afternoon. I checked with the team at Children's Hospital, and Dr. Carter has everything ready for the experimental procedure. Her room there will be on the third floor of the main building. Tianna is being prepped for the move now, and should be there within thirty minutes. I suggest going over now and checking in at the main reception desk. There will be papers for you to sign, and they will guide you to her room."

"We'll do that, Dr. Kohl. Will you still be taking care of my daughter?"

"I will be her doctor until she leaves the hospital. I plan to be there this evening. Dr. Carter will start the procedure as soon as Tianna's moved and all they test the equipment."

The doctor stood, as did Clarence and Thelma. He shook Clarence's hand and then hugged Thelma. "I feel good about this experimental treatment. I know I shouldn't say this, but I think your daughter is a fighter and has."

"Thank you, Dr. Kohl," Clarence said. "We have those same feelings."

Thelma walked past her daughter's cubical and saw she was ready to move. With the nurses' blessing, she took Tianna's hand and told her she would see her in half an hour. The nurses then wheeled the gurney and all the attached machines down the hall to the service elevator.

Thelma turned to Clarence, and the two headed to the main elevators. On their way, Thelma took her cell out and called Alice to let her know what was happening.

"Alice, Tianna's being moved now. I wanted to know how Amber is doing," Thelma said.

Alice looked in the back seat at Amber and said, "She's calm. She said Tianna came to her and told her she would be OK."

"Strange, but I'm glad she is doing better. Do they have her on anything to calm her down?"

"Yes. They gave her something for the pain several hours ago. The doctor prescribed anxiety medication, but I'm not sure she will need it," said Alice. "We're on our way home now. When would be a good time for us to come up to Children's Hospital for a visit?"

"Well, like I said, we're on our way over there now. Dr. Kohl said they will start the treatment in a few hours, so perhaps you could stop by in the morning?"

"Yes, for her birthday party. Not as planned, but we will be there about nine. I don't know about Lester, he said something about wanting to get back to work ASAP, and that will mean he'll work all day Saturday again," said Alice, with a sigh.

"I have to go, Alice. We're in the car now. Damn, I have a ticket. Tell Lester I might need his help on this one. I hate tickets," Thelma said, laughing.

"Thelma, just pay it," was Alice's response. As she put her phone back in her pocket, Lester pulled into the driveway of their home on Charlevoix Street. Amber jumped out and started for the front door. She stopped when she realized she didn't have her backpack with the house key.

"Mom, my backpack disappeared. My phone and all my books were in it."

Alice walked to the back of the car and opened the trunk. One of the EMT nurses at the hospital asked for her keys so they could put the backpack in the car. It was in a black plastic bag, and Alice never saw what condition it was in. No longer white and blue, it's now soaked in red blood. Tears welled in her eyes, and Lester took the bag and told her to go in. "I'll clean this up and bring her things in. I don't want her to see this," he said.

Alice told Amber that her dad would get her things for her, but her backpack got destroyed. "The police must have cut it open, so Dad will get your phone and books. Come on, let's get in the house."

Lester went through the contents of the backpack. The blood did not work its way inside, and her books, papers, and phone were clean. He put Amber's belongings in another bag and threw the backpack into the garbage can. With everything that Amber had seen today, he was not ready to let her see this bloody mess. It was bad enough he had to deal with it. But as a police officer, he had to get used to working in blood. It came with the job of a homicide detective.

* * *

Thelma and her father-in-law checked in at the Children's Hospital main registration desk, where she filled out the required papers. The receptionist told her Tianna would not be in the room for about an hour because the doctors were using a CAT scan while injecting her with the nanobots. The scan would show if the nanobots were going to the correct area of her brain. Clarence suggested they go to the cafeteria for dinner as neither of them had eaten since breakfast. Before they left, the receptionist took Thelma's cell number and said she would have a nurse text her when Tianna was in the room.

During dinner, Clarence asked Thelma if she planned to spend the night at the hospital.

"Yes, if need be, I'll sleep in a chair or on the floor until my daughter is out of the woods. I want to be at her side. Do you know how I would feel if she passed during a period when I was at home? The guilt would be unbearable," she responded.

"I understand, but you realize that I'm way too old to do that. Let me go home before it gets too late. In the past, I spent many nights with my wife when she was dying in the hospital, and I'm glad I did, but I can't do that now."

"Dad, I don't expect you to stay longer than you feel comfortable doing. I know you care and would do anything for Tianna. Never feel you're not doing enough."

"Thank you. Once she's on the mend, I'll stay with her so you can get some of your work done. I would do better in the late morning and early afternoons."

"Deal. Now eat your dinner and let me make a few calls. I will arrange time off from work."

After finishing their meal, Clarence refilled their coffee and cleaned the table. Thelma checked her phone and saw a message from the neurology nurse. Tianna was in her room, and Dr. Clark and his team were starting the procedure.

"Let's go, Dad. We can see Tianna now," Thelma said.

"Great timing. I'll get lids for our coffee," he said. "When will they start the treatment?"

"They've already started."

"Man, they aren't wasting any time, are they?"

"No, thank God," Thelma said as she started for the exit.

It took about ten minutes to make their way to the third floor neurology department. At the nurses' station, Thelma asked for Tianna's room. The nurse said Dr. Clark would be with them in a few minutes, as soon as they started the procedure. Clarence and Thelma walked around the nurses' station, looking at the creative artwork decorating the hallway and floor. These were the same decorations that Thelma remembered, and the area made for a relaxing experience that children would love.

Dr. Clark stood in the doorway of Tianna's room. Seeing Thelma and Clarence, and asked, "Why don't you two come down to the room with me?"

As Thelma walked to the door of Tianna's room, she saw three doctors and a nurse standing around the bed. There were several bags of solution hanging next to her with tubes leading to Tianna's arms and neck. She was still hooked up to a breathing ventilator and heart monitor.

The doctor advised, "We won't be able to enter the room or stay long, as it's important that we don't impede the staff. I wanted you to see what we are doing," the doctor said. "I didn't have time to explain the procedure when we talked in the emergency room earlier today."

The doctor walked a few doors down from Tianna's room with Clarence and Thelma and entered an empty room. "Let's talk here. We can relax a little as I explain the procedure. I see you have coffee, which looks so good."

Clarence offered to get the doctor a cup from the waiting room, and the doctor agreed.

"Yes. It has been so busy here. We had to move our equipment and supplies as soon as we knew the procedure was a go."

Thelma sipped her coffee and smiled. "I'm thankful you can help my daughter."

"Remember, Thelma. This procedure is experimental, and there are no guarantees it will have the results we all want."

"I understand, but I have a good feeling. I know Tianna is a fighter, and God is on her side."

Clarence walked into the room and handed the doctor a cup of hot coffee along with some sugar and creamer. As the doctor fixed his coffee, he said, "You know the gunshot wound entered the back of Tianna's head. One bullet entered and exited the lower back of the head. That bullet did minor damage to the medulla in the brainstem. The second bullet became lodged in the cerebellum. Dr. Kohl removed the bullet and repaired the damage as much as he could. That damage is preventing Tianna from breathing on her own. It is also interrupting her heartbeat. We are not sure if her spinal cord suffered permanent damage because she has limited feeling in her arms, back and legs, showing we are not dealing with complete paralysis."

Clarence asked, "Why did Dr. Kohl say she is dying?"

"Because if the damage isn't fixed, Tianna's organs will fail. Her heart and lungs, even with our help, cannot perform their job and if the lungs are not functional, everything will fail. It could take a few days or a month, but eventually she would die. That's why we hustled to start treatment," Dr. Carter explained.

"OK. I understand that, but I'm not sure what these nano-things are and what they will do to help my daughter," said Thelma.

"Well, in the past we believed there was nothing that could repair neural transmitter damage in the brain. We have now found several techniques that can help the brain repair itself. The problem is, if not done quickly, the brain tries to save itself by preventing outside help. One technique is the use of neural stem cells. These stem cells can generate many, if not all, types of cells found in the brain, including neurons." The doctor took another sip of coffee.

"Our technique uses micro-particles that can attach themselves to the ends of the broken neurons and deliver a neural stem cell. These nanoparticles then dissolve, and another stem cell is delivered. The method is quick because the stem cells go where we want them to go. We are using both fetal stem cells and stem cells we harvested from your daughter. The adult cells take more time to produce, but we think they will prove more stable over time, since they are not foreign to her system. We are using fetal cells first. As we produce your daughter's stem cells, we will use them."

The Doctor paused, allowing Thelma and Clarence to absorb this information. "I'm sure you have a lot of questions."

"My first question is, when will we know if this procedure is working?" asked Clarence.

"We should have results by morning. If it doesn't work, we will make adjustments to our technique. There are several ways to approach this brain damage."

Thelma stood and walked to the window. The sun was setting over Detroit, and she was growing weary. "Can I stay the night with my daughter?"

"Yes, I requested a cot in Tianna's room for you to sleep on. I realize how important it is for you to be with your daughter, and I would never refuse you."

With a sigh of relief, she returned to her seat, next to Clarence. "Thank you, Dr. Carter." She turned to Clarence and said, "You need to go home and get rest. I'll call you in the morning with a report, and I'll also call Alice and Lester, so they will know what's happening."

Clarence agreed with her plans and thanked the doctor for helping them to understand Tianna's treatment. He reached out with his weary arms and hugged his daughter-in-law. "I love you, Thelma, and I'll be praying all night for our little girl."

"Thanks, Dad. I think there will be many prayers for God's help tonight."

As they walked out of the room, Thelma noticed that Rev. James, the minister at her family church, New Harmony Baptist Church, was waiting to talk to her and Clarence. She called to him, "Rev. James, thank you so much for coming. Tianna is getting treatment now. We can go into the waiting room and talk."

The three of them walked to the room and sat in a corner space. There were others in the room laughing and enjoying themselves.

"Thelma, we are all worried about your daughter. I have been praying since I heard about the shooting, and I started a prayer vigil for her."

"Thank you. She is in critical condition, but we feel God will bring her through," Thelma said. "I am glad you are here for another reason. Dad took the bus here this morning, and he's planning to go home soon. Could you arrange for someone to drive him? I hate to see him on the bus after dark."

"I'll take him home," responded Rev. James. "Clarence, I imagine it's been a long and stressful day."

"Yes, one of the longest days in my long life, and I appreciate your help."

Rev. James took Thelma's hand and offered his other hand to Clarence. "Let's say a prayer for Tianna."

In a low voice he said, "Lord, we know that your love is always within our grasp. Today we pray for a special love, the love we have in our hearts for Tianna Gulliver, a beautiful Christian girl who is strong. Lord, an evil has struck Tianna today. An evil not of her making, but this evil has threatened to take her from us. Lord, we believe in the healing power of prayer, and we believe you can and will intervene in this matter. Lord, put your arms around our little girl and breathe life into her small body. Let her reach her sixteenth birthday and let there be many more for her to enjoy. We pray in our Savior Jesus' name, Amen."

When Thelma opened her eyes, she saw that everyone in the waiting room had their heads bowed in prayer. A warm feeling of love filled her heart as she thanked the Reverend for his kind words and for giving Clarence a ride.

CHAPTER 6

Lester heard his cell phone ring several times during the early morning. This time when it rang, he picked it up to see who was calling. It was his partner, Jim Lee. Seeing he had missed three of his calls already, he decided he should answer.

"What's so important that you would wake me on a Saturday morning before six o'clock?" Lester asked.

"The police chief called a press conference for noon. He tried to call you, but you didn't answer," said Detective Lee.

"Damn, I hate press conferences."

"And the good part is the Chief said you and I are in charge of it, because he's going on vacation. His exact message was, *Tell Thornson that he has to have this mess wrapped up by noon. The mayor doesn't want to face Monday morning with a bunch of questions about an unsolved shooting. So come up with an answer today!*

"Jim, that sounded just like the chief. Since I last talked with you, have there been any new answers?" Lester asked.

"There was another shooting this morning, and it was also of a fifteen-year-old girl who was just turning sixteen. The Eleventh Precinct sent the report to the office. The shooting happened on Adeline Street."

Walking into the bathroom, Lester said in an angry tone. "Another shooting to have wrapped up by noon? Son of a bitch. I hope Jason has answers."

"Jason says there are more questions than solutions, Boss."

"Oh, because we have to face the press, I'm the boss?" Lester asked.

"You know I no speak so good English," Jim said with an exaggerated Chinese accent.

"Don't give me that crap; we all know you're the smart one," said Lester.

"So sorry, no understand."

"OK. So, I'll be at headquarters by eight o'clock. We'll have four hours to solve these two homicides, and then we can face the press."

"Sounds good, Boss," replied Detective Lee.

Lester opened his drawer on the bathroom vanity and pulled out a razor, shaving cream, comb, deodorant, toothbrush and paste. He then jumped into the shower and turned on the hot water. The blast of cold water shocked him awake, and then steaming hot water relaxed his tired muscles. It was a routine he enjoyed.

As the water ran across his muscular form, he considered the facts of the case. *How the hell am I going to solve this one?* He asked himself. He remembered the advice his dad gave him when he was studying to be a detective, *Just go with the facts, and the solution will present itself.* This is one case he would love to share with his dad, but he passed away two years ago. He was a great Detroit police officer during his time and inspired Lester to become a detective. His dad still inspires Lester to push for the truth.

After Lester dried off and finished his bathroom business, he checked the hall to make sure no one was there. He then streaked down the hall and into the bedroom. His wife was sitting in bed, and when her naked husband came through the doorway, she smiled.

"Sorry, dear, I have to take Amber with me to see Tianna this morning. But you look like you would be a pleasant distraction."

As Lester pulled up his dark black slacks, he smiled and said, "Sorry, dear, I have to be at headquarters by eight, because our wise Police Chief decided Jim and I will host a press conference at noon. He insists we have the school shooting and last night's shooting of a fifteen-year-old girl in the eleventh precinct solved by noon."

"Oh no. Not another shooting. What's happening to your city?"

"No, the real question is, what happened to our city? It isn't an additional problem because it's been with us forever. I call it the curse of Detroit. But somehow, I'll have an answer for the mayor. It won't be the correct answer, but we'll make it work."

Lester finished putting his tie on and then slid his muscular arms into the sleeves of his dark blue suit coat.

"I used to miss your patrol suit, but now I love seeing you in your detective uniform. You look nice, dear."

"Thank you," Lester said as he bent down and kissed his wife. "I'll let you know after the press conference if I can make it to the hospital."

"I will call Thelma and see if she needs me to bring anything. Also, I plan on picking up Clarence and giving him a ride."

"Great! Love you and see you later," Lester said as he stepped into the hall. He stopped at Amber's room and pushed the door open. Amber was still sleeping, so he bent down and whispered, "Love you, honey," as he kissed her forehead.

"I love you too, Daddy," she replied.

"You little sneak. You're awake."

"Yes, and I heard you and Mom talking. I can't wait to wish Tianna a happy birthday," she said.

"Well, I don't know if she'll even be aware you're there, Amber. She is in a coma, you know."

"Yes, but she'll know I'm there," she insisted.

Lester grabbed a bagel and made a mug of instant coffee. He sat down and checked the messages on his phone. There were over twenty missed calls. Some from the Police Chief, a few from Detective Lee, some from a news reporter he knew, and a slew of calls from numbers he didn't know. He decided not to return any of the calls. *It's Saturday. I shouldn't be working today, so why bother with these calls?*

* * *

Detective Thornson pulled his unmarked patrol car into his reserved space. As he walked toward the police headquarters, a small red-headed man ran up to him while holding his telephone microphone. It was Fredrick McDougall, a young city homicide reporter from The Detroit Free Press.

"Detective Thornson, how are your daughter and Tianna Gulliver doing? We hear she may die today?"

"No comment, Fredrick. You should know better than to wrangle a story out of me," Lester said.

"I know, Lester, but I care about the kids. And besides, I thought we had an understanding."

"We do. If you help me, I'll help you. Do you have anything for me?" asked Lester.

"Just things you may already know. You found a gun in the cemetery, and it was used to shoot both girls. Someone shot Tianna in the head, and the hospital told me her condition is critical. The mayor is eager to get this out of the news. And now there was another killing of a fifteen-year-old girl near the old State Fairgrounds. I also hear the gun was involved in the 1967 killing of a black fifteen-year-old girl. It sounds like you have a serial killer on your hands."

"Fredrick, you could get fired from your Free Press job because you don't have crap to report. Come to the press conference and learn something," said the Detective as he entered the building.

Fredrick stood at the door, looking downtrodden. He could count on Detective Thornson for come crumbs, but not today.

When Detective Thornson reached the Homicide unit, the other detectives were waiting around the round table. Leaning against the wall was Lt. Carl Ellington. He turned to Lester and said, "You're late, and how's your daughter?"

"She's home doing well, and the press is already on my ass with questions. That's why I'm late."

The lieutenant turned to the group and continued, "So, like I said.

DEADLY SIXTEEN

You guys will work miracles this morning because the mayor is in an uproar about these shootings. No excuses; he wants an answer for the press at noon. Let's get busy, men."

He turned, shook Lester's hand and whispered, "Do the best you can with this. We all know we can only do so much. At least we know it. It's just the mayor who's clueless."

Detective Thornson turned to his team and said, "How the hell does a Free Press reporter know the gun links back to the 1967 killing?"

"Sorry, boss, my bad. I called The Free Press for help in digging up information. I'm not sure, but I may have mentioned the gun," explained Jason.

"OK. Did you get any information?"

"Yes, I got the newspaper report about the killing. It matched the old records I dug up here. It was difficult to find the records. Since the move to the new headquarters, some records seem to have vanished. That's why I wanted to verify that I had all the facts."

"Well, Jason, you can give your report now. We need something here."

Jason opened his computer and lowered the lights. On the large screen, his desktop became visible. "Starting from the beginning, the shooting took place just north of the school entrance, and the shooter was behind this tree, in the Elmwood Cemetery. We found the gun, a Remington M40 Rifle. Tests confirmed it is the weapon used in the King School shooting. The ballistics matched the bullet found in the school exterior brick and the one taken out of Tianna's head wound. As you can see from this illustration, the gang members over here were not in-line with the girls. Therefore, they were not the target. The girls were. In fact, only Tianna was the target. Detective Thornson's daughter, Amber, was just in the way."

Jason stopped and took a sip of coffee. "The first shot hit Tianna in the back of the head. She turned, so the bullet went across the back, not into the skull. The second bullet hit Amber's upper arm, grazed the bone and then went into Tianna's skull. If it had not hit Amber first, it would have been a kill shot."

"You mean Amber could have saved Tianna's life?" asked Lester.

"Yes. That is if Tianna lives," said Jason. "When we checked the gun, we discovered it had been used to kill a fifteen-year-old girl, Amanda Carson. Amanda and her mother and father lived in the Brewster-Douglass projects. Dad worked at Dodge Main and Mom, at Hudson's downtown. The gun had three fingerprints on it, but there was never a match. We do not know what happened to the gun. As with a lot of evidence, it disappeared from the evidence room."

"Until now," said Detective Lee. "Have we tried to trace those old prints?"

"We have, but there have been no results so far," said Jason.

"Could it be the same person doing both shootings? Someone with a thing for shooting young girls?" asked one detective.

"If it is, the shooter would have to be in his or her sixties, and have steady nerves and good eyesight for a person who is old."

"Lee, what about the killing in the eleventh precinct? Are the shootings related to this case?" asked Detective Thornson.

"No. The shooter was the girl's uncle. He assaulted the girl last week, and she reported him to the police. He made bail, got drunk, and came after her. The girl's father shot the killer when he saw him shoot his daughter in their living room. Case closed... no charges against the father."

Lester sighed. "So, unless our shooter is sixty-something, we don't have a serial killing."

"Ann, did you go over all the video we collected at the scene?" asked Detective Lee.

The young assistant detective gathered her paperwork and said, "Yes, sir, we completed viewing everything. Other than a mystery car appearing on one security camera, a bunch of students and a lot of blood, we saw nothing that would help the investigation. Also, the interviews showed the gang had no involvement in the shooting. The shooter tried to kill Tianna."

Detective Thornson looked at his watch. He considered all that findings and said, "We have shit. That's what we have. Now, what am I to tell the press at noon?"

"The spin should be honesty. Tell them what we know, and what we don't know," suggested Detective Lee. "The mayor can't change facts, and we shouldn't lie about them either."

"We must keep digging. Is there a reason someone would want to kill Tianna? Can we find the 1967 shooter after all these years? Are these two shootings intertwined?" Lester asked. "We have other pressing crimes to solve, so I don't want everyone on this. Detective Lee and I will continue to investigate this one when we have time. Jason, if you can put some time on it, I would appreciate it."

The homicide detectives agreed on the goal and then dispersed. Jason asked Detective Thornson if he could speak with him in private. When the room was empty, Jason said, "I'm sorry about talking to The Free Press, but I would like to continue my investigation using their archive. It amazes me that the same gun is involved in two shootings that are forty-seven years apart, so similar, but with no kind of link."

"That's fine, Jason. You can keep digging. I wasn't upset about your leaking information about the gun. Besides, in an hour I'll be bleeding all over the media."

Jason laughed. "I hope it's not that bad, sir."

"It will be."

CHAPTER 7

Alice, Amber and Clarence kept driving around the parking garage at Children's Hospital looking for a parking spot. Since this was Saturday, there were many parking spaces close to the elevators already taken. Clarence kept saying he could walk the distance, but Alice insisted she would find a closer spot. As she made her third drive around, she spotted the perfect parking space.

"See, it takes a little persistence to get a good parking spot. It looks like this will be a good day, doesn't it?" she said.

"Yes, Mom. A great day. I had a dream last night, and Tianna said she was OK."

"Well, dear, remember that it was just a dream. Sometimes we become disappointed when life doesn't live up to the dream," said Alice.

Clarence chimed in, "Not today. Today we will get good news. My bones feel it, and so does my heart. Yep, a great day."

Once they made their way into Children's, the receptionist directed the group to Tianna's room on the third floor. Amber loved the colorful artwork on the hallway walls, and when she looked into the rooms, it looked like everyone was happy. Then she saw a room with a little girl who had sunken eyes that reminded her of the pictures she had seen of the German death camps.

"Mommy, is that girl going to die?"

"She may, Amber. They make it comfortable here for children, but some of them might die because they are beyond the doctors' ability to cure them. All we can do is pray that God will save them."

"I will," Amber whispered.

Once the group reached Tianna's room, the nurse told them to find a seat in the waiting room. The doctors were still in Tianna's room and would take a while to finish. Alice checked her phone for the time and to see if there were any messages. There were no messages, but she had several bars and free hospital internet, so keeping track of her husband's press conference wouldn't be a problem.

"Clarence, do you want coffee?" she asked.

"Yes, but let me get it. I have too much energy to just sit and wait," he said. "Amber, do you want anything?"

"Hot chocolate would be nice," she said.

Clarence checked and there was hot water and a small packet of cocoa, so he made that for Amber. As they waited, Clarence watched cartoons on the small television in the corner. Amber played with her iPhone, and Alice read a magazine about neuroscience. It made her feel smart when she understood some of it.

When Thelma walked into the room, no one noticed. She walked over to Amber and said, "Honey, I'm so glad you're doing well."

Amber jumped up and hugged Thelma. "Thank you. Is Tianna OK?"

"They haven't said yet. They kicked me out an hour ago, and I was down in the cafeteria having breakfast."

Clarence stood and approached his daughter-in-law. "Any word on how she's doing?"

"Dad, they worked on her all night. I would fall asleep while they were there, and a few hours later, they were still there. And they would only whisper to each other, and I know they didn't want me to hear. It's so damn frustrating. I ask for info and they say, *Nothing for you yet, sorry. Dr. Kohl will talk to you later this morning.* Then, like I said, they kicked me out. Something about having to do another MRI and an EEG."

"Don't worry, Thelma. I think it will be good news."

Every fifteen minutes, Thelma would walk down to the nurses' station to see if Tianna was back in her room. The nurse kept saying, "We'll have someone call for you when she comes back," but Thelma couldn't stand sitting and waiting. Being separated from her daughter was driving her crazy.

Clarence said, "Thelma, you're wearing out the carpet. Sit down and drink your coffee." As he finished his sentence, the nurse entered the room and said, "Thelma, you and your family can return to the room now. Dr. Kohl wants to talk to you."

"Oh, God," she gasped. Her nerves were getting to her. No matter how she told herself that everything would be fine, deep down she feared the unknown.

"Is everything OK?" she asked.

"I can't say. Please follow me," the nurse insisted.

Alice said, "Thelma, Amber and I can wait here."

"No! Please come in with me for moral support," insisted Thelma.

They entered Tianna's room, where Dr. Kohl and Dr. Carter stood next to her hospital bed. Dr. Kohl offered his hand to Thelma and Clarence. "Well, I'm sure you're eager to learn what's happening." He saw Amber and added, "You're Tianna's best friend. It looks like you have recovered nicely, and you are calmer than the last time I saw you."

"That's because I know everything will be OK," Amber said.

"Yes, I agree," said Dr. Kohl. "Dr. Carter, I know you are eager to let Tianna's family know how your experiment is working."

Dr. Carter had a huge grin glowing on his face. "Yes. Yes, I would love to explain what happened last night. I had expected slow but steady improvement. I thought this morning we would see a slight increase in your daughter's ability to breathe, and perhaps an improved heartbeat. Would you believe your daughter can now breathe on her own? I mean, it's unheard of. Your daughter can breathe unaided, and we no longer need to assist her heart."

Thelma was sitting with Clarence's comforting hand on her shoulder. She was crying, laughing and praising God. "Was it because of your nano-things?" she asked.

"Yes," Dr. Carter continued. "The scans we took today showed that the area damaged is almost back to normal. The damage is only barely visible. Like I said, we didn't expect such a rapid improvement. Your daughter is almost recovered. The only damage that is still apparent is paralysis in her legs. We are not sure about her ability to walk."

"When will Tianna come out of the coma?" asked Clarence.

Dr. Carter smiled and said, "It could take up to a week. We need to bring her out slowly. She had a tremendous trauma to her system, and now that her vitals are improving. She will recover while in a coma."

Alice and Amber were staying back, so they wouldn't interfere in the conversation. But Alice had to ask, "Will she remember everything that happened?"

"That we don't know. I know from the EEG that her brain is active. In fact, it is more active than most people in a conscious state. We aren't sure why, but it's not something to fear. I think it's important that you talk to her. In the state she's in, she will know you are there. Talk to her, hold her hand, and let her know you are there for her. That way, as we bring her out of the coma, she will remain calm."

Clarence smiled. "I can give her my famous history lessons. She always enjoyed hearing about Detroit's history."

"Great," agreed Dr. Carter. "And Amber, if you could bring some of her friends in to talk, that would help. She will want you to talk to her, being that you are her best friend."

"Mom, can I stop Monday after school?" Amber asked.

"Yes. We can set up a schedule so that everyone will be here at a set time."

There was a magical feeling in the hospital room. Everyone was talking back and forth, laughing, and making plans for their time with Tianna.

Dr. Carter cleared his voice for attention. "Remember, she's not out of the woods. She may not walk, and we are not positive that there hasn't been other brain damage. But it looks positive, and I feel

Tianna will have a complete recovery. With that said, Dr. Kohl has a press conference to attend, and I have work to get done this morning in Ann Arbor."

The two exited the room as Tianna's family continued their celebration.

* * *

The party in Tianna's room continued for over an hour. Each one of the group took turns holding Tianna's hand and talking to her.

When it was Amber's turn, she inched up to the bed, took Tianna's hand and with tears in her eyes said, "I was so afraid you would die, Tianna. It was the most awful thing I have ever seen. But now I know you will be OK. So, did you get the iPhone for your birthday? Remember when I told you if you left enough hints, they would break down and buy one for you? I texted Eddie, and he's praying you get well. God answered all our prayers. Yes, I know. You could answer some of Eddie's prayers."

Amber laughed and looked at Tianna's mother. "Sorry, Mrs. Gulliver. It's an inside joke."

She continued to talk to her friend until the nurse came into the room and said, "Sorry, honey, there are things I need to do, so you will all have to wait in the hall or the waiting room until I'm done."

Alice said, "Amber and I will go down to the waiting room. There's a television there, and my husband should have his press conference in less than half an hour."

Clarence chimed in, "I want to see that, too. You coming, Thelma? That's where Dr. Kohl was heading. It should be interesting. I hope they found the creep who did this to our girls."

Thelma agreed. She told the nurse that if there were any changes to Tianna's condition, she would be in the waiting room.

"Mrs. Gulliver, I know you're afraid that things will fall apart or go downhill. Your daughter is getting better every minute. You don't have to fear for her. She's our miracle, and we love her like she were our own. Thelma, it's these miracles that make our jobs so fulfilling."

"Thank you for making me feel better. I'm going with my friends now, and I'll be back later."

"You do that, and I'll take care of Tianna."

Clarence asked at the nurses' station for a remote control so he could change the channel on the television in the waiting room. At first, the nurse didn't think they should change the channel. Then, when she heard why, she brought in the remote and changed it herself. Soon there were several nurses in the room, and others were standing in the doorway.

It was the noon report on Channel 7 WXYZ. The newscaster announced that the press conference was just starting and then cut to a live report from the press room at Police Headquarters.

"Look, it's Daddy," said Amber.

Detective Lester Thornson tapped the mike to make sure it was on and said, "There will be a few brief comments we need to make before we take your questions. As you know, there was a shooting yesterday morning at King High School. Two fifteen-year-old girls suffered gunshot wounds. My daughter was one victim. She is now home and has recovered. Her young friend did not fare so well. As of last night, she was in critical condition. I would like to introduce Dr. Kohl from Children's Medical Center. Dr. Kohl, you have the microphone."

The doctor stepped up and began, "When the young victim, Tianna Gulliver, came to the emergency room, she was almost dead. It was the fast thinking of Mr. Ewald, a teacher at King High, that saved her life. I understand he was a medic in Iraq, and his training came into play. The girl suffered two bullet wounds in the back of her head. Her injuries made it impossible to breathe on her own. Under the circumstances, we felt she had only a few days to live."

The reporters gasped and typed into their electronic devices as Dr. Kohl continued, "Ann Arbor's Nano-Technology Department, supervised by Dr. Jerome Carter, was called in because they offered an experimental procedure using nanoparticles. It was a miracle recovery because the treatment last night had saved the young girl. She is no longer listed as being in critical condition, and we expect a full recovery."

Lester stepped forward and said, "Thank you, Dr. Kohl; we are pleased Tianna Gulliver is recovering. During our investigation of this shooting, there was talk that it was gang related. All the evidence leads us to the conclusion that it was not. Someone deliberately shot these two girls. We are searching for the shooter, and we are looking for a motive. Because this is not a homicide, our department will limit its time on the investigation. Are there questions?"

The reporters all spoke at the same time.

"One at a time," said Lester. He pointed at the WXYZ reporter.

"Sir, there was another shooting south of the old State Fairground. It is like this shooting. Could this be a serial shooting?"

"No! The shooter in the eleventh precinct was a family member. There is no relation to the King School shooting because the killer had a valid alibi for that time period. Next question."

Lester pointed to a Free Press reporter who he knew and said, "Jimmy, your question?"

"Detective Thornson, I understand the weapon linked to the 1967 killing of a young black girl who was just turning sixteen. I also understand that the gun was in the custody of the Detroit Police Department. Are these two shootings related, and how could this gun have gotten out of the Department's evidence room?"

"Because the shooter would now be an old man, I'm sure he isn't the serial killer. If he is, why did he wait so long time for his second shooting, because we have no other cases with the same M.O. As for the gun, I don't know what happened. We think the gun was stolen or lost during the move into the new headquarters."

A reporter from The Oakland Press asked, "Detective, you said will not investigate this case as a homicide. Does that mean it will be like so many shootings that go uninvestigated?"

"We are short handed, as you know. Our team investigates every case, but we have to prioritize. I will continue to look for the shooter, to get him or her off the streets. But it will not be a top priority."

"Then, like so many shootings, it will just be unsolved?" another reporter asked.

"Yes."

"I thank you, but our time is up," said Detective Thornson as he stepped away from the microphone. The reporters tried to follow him with questions, but he slipped into another room and shut the door.

The newscaster concluded, "That was Detective Lester Thornson, of the Detroit Police Department. We now return to the station."

Clarence turned the television off, and the nurses returned to their duties. He put his hand on Alice's and said, "Your husband did a good job; it's just too bad they don't have more evidence. I hate to see crimes like this go unsolved in our city."

"So does he, Clarence. I know Lester, and he won't let this case get cold. He'll be working on it even if he's the only one investigating."

"If he needs help, you tell him to call me," he said with a laugh. "Can we get back to our little girl now?"

The nurse walked through the doorway and smiled. "Yes, Clarence, I'm done, and you can see her again. Lord, every minute she is getting stronger. Her blood pressure is perfect. She has good oxygen levels and a strong heartbeat. It's like God pulled her through this time. Dr. Carter said he wouldn't need to use more nanoparticles unless she goes into a decline this morning, so it looks like they are done with the treatments."

CHAPTER 8

It was Tianna's birthday today, so Amber suggested they organize a party for her.

She said, "I have my gift for her, and I brought Mom and Dad's with me too."

"I have her gifts in the car," said Thelma. "But I'm not sure about a party. What kind of party do you have when the party girl can't open her own gifts?"

"We can open them for her," said Amber. "She'll know it's a party by our voices."

Sienna Williams, Tianna's afternoon nurse, was standing in the doorway listening to the discussion. She said, "I'll order cake and ice cream, and I know where there are decorations. We have them for the kids. This sounds like it will be fun. We love parties."

She turned and bumped into Detective Thornson. "Were you the guy on television an hour ago?" she asked.

"Yes, but what did I hear about a party?" he asked.

Alice stood and hugged him. "We're having Tianna's birthday party. Sienna, the nurse, is ordering cake, ice cream, and some party decorations. And yes, you are invited," she said and then gave him a quick kiss.

"Great idea. I take it you all saw the news conference?" he asked.

Clarence said, "Yes, but it's too bad you didn't catch the creep. Don't you have any idea who it was? I mean, there must have been a reason someone would shoot our Tianna."

"Not a clue. We will continue to dig for evidence and leads, though. But we can talk about that later. I'm just so happy that Tianna is recovering. I afraid for her," he said. Lester thought how much better it was that they were celebrating Tianna's birthday and not preparing for her funeral. He hated funerals, especially when they were for children.

"We were all afraid for her," said Thelma. "But my little girl will be fine. Thank God."

Amber said, "I was afraid at first, but I knew she was better."

"Honey, you have to be careful. I know you think Tianna came to you in your dreams, but if you tell everyone you were chatting with her, they might think you need help. Do you need help?" asked Alice.

"No, Mom. It was just such a vivid dream." Amber walked over to Tianna and took her hand. In her mind, she told her, *Happy birthday, Tianna.... Yes, we're having a party for you.... Just like you asked me to have.* She knew Tianna could hear her, or at least she felt she could. The two girls had been this way since they first met. Amber would say something, and Tianna would complete her thought. It was like they were on the same wavelength. As Grandpa Gulliver would say, *Two peas in a pod*, whatever that meant.

Sienna brought in the decorations. They included two signs that said *HAPPY BIRTHDAY*, some streamers for the door, and a bunch of balloons.

As Thelma and Alice put up the signs, a girl from the kitchen brought in a cart of cake and ice cream. It was a party. By the time they had sung the songs and opened the gifts, everyone felt joyful and exhausted.

Alice asked Thelma if she wanted to go home for a while. "Friend, we need to set up a schedule. The doctor wants us to talk to Tianna, so you shouldn't have to be here around the clock. She's safe, Thelma! You don't have to be here every minute."

"I know, Alice, but it's hard to leave my little girl here alone," sighed Thelma.

"She won't be alone. Let's set a schedule now. We can take turns and make sure someone is here."

The nurse suggested that they allow Tianna time to rest between ten at night until nine in the morning. "She will need that quiet time to let her mind rest. And besides, we are always here. Should we need to get a hold of you, Thelma, we will call."

Thelma relented. She knew Tianna was safe now, and she needed some rest. "That sounds good, and I need rest, and I also need a shower."

Alice laughed, "We didn't want to hurt your feelings, so we didn't mention it."

"Mom, that's not nice," laughed Amber. "Mom's just kidding, Mrs. Gulliver."

"I know, and I love you for that, Alice," she said as she hugged her. "Now, who stays here, and who goes home?"

Lester took his telephone out and said, "It's five thirty now, so we have four and a half hours until lights out. I can stay for that time, but I won't get a lot of time during the week, and I need quiet time myself. Alice, you can drive Amber home?"

"Good," said Clarence, "I can take the bus to the hospital at nine in the morning and stay until one. Then who?"

Alice said, "That would be great, Clarence. Amber and I could be here during the afternoon and stay until six o'clock, and Thelma, you could spend the evening with your daughter. That way you will get a day's rest, and we have one complete day planned."

Thelma frowned. "Alice. I don't know if I can stay away all day."

"No problem, Thelma. If you stop in during the afternoon, we can take turns snacking in the cafeteria," suggested Alice.

* * *

As everyone said their "goodbyes" and left Tianna's hospital room, Alice hugged her husband and said, "Are you sure you don't want me to stay this evening?"

"No, I need to do this. Dr. Kohl told me it would be good for the soul to talk to Tianna. God knows I carry a lot of my job around as guilt and whatnot, but this case takes the cake. Our daughter and her best friend...... I need time to think about it, and the best way to think sometimes is to talk. Even if the listener can't talk back.... Do you understand, honey?"

Tears were welling in Alice's eyes. She loved her husband because he was hard as nails on the outside, and a teddy bear inside. "Yes, I understand."

She kissed him again and stepped out of the room. Amber was at the nurses' station, laughing about something. Alice called her, and she came.

"Mom, should I become a nurse?" she asked.

"Why do you ask?"

"They have such a loving job. They take care of people when they need it the most."

Alice was proud of her daughter and said, "You can be whatever you want to be, Amber. Just make sure it's what you want, because it's hard to change your mind about something that serious, and you change your mind every day. Let's go, honey. We have to get home."

Lester kissed his wife and then his daughter. "See you around ten o'clock," he said. Watching his pride and joy walk down to the elevators, Lester turned back into the hospital room. The scene reminded him of the times he visited his mom and dad when they were in the hospital. His mother died when he was eleven, and his dad died last fall. The memories were still fresh in his mind, and today, they still hurt.

"I guess I'm your speaker for the evening, so I hope you don't tire of hearing me ramble on like Amber does sometimes. Anyway, where do I begin?" He pulled up a chair and sat next to the hospital bed as close as he could. He didn't want to get tangled in the wires and tubes, but he wanted to hold her hand. Dr. Kohl told him that hearing family voices and having tactile stimulation, such as the touch of a hand, would help ease her unconscious anxiety. Or at least that is what they hoped would happen.

The detective cleared his throat. "OK. Tianna, I'm sorry this happened. I'm sorry we haven't caught the person who shot you. I wish I knew why someone would want you dead. Is there something I should know? No, I didn't think I would get an answer to that one."

Lester felt uneasy. It was difficult to communicate without thinking like a detective, and he felt guilty for not solving the case. "I want you to know I won't give up. I'll hunt for the shooter until I solve this. You know, you could be dead, and Amber could be dead. It's the one situation I know I could never handle. Parents aren't supposed to see their children die. We're supposed to see them grow up, have families of their own, so we can retire as babysitters."

Sienna, the nurse, came in to check the reading on the monitors. She smiled at Lester and said, "Kind of hard to talk to someone who can't talk back, isn't it?"

"Sure is. I'm used to talking to people who yell back at me, cuss me out, and then call me all kinds of names. But it feels good being here. I know she understands what we're trying to do. Somehow, I can feel it."

"That's funny, Sir. All the nurses love Tianna because they can feel her spirit talking to us. She is special. I hope that doesn't sound corny," she said.

"Not at all. Tianna has a powerful spirit. She can walk into a room and have everyone swoon over her. But she doesn't use it to lord over people. She uses it to make friends with everyone. That's why it's so perplexing that someone would want to kill her," Lester said.

"I don't know; I'm not a detective. I'm just a nurse, but I know that love can sometimes turn into hate. And hate can turn into violence," Sienna said, as she checked Tianna's I.V. line. "Everything is fine here. I'm going off duty in fifteen minutes. The night nurse is Martha. She can help if you need anything."

"Can she make me a better speaker? I seem to have trouble figuring out what to say to Tianna."

"No, but I think you're doing fine. More important than what you say is that you're saying it. She needs to know you're here, and that you care. I'm sure she knows that."

"Thanks, Sienna. Your parents must be proud of you."

"They are, Sir. They are," Sienna said as she walked out of the room.

Lester told Tianna all about the press conference. He told her what evidence his team had found and that the gun was the same one used in the 1967 shooting of a young girl, who was also just turning sixteen. His voice grew a little angry when he talked about the violence he sees every day he works homicide, and softer when he talked about how proud he was of his daughter and his wife.

After he had talked for two hours straight, he felt almost relieved. It was comforting being here with Tianna. Somehow, it was as if she were making him feel better. *Yes,* he thought, *this young girl is special.*

The night nurse wasn't as friendly as Sienna. She said she had not been in Tianna's room before, but she heard the other nurses talk about her, like she was a princess. She didn't appear to have bad feelings toward Tianna. It was more of a sense of wonder.

"I think they are happy she made it through the night. It was a miracle she survived," Lester said.

"Yes, it was. Sienna said it was touch and go until Dr. Carter's team did their magic," she said.

"It was magic. I still don't understand it."

"I'm not sure what they did. Someone said it was nanoparticles. I heard about them, but I didn't know they were using them yet."

"It was experimental, and they did the job," Lester said.

The nurse finished her duties and left the room. Lester considered each nurse's outlook. The day nurse was uplifting, and this nurse is subdued. *Odd,* he thought. *Kind of like the homicide department. Some detectives have an upbeat outlook, while other guys are about to give up the battle.*

When ten o'clock arrived, Lester recalled he hadn't thought he could talk for so many hours, but he found himself with words still unsaid. *Few... but some.*

As he left the hospital, he called his wife, Alice. "Hi honey," he said. "I'm leaving now. Do you want me to pick anything up on my way home?"

Alice said that she and Amber went shopping, so he could come home. She reminded him they were going to church in the morning, and he volunteered to teach Sunday school.

"Yes, I remember," he lied. "I think I know what I'll talk about."

"God's miracles?" she asked.

"You got it, honey."

CHAPTER 9

After a long night of rest, both Clarence and Thelma were eager to get on with their day. Over a hot breakfast, Thelma suggested driving Clarence to the hospital for his visit with Tianna, but he insisted he would take the bus.

"You need to go to church and thank everyone for their prayers. I'll be fine, Thelma," he said.

"Fine, we'll do it your way, Dad," she relented.

After breakfast, Thelma called Alice and Lester to see if they would go to church. The two families were members of Bethel New Harmony Baptist Church on Mt. Elliott. Situated only a few blocks from their homes, it was their neighborhood church. The church held both happy and sad memories; it was where she married her husband and buried him.

"Lester, are you and Alice going to church this morning? I figured you were. If you're driving, I wouldn't mind a lift. Dad is heading to the hospital to see Tianna, and I can be ready in about an hour or whenever you want. Great, I'll see you then."

It was a strange feeling getting ready for church in an empty house. Her home is always so alive with Tianna and Clarence chattering and Amber often over to visit. Now, it's just street noise, and the creaking of the old house. Thelma went upstairs and slipped into the shower. The warmth of the water felt heavenly. She almost forgot all of her problems until the hot water gave way to an icy blast.

She dried off and began making herself presentable. Church was the one day when her friends and neighbors put on their Sunday best. Some came as they were, but it was so much fun to dress up. She picked the red suit she reserves for special occasions and matched it with black patent leather shoes and purse. The pearls her husband gave her on their second anniversary and the large silver earrings Tianna gave her for Christmas made the look complete. *Looking good*, she told herself as she went downstairs to wait for Alice and Lester.

Lester pulled his car into the driveway, and before he could get out, Thelma was walking down the steps. He got out, dressed in a black vest and suit, white shirt, a metallic gold tie and matching silk pocket square.

Opening the back door of the car, he said, "Thelma, you look like you will rock the church this morning."

"I am! The Lord gave me back my daughter, and I will give Him the loudest thank you I can," she said.

"Amen! We all are giving thanks today."

As the group walked into the old red church, Rev. James and his family were greeting the parishioners. His face became a beam of light when he saw Amber, her parents and Thelma walking up the steps.

"God bless us all. Thelma, tell me that Tianna is recovering. She must be for you to be here with us, in that beautiful red dress, wearing a smile that could warm the entire church."

"Yes, Rev. James, she is out of the woods. Her grandfather, Clarence, is with her this morning, and we want to give our thanks to God and our church family for all of their prayers," said Thelma.

"And Lester, you're working with the children in Bible school this morning?" the Reverend asked.

"Yes, Rev. James," said Lester. "I always look forward to the days I can share with the young ones."

Amber wore a flowing black skirt with a red blouse and a short black jacket. Reverend James kneeled down to her level and said, "We are all so proud of you, Amber. You have faced evil, and yet you are strong in the Lord. Bless you for your strength and courage."

* * *

Since giving up driving two years ago, Clarence has enjoyed the busses of Detroit. The only thing he doesn't like is waiting for the bus when it's cold, but today the weather is moderate for November. Wearing a light winter jacket, he wasn't cold today, but he remembered last winter when the temperatures stayed below zero until well into March. And the snow? *Unreal,* he thought. *There was more snow than I can remember ever falling on my city.*

From home, he walked to the corner of Mt. Elliott and headed north to Mack Avenue. He got on the bus at stop 31 and stayed on Mack until it reached Beaubien, where he departed and walked north to Children's Hospital. He spent eleven minutes walking and eleven minutes on the bus.

Feeling a little winded when he finally reached Tianna's hospital room, hand talked to the nurses, who relayed good news about her recovery.

"We talked to your daughter a while ago. Everything is going well, Clarence. Tianna is now off life support, and Dr. Kohl plans to bring her out of the induced coma in three days. She might even go home by next weekend," the nurse said.

"That's amazing. I expected I'd be riding the bus here a lot more than a week. I thank you very much, and now I will talk to my granddaughter."

"Enjoy yourself, Sir. She is a wonderful young woman. Somehow, she makes all the nurses love her, and we have never even spoken to her," the nurse added.

"She's like that. She has always exuded love," Clarence said as he started down the hall to Tianna's room.

It set him back when he saw her again, lying so still in the hospital bed, with tubes from her arm and neck, and wires connected to the various monitors. It reminded him she still had not fully recovered. The good news of yesterday put everyone in a state of euphoria, but this is reality. Seeing her like this brought that back home for him.

"Well, honey, Grandpa's here with your Sunday morning history lesson. I hope you're ready to learn," he said as he patted her hand and pulled the seat closer to the bed.

"Your mom and the Thornson family are in church this morning. I know you would rather be there than here, but life is what it is. Did I ever tell you about the first African American church in Detroit? Well, even if I did, that's where we will start today. In church."

"In the mid-1700s there were few black people living in the Detroit area. Some of them were free black and one or two were slaves. The French, who ruled Detroit back then, took a census in 1750 and recorded thirty-three enslaved Africans and Indians, but they didn't say how many of each."

"On July 13, 1787, the young United States enacted the Northwest Ordinance, which prohibited slavery in the Northwest Territories, which included the Great Lakes area. This would later prove crucial in making Michigan a safe place for African Americans. However, the rule was tested several times in Michigan courts. One incident was when a black couple's owner set them free when he died, but he gave the black couple's children to his brother. The couple, Peter and Hannah Denison, were working for Elijah Brush, a wealthy land-owner. They named Brush Street in his honor. Mr. Brush told the Denisons to sue for the return of their children because it was illegal to enslave people in Michigan. Judge Augustus B. Woodward ruled that the Michigan Territory had no obligation to return slaves freed by establishing residency in Canada, even if they then came back to Michigan at a later date."

"Because of this ruling, Michigan became the ending point of what would become known as the Underground Railroad. It wasn't a railroad, but a secret route that runaway slaves could take from the South to escape slavery and move across the Detroit River to live in Canada." Clarence cleared his throat and took a sip of coffee.

"So, Tianna, that brings us up to the early eighteen hundreds as more free African families settled on the eastside of Detroit. In 1825, there were 67 African Americans in Detroit. That number doubled by 1830 when the total population of Detroit was 2,222 people. In 1837, Michigan became a state, and its constitution prohibited slavery. However, that didn't mean that African Americans had the same rights as their white counterparts."

"Since it's Sunday, Tianna, I want you to know the first Blacks in Detroit attended the First Baptist Church. They were free to attend the church, but they could not sit on the main floor, which was reserved for white parishioners."

"Several African American members demanded an end to this segregation, and thirteen families left the church and formed their own Colored American Baptist Church, which they later called the Second Baptist Church. They located the new church on Monroe Street just north of East Lafayette Street."

"These African-Americans worked for the freedom of all blacks in America. They held meetings to fight slavery in the South and segregation in the North. Their biggest adventure was their participation in the smuggling of slaves from the South into Canada. The Underground Railroad brought slaves north, and when they reached Detroit, many of them hid in their church basement until they could cross the river at night. Bounty hunters would try to catch the runaway slaves, and it was always a risk to the safety of the church members. Faith in the Lord and a strong desire to set their brothers free gave them the strength to overcome their fear of being caught. Yes, Tianna, freedom is never free. We must work and fight for it."

* * *

Reverend James stood in front of the congregation singing along with the choir. It was a rousing rendition of *Down Through the Years* that ended with everyone singing and clapping their hands.

"Brothers and Sisters it has been a long ride, *down through the years*. We have faced sadness and joy, poverty and wealth, weakness and power. And through all our tribulations, we have walked hand in hand with the Lord, our Savior."

"Amen!" came a call from the congregation.

"We let the Lord be our shepherd, and we open our hearts and let his forgiving words comfort our fears. And now, we celebrate the power of our prayers to change the lives of those we love."

"Amen, Reverend James," cried Lester.

"*Down Through The Years...* since our brothers and sisters first stepped foot in Detroit, almost three hundred years ago, we have been in pursuit of God and freedom. Freedom for ourselves and our brothers from the South, whom we guided along the Underground Railroad to a promised land. We have found freedom from slavery, and we have found the Lord who gives us the strength to continue through difficult times. But freedom cannot protect us from evil. Our daughters, Tianna and Amber, have faced the evil within our community. I ask you, brothers and sisters, what kind of evil targets the lives of our children, and sows the seeds of drug addiction to our young ones? It is a cancer we must ask God to cure. But sometimes the Lord asks that we should heal ourselves. We must seek solutions through God and our community to fight this evil. We may be the victims, but we, with the Lord's help, are also the solution."

"Amen," cried the congregation.

"Let us pray," said Rev. James. "Lord, thank you for the strength you give us every day to battle the evil surrounding us. We thank you for the bonds of love that are our family and our community. We come to you, Jesus, because you are our salvation. With love and courage, we will overcome the obstacles of life. Lord, thank you for giving us back our loving daughter, Tianna. Let her continued recovery be an inspiration to us all. For we too can recover from the despair that can sometimes overwhelm us. Amen."

"Amen..." repeated the congregation as the choir broke into the hymn *Let the Church Say Amen*.

* * *

Clarence stood up to keep his legs from cramping. He walked to the window and looked out toward Harper Hospital, built in 1863 to care for wounded Civil War soldiers coming home from the war, wounded and broken. The hospital later joined Wayne State College to form a teaching hospital, and today it's one of the oldest U.S. medical teaching institutions. Clarence reflected on how he had started college at Wayne State in 1966 and graduated with a doctorate in history in 1974. He continued teaching at Wayne State until his retirement several years ago.

"Tianna, did you know there were once thousands of Indians living in this area? Yes, you do, since I've told you these stories so many times. But I'll repeat myself one more time."

Walking back to Tianna's bed, he took her hand and said, "Your grandmother was part Huron Indian, French, and African American. I used to tell her she was the ultimate melting pot, just like America itself. When Grandma's French ancestors came to the New World, they started a settlement in what is now Canada, near Montreal. They came looking for animal fur. The fur was precious in France, and many voyagers came to the New World to make their fortunes trapping these animals. When they got here, they found Indian clans throughout the area. Over two hundred thousand Indians once lived in this area in the early years."

"Sometime between 1534 and 1543, Jacques Cartier, the French explorer, found the Huron Indians, an Iroquoian tribe comprising four groups living around Lake Simcoe in the Georgian Bay area. These clans, known as the Bear, Cord, Rock, and Deer, lived in the St. Lawrence Valley for two hundred years. The Iroquois Indians, who live to the south, drove them out of the area," Clarence said. He stood and again walked to the window.

"The different clans could communicate with each other because they shared a common root language of the Algonquian. They also shared the warrior instinct and waged many wars against their enemies. The French and British used this warrior trait against the Indians in the 1700s by convincing them to help fight against other clans to aid in their fight."

"By the 1650s, the number of Indians had dropped by one half. Many died in battle, while even more died because of the diseases that the white man brought into their new world. Diseases that the Indians had no defense against."

As Clarence told his story, two nurses stood in the doorway. They listened with interest. He then told Tianna, "The Huron Indians trapped beavers, a prized fur. They became friends to the French and helped teach them how to survive in the new world. The Hurons hunted beaver skins and traded for things the French brought from Europe. Things like knives, guns, tobacco, and tools, which they couldn't make themselves. Many of the French explorers were Catholic priests known as Jesuits. These preachers and missionaries brought the word of Jesus to the Indians. They didn't look down at them as lesser humans, and some Frenchmen even took female Indians as their wives."

"Today, some think the Indians were savages. Perhaps in war they were, but they lived in homes built like large bark huts. In their villages, they had vast fields of corn and other vegetables, and they were excellent hunters. Living by rules, they considered it wrong to steal, murder, maim, or commit adultery. They removed those found guilty and treated them as outlaws."

"So you see, Tianna, your grandmother and you have a rich background. The French and the Indians are an important foundation of the history of Detroit. They suffered like all of us today, but they worked hard, loved their families and community, and they loved the Lord Jesus. Like our community, today they would attend church. And, like your dad, Joe, they went to war to protect their way of life. Yes, they were just like us."

One nurse listening to Clarence's story said, "Amen. You make our history so rich. You should be teaching."

Clarence laughed. "I used to teach at Wayne State University, but they decided I was too old and needed to retire."

"Well, it's their loss," the nurse said. "I hate to interrupt, but I have work to do, and I need you to step out for a while. It will take over one hour. We have another MRI and E.E.G. to do."

"OK. I'm sure Tianna grows tired of my lectures, anyway. I'll get a bite of lunch at the cafeteria. It's almost noon, and I had a very early breakfast. Besides, my legs are stiff and need exercise. It's hell getting old."

"Old? You're just getting started, Sir," the nurse said as she adjusted Tianna's wires and tubes.

CHAPTER 10

A lice knew her best friend, Thelma, could not stay home on a beautiful November Sunday afternoon while Tianna was in the hospital. As they walked out of the church, Alice asked, "Do you want to come with us to the hospital after lunch? I know it's killing you to be away from her."

A look of joy raced across Thelma's face. "Oh, God yes!" she sighed. "I'll tell you what, we can both drive and then I'll come home and make dinner for Clarence around five, before I return for the evening."

"That sounds good. Have you called to see how she is doing?"

Thelma replied, "Every hour since I left the hospital. And she's doing great. The nurses are taking her for more MRI tests now. They said Clarence has been giving her a rousing history lesson, but now he's having lunch."

Lester turned and said, "And that's what we should do. I'll bring the car around and we can head to the IHOP on Jefferson for brunch."

Amber laughed and said, "That's what I was thinking, Dad. How did you know I was hungry?"

"I won't answer that. I'll just get the car," laughed Lester.

After a quick lunch and a trip back home, Thelma was on the road, followed by Alice and Amber. There wasn't a lot of traffic; so they pulled up to the Children's Hospital parking ramp by one o'clock. The trio had changed from their Sunday best and now wore comfortable clothes.

As they walked out of the elevator, they saw Clarence walking toward the nurses' station.

"Dad, we're here," said Thelma. "How is Tianna?"

"She was doing well. I went to the cafeteria, so I don't know the results of the tests yet," he said. "You girls look nice and sporty. Are we going to a marathon today?"

"Mom suggested wearing something comfortable. I thought our church clothes would be better, but that's OK. At least we're here."

"You'll thank me after you've sat around for four hours, Amber," said Alice.

"Perhaps, but when can we see, Tianna? I have a bunch of news to tell her."

Thelma had stepped up to the nurses' station and was talking to the head nurse about her daughter.

The nurse said, "I can't tell you what the tests say, since they don't tell me that, but Dr. Kohl is in the building and he should be here in less than an hour. I'll call him and inform him you are here."

"That would be great. Can we see my daughter now?" Thelma asked.

"You sure can, but I suggest you try to take turns. You can all go in, but only two or three of you should stay for any period. There just isn't enough room for the nurses to do their jobs."

"I understand," said Thelma. "Clarence will head home soon, so there will only be three of us this afternoon. And my friend will try to convince me to go home for a nap too. It's my turn to stay with Tianna this evening."

Everyone talked to Tianna at the same time. Clarence said, "Ladies, I will catch my bus, and I suggest you take turns and be nice. Tianna had a long history lesson, and her mind is full of beautiful historical images. If you mess that up, you must deal with me," he said with a chuckle.

He kissed Tianna's forehead and hugged Thelma. "No, I don't need a ride home," he said, without her having to ask.

"OK. Be careful, and I'll be home around four with dinner."

"If you want to stay, you can, Thelma. I know how to cook, you know."

"I'll call and let you know what I'm doing," Thelma said.

Clarence walked out and turned back. He loved his family and friends, and now he felt everything would have a positive result. *It's strange*, he thought. *One minute your world is falling apart at the seams, and the next, it couldn't be better.* Clarence had always could sense when trouble was at hand. Some would call it intuition. He called it... his gut feelings.

After Clarence left, Alice, Amber and Thelma took turns telling Tianna what was happening in their lives. Then Dr. Kohl walked into the hospital room. Thelma jumped out of her seat and asked, "What's the word, Dr. Kohl? Is everything going well, or are there some additional problems?"

"You worry a lot, don't you?"

"Yes, but I am a mother," responded Thelma.

"Well, don't worry. It looks like our miracle is permanent. The MRI shows that the internal injury has healed. There will be weakness in her legs, but there is no permanent damage, and she will just need therapy to help her walk. The bullet almost severed the nerves connecting her spinal column, but the nanoparticles did their job," he said as he picked up Tianna's hand. "We never expected this much success when we took the gamble to use this new treatment. It is a miracle," he said.

"I can also confirm her brain activity is back to normal. After the procedure, there was a tremendous spike in activity. We thought it was because of the trauma she suffered, but now it's back to normal. I would guess that your conversations with her have helped her relax. So keep it up, and I'll talk to you on Monday. Tianna might be home before next weekend."

* * *

When Dr. Kohl left the girls alone with Tianna, they each took turns discussing a variety of subjects, but Amber seemed to hold something back.

"Honey," said Alice, "is there something you want to say to Tianna alone?"

"Wow, Mom, you're a mind reader too. Yes, if you and Mrs. Gulliver don't mind, I had things I wanted to tell Tianna that are personal."

Thelma reached over and hugged Amber. "We understand. You two are best friends. We can get coffee. How's that sound to you, Best Friend?"

"Sounds great," Alice said. She hugged her daughter and added, "We'll give you a half hour. Is that enough time?"

"Yes, thank you, Mom."

When the coast was clear, Amber took Tianna's hand and started, "Tianna, I have news. I've been talking to everyone at school. They keep calling and texting me about what happened. No one knows who shot us, but Eddie is trying to find out. He wants to impress you, even if he can't talk to you. You know he has genuine problems. He's like that guy on The Big Bang Show, you know, the Indian guy. Just can't talk to girls... except he can talk to me. So what does that say about me? Oh God. Am I like a guy to him? No... No! It's just that he doesn't have a thing for me. It's only you he can't talk to."

"Anyway, Eddie is asking around to see if someone hates us for some stupid reason. Did you piss-off someone? You didn't tell a guy to get lost, did you? You know one of those gang members? I didn't think so. You are the only girl I know who can insult a guy and tell him to get lost and make him like you even more. You got that magic. Everyone likes Tianna. Everyone except the guy who shot us."

"I heard Dad talking to his partner, and my Dad said the shooter may still want to kill you. If so, then we have to be careful. I almost lost you once; I will not let that happen again."

Amber stopped and watched a young girl walk past the door. She was struggling to walk as she pushed her I.V. stand along, and she looked like she had had her head shaved. There were white bandages wrapped around the top of her head. *Damn*, Amber thought. *I'm sure glad that isn't me.*

Then she thought about Tianna's wound and how bandages covered her head. "Tianna. Did they cut your beautiful black hair off? Oh My God! I bet they did. You will look so hot with your head shaved. I might just have to get mine done to match it. Wouldn't that be hot?"

Amber laughed. "I know, Tianna. I understand. But it would be my way of showing how much I love you. You know, when I first saw you across the backyard ten years ago, I felt like I knew you. It was like we had been best friends forever. You know, for all time."

"Oh, the reason I wanted to get Mom out was to let you know Eddie will come over after school tomorrow. He says perhaps if he talks to you, when you can't talk to him, he can get over not being able to talk to you. Yes! It's crazy! But he is such a sweet guy. And he will be someone important. I can tell because he's smart and ambitious. He'll be a doctor or something. And that's what you need. A doctor to take care of you for the rest of your life."

Amber couldn't stop laughing. "He'd be able to keep you in stitches your entire married life. Isn't that a funny play on words because he's got a great sense of humor and he would be a doctor? OK, it's dumb. But he is nice. You know that."

Amber hadn't noticed that a man was standing in the doorway. It was Mr. Ewald, the English teacher, who helped save Tianna's life at school. He coughed to get their attention.

"Oh God, you startled me," she said as she stood and started for the door. Amber threw her arms around the handsome teacher and added, "Thank you so much for saving my best friend's life. II will always remember that."

"Hey, I did what they taught me in the Army. When I saw what happened, it was like I was back in Iraq. So, Amber, how are you and Tianna?"

"I'm great. My arm is still a little sore, but if I don't move it too much, it's OK. And Tianna is getting better every day. Did you hear that those nano-things they used worked wonders? She was almost dead, and now she is alive. Thank you, Jesus."

"Wonderful. I had to stop. The two of you have been on my mind, and I needed to see you both. Is your mom here? The last time I saw her was at your softball game last spring. Are you trying out again this year?" he asked.

"Yes, and I don't know. Yes, our moms are in the cafeteria getting coffee, and I'm not sure what sports I'll do this spring. I enjoyed softball though, and you were a great coach. Are you coaching again next spring?" she asked.

"I'm not sure. It was fun, but I'm trying to write a book, and I don't know if I'll have time."

"A book! That is so exceptional. What will it be about?"

"I've been working on a romance novel that takes place in Iraq. A *Guns and Roses* type of story about two soldiers who fall in love. Male and female soldiers," he added.

"I want to read it when you're done. That is so great. I wish I could write like that," said Amber.

"Hey, I've told you many times, you write like that. Your prose is better than any student I've ever had, but you need to focus," said Mr. Ewald.

Alice and Thelma walked into the room, and Alice recognized the teacher. "You're Mr. Ewald, aren't you?"

"Yes, Mrs. Thornson. I wanted to stop and see the girls. I hope I'm not intruding."

"No way," Alice said. "You saved Tianna's life and perhaps my daughter's. You are now part of our family... forever! So, you better call me Alice, because Mrs. Thornson was my mother-in-law."

Thelma walked into the crowded room and said, "We have a guest? I know I've seen you around. My name is Thelma Gulliver, Tianna's mother. And you?"

"Carson Ewald, Tianna and Amber's English teacher."

Thelma put her arms around the tall black man, and said, "God bless you, Carson. I want you to know how much I appreciate you. Damn, I'm tearing up, and I hate crying."

"So do I, Thelma," said Carson. "And I only did what I could. It was fortunate that I was there to see what happened and could help."

Amber laughed, "OK, you two. You can stop hugging now."

"Oh," laughed Thelma. "You met Alice and you know Amber."

"Yes. You and I met once at a school meeting. I remember how young you were. Almost too young to be a mother of a fifteen-year-old girl."

"Well, aren't you sweet? And how many years have you been an English teacher?"

"Only five years. After I got back from Iraq, I became a teacher," said Carson. "I understand your husband died in Iraq. I'm very sorry. So many guys lose their lives on the streets of Baghdad. Too many."

"They said you were a medic. That must have been very traumatic for someone sensitive, like I feel you are," said Thelma.

Alice and Amber watched the two talk. They could both tell that something was happening between Thelma and Carson. There was a spark that lit both of their faces with joy. Amber pulled on her mother's sleeve and whispered, "Mom, can we go down for some hot cocoa?"

Alice laughed, "Great idea, Amber. I could use a cold drink. It's getting a little warm in here." She patted Thelma on her shoulder. "Thelma, Amber wants me to take her to get a drink. We'll be back in a while. Carson, I hope to see much more of you."

Thelma and Carson talked for about an hour about Tianna, Thelma's deceased husband, Carson's struggle with post-traumatic stress disorder, and his plans to write a novel. They discovered that at one time they had attended the same middle school, couldn't remember each other, but there were people they both knew.

Carson looked at his watch and said, "It's getting late, Thelma. Is there any chance we could get together again? Perhaps for dinner sometime?" He didn't want to push, but he knew he wanted to get to know her better. As it was, he felt more comfortable with her than other woman he had known.

"Yes, I would love that," she said. Taking out her cell phone, she said, "Give me your number, and I'll call you now, so you'll have my number."

They exchanged numbers before he started down the hallway, just as Amber and her mom walked out of the elevator.

"Bye, Mr. Ewald," yelled Amber. "I'll see you at school tomorrow."

"Bye Amber, and don't worry about the homework I assigned on Friday," he said, laughing. "I think you have a valid excuse."

CHAPTER 11

Sunday afternoon slipped away. After Alice and Amber headed for home, Thelma talked to her daughter about her birthday presents. She opened her purse and took out Tianna's new iPhone and attached a set of Bluetooth speakers. Tianna had mentioned wanting to read the book called *Rapture* by Lauren Kate. She had already read the first two books and was eager to start the third. The audiobook was to be a part of Tianna's birthday present, including the iPhone, speakers and a subscription to an audiobook club.

Thelma told her daughter that they could listen to the story together. Because Thelma hadn't read the first two books, she read as many reviews as possible to catch the storyline. At one point, she got lost and asked Tianna about an incident mentioned that happened in a previous novel. Tianna didn't speak, but Thelma could swear that she heard her answer.

When Thelma reached home, Clarence was still up, reading his favorite Detroit history book. His library had books covering the entire world, but Detroit was his favorite subject. Toward the end of his teaching career, he taught a specialized class on the *black history of Detroit*. Students from all over the country would vie for the chance to attend his lectures, either as a student or to just audit the class.

"Hi, honey. Was it a busy afternoon at the hospital?"

"Yes. I met Tianna's English teacher, Carson Ewald. He's the man who saved her life. I think you would like him. In fact, he reminds me of Joe and you," Thelma said. She wasn't sure how to Clarence she liked him and planned to have dinner with him. It had been many years since her husband had passed, and she seldom went out with another man.

"Well then, get to know him better," hinted Clarence. "He's an ex-army medic. He served in Iraq the same year Joe did. You know, Thelma, I have no reservations about your getting involved with other men. My son would have wanted you to find another man to share your life with. I know it's your decision, but you have my blessing."

Thelma walked over to Clarence, bent down, and gave him a big hug. "How did you become such a wonderful man?" she asked.

"My wife trained me well, I guess," he said with a twinkle in his eye.

"She sure did. I'm going up to bed. I've put in for a week of family leave, so I won't be going to work in the morning. We can go in together at nine to see Tianna, and Amber will visit her right after school from three until her dad picks her up at six. Then Alice and I will go down for the evening."

"You've got it all planned. Did Dr. Kohl say when she will regain consciousness?" he asked.

"Yes, he did. Depending on how she is in the morning, they will bring her out of her coma, and she should be awake perhaps by Wednesday or Thursday. I can't wait, Dad. There is so much I want to tell her," she said.

"You've been telling her all weekend. What more do you have to say?"

"Dad, it's different. I don't know if she will remember what we talked about while she was unconscious."

"Well, she better not forget her history lesson, because I will test her next week," Clarence laughed and put his book down. "I'm heading for bed too. Do you want a snack?"

The two sat for half an hour at the large kitchen table eating cookies and drinking milk. They wished Tianna were there for her favorite treat. It was a comfort to know she would soon be home.

* * *

Detective Thornson didn't want to answer the telephone call, but it was time to get up, and he figured it might be important. He checked the number, and it was not one he recognized.

"Hello, Detective Thornson here. How can I help you?"

"Detective, this is Fredrick McDougall. You said if I found anything about the King High School shooting, I should call you. Could I stop in at the police headquarters this morning? I have things to show you."

"Fredrick, this better not be a ploy to get more information out of me. I told you at the press conference, we are no longer investigating the shooting as a homicide, and there isn't anything new about the case," Lester said. He had worked with Fredrick on several cases in the past. Fredrick is notable for digging up information that the police are unable or unwilling to find. Sometimes, a newspaper reporter can do things and ask questions that a police officer could never do.

"Sir, I know the case is going cold, but I also know I have information that may be helpful. I'm not doing this to get a story, since I already have the story and I'll be running it in today's edition," Fredrick said.

"OK, I'll be at headquarters before eight o'clock. Try to be there then. I don't know where I will be after that. God knows who killed whom last night."

"You want me to tell you, Sir," Fredrick said, laughing.

"No! I want breakfast. Bye, Fredrick."

Alice was sitting in bed listening to the conversation. "That sounded interesting. Good news or bad?"

"I'm not sure. Should I wake Amber for school? Perhaps we're sending her back too soon."

"Lester, it's amazing. She acts like it were nothing. Just another day in the neighborhood. That's the scary part," said Alice.

"I agree. But you know Amber, nothing has ever fazed her. She's one strong woman, like you," Lester said as he bent down and kissed her.

He walked by Amber's bedroom and saw she was awake and sorting out the clothing she planned to wear today.

Lester smiled and said, "Honey, do you need a new outfit for school?"

"Yes, as a matter of fact. My school clothes got ruined, so I'm trying to figure out what to wear until I can get a new uniform."

"Check the bag in the corner. I picked up a new uniform on Saturday after the press conference. I need a few minutes, and then the bathroom is all yours."

"Thanks, Dad," Amber said as she took the tags off her new uniform. "It will be lonely at school without Tianna there to pester."

"I'm sure you will find someone to play with, Honey," he said.

* * *

It was hard for both Amber and Lester to stop at the exact spot where she and Tianna got show just two days before. For a few minutes, they talked about their feelings.

"You must feel this way a lot, Dad. I mean, you've seen a lot of murders, and then you have to go back to those places where they happened later. Does it hurt like it does now?" Amber asked.

"Yes. But the spot where a shooting took place is only a place. It's the human suffering that troubles me. In your case, it was personal. I can keep my emotions away from the victim and their families. But there's always the thought, *boy I'm glad that wasn't my family*, but now it is my family, and yes, it hurts."

"I love you, Dad. I'll be OK today. It's just the place where bad things happened last Friday."

With that statement, Amber got out of the car and caught up with a student she knew. By the time she was at the school door, she was laughing. She looked back and waved goodbye to her dad.

Lester stopped for a large coffee at a drive-thru and then went to police headquarters. On his way in, the police chief stopped him.

"Detective Thornson, I want to say you did a great job with the press conference on Saturday. The mayor reports there haven't been a ton of questions this morning. Is it true you plan on doing the investigation on your own?"

"No, it's still an open crime case, so my men will investigate when they have free time. We aren't putting a lot of effort into it, though. Just the usual," said Lester. He still needed to find the shooter, but he wanted to be careful about what he said to the Chief. "Remember, sir, the killer may still want to finish the job. And until we catch him or her, we owe the victims some protection."

"OK, but be careful. People may think because it was your daughter and her friend that got shot, we consider it more important than all the other unsolved shootings in Detroit," the Chief said in a stern voice.

"Understood, Sir," said Lester, as he started down the hall. The homicide bureau was busy, and it took a while for Lester's partner to notice he was there.

"Hey, Lester, there's a little newspaper reporter here. I put him in the interrogation room so he would feel nice and comfortable," said Detective Lee.

"Jim, you're terrible, but that's a good place for the little rat."

Lester checked his messages, sent off emails, and walked to the interrogation room where Freddie McDougall had been sitting. There was an envelope in front of him. When he saw Detective Thornson, he laughed. "Nice place to put me, Sir. I felt right at home. You know, this room reminds me of the office of our news editor at The Free Press. Very Spartan."

"Great, Freddie. So what is this fantastic story you're printing this afternoon?" asked Lester.

"Well, most of it is about the shooting, with background information I got from our sources, students, and your press releases. The slant of the story is the relationship to the 1967 killing of Amanda Carson, the fifteen-year-old black girl killed with the same weapon used in the King High School shooting," said Freddie. He had a beaming smile, like he had one up on the detective.

"So, that's old news. We dug that up already."

"Well, did you know Tianna's grandfather knew Amanda Carson? Did you know they lived on the same floor at the Brewster-Douglass projects? That is more than a coincidence. That smells like a serial killer. We are looking in The Free Press archives for any other killing like it in the Detroit area," added Freddie.

"I hope you aren't trying to pin this on Clarence Gulliver, Tianna's grandfather. He's not the killer type, and the last thing he would do is hurt his granddaughter."

"No, he was in Europe at the time of Carson's shooting. The Free Press interviewed him in 1967 because he knew her well. I'm clear on the fact that he is not a suspect. It's just that this case is so strange. What would be the odds that Clarence would know the girl killed in 1967?" asked Freddie.

"I don't know, and I agree with you, Freddie. This is the strangest case I have ever seen. We even have a video of a car that disappears at the scene. How's that for mystery, or should I say, magic?"

Freddie's ears perked up. "Car? What car?" he asked.

"Never mind. We think it was a glitch in the surveillance camera," suggested Lester.

"Well, I hope my sharing this with you will help," said Freddie, as he handed the envelope to Detective Thornson.

"Look, I thank you for the info, and if you get more, please let me know before you put it to print. We can't have innocent people like Clarence Gulliver getting a bad rap. Lord knows, it's hard keeping the lies from spreading like wildfires."

"Sir, all I wanted to do was ask questions. That's what my story is all about. It's a mystery we are all trying to solve," Freddie said as he stood and started for the open door. "I'm glad Tianna is doing so well, and I mentioned that in my story too. The doctors and nurses were eager to share, and this story will put their experimental procedure in the news, big time."

After Freddie left, Lester Thornson, Jim Lee and Jason Arborsen went over Freddie's story. Lester asked if any of this information was in the file from 1967. Jason said he knew everything except that Clarence knew the victim.

"He didn't show up in the report because when the shooting happened, he wasn't a suspect. In fact, there were no suspects. They thought it was one of the random snipers that was shooting at everyone during the riot, just for fun," said Jason.

"Look over this material, and if you or one of your men get time, try to find any other shootings that fit this M.O."

Lester handed the envelope to Jason. "I know you said before that you would like to investigate this mystery. Well, here's your chance. Please keep this under wraps. I don't want the chief knowing what we're up to."

CHAPTER 12

Throughout the entire day, Amber had to answer a constant stream of questions from her fellow students. Even the gang members came up and wanted to know how she and Tianna were doing.

She told one friend, "If I had known this is what it takes to be popular, I would have had myself shot long ago."

She was only kidding, but it made her aware of how bad news travels so fast. *If a student does something good, like win an award in science, who cares? But get hit with a bullet at school and you're special. Everyone wants to be your friend. Now that's crazy*, she thought.

She didn't have time to see Eddie until the last hour. She told him that her mom would pick them up and drop them off at the hospital.

"Do you know what you will tell Tianna?" she asked.

"Somewhat. I hope I can. Amber, why am I so afraid to talk to her? I mean, I can talk to you, and most of the other girls here at school."

"It's because you like her. You don't want to take me to the dance. It's Tianna that you're interested in, and what's wrong with me?" she asked.

"Nothing. You're my friend, Amber. My best friend. I love you as a friend."

"Like I said, what's wrong with me?"

"Nothing's wrong with you, Amber. It's me. I'm the guy who's messed up."

"Messed up or not, I'll see you at the north entrance after school. Mom will be there. Don't be late!"

Alice picked Amber and Eddie up at the King High School entrance. Amber jumped in the front seat and let Eddie sit behind her.

"Mom, you know Eddie, don't you?" she asked.

"Sure do, Honey. Hi Eddie. Are you still in the science program?"

"Yes Ma'am. I want to become a medical doctor if I can find enough scholarships. Mom says without scholarships I can't afford it. I'll attend Wayne State University. They have an excellent program."

"Great. See, Amber, it's important to make your plans now."

"Yes, Mom. When I decide what I want to be, I'll let you know."

"Amber should become an author. She has a lot of talent," said Eddie.

"I checked into that, Eddie," said Amber, "and unless you're famous, it's hard to make a living as an author. I want to make money, and that means something in business, or I can become a movie or rock star."

"How about a comedian, Amber?" joked Alice.

"Hilarious, Mom. Are we there yet?"

Alice dropped the two off at the main door and said, "Be here at six o'clock, and tell Thelma and Clarence I said hello. Love you and have a pleasant visit."

"Love you too, Mom."

"Thanks, Mrs. Thornson. We'll be here at six," said Eddie.

The two teens bounded up the sidewalk to the door and disappeared. As they got off the elevator, they saw Thelma at the nurses' station. She was talking to Dr. Kohl, and it looked like she was thrilled.

"Hi, Mrs. Gulliver. Is Tianna doing well today?" Amber asked.

"Yes! Dr. Kohl just told me he will wake her in the morning."

"Great news! This is Eddie. I think you've met him before. I brought him to talk to Tianna. He's the guy who wanted to take her to the dance, but he has a problem talking to girls he likes," said Amber.

Eddie cringed at her words. "Amber, you didn't have to tell her that. You're making me sound like a nerd."

Dr. Kohl laughed. "Son, you'll get over that shyness soon enough. It takes practice. Well, Thelma, I have my rounds to finish. I'll see you tomorrow morning. Kids, you may as well talk to Tianna. I'm sure she wants to hear you."

Amber pushed Eddie to the door of Tianna's room, where Clarence was sitting next to her bed. He was talking about the 1920s in Detroit. When Clarence noticed them, he said, "Sorry, I guess it's your turn."

Eddie extended a hand to Clarence and said, "Sir, I'm Eddie, from Tianna's school. It was interesting what you said about the Black and Jewish people living in the same areas of Detroit. My mom likes to talk about the stories her grandfather told her. I guess he worked at some nightclubs on Hastings Street as a band member. Mom said it was wild back then and her grandfather played with a lot of famous jazz singers."

"That it was, Eddie. I would love to talk to your mom about her stories. I'm a historian, and I can't get enough of it. As you heard, I've been telling Tianna all about Detroit's history. We were just finishing up talking about the Purple Gang. They were as bad, if not worse, than any gang today."

"Outstanding. Were they African Americans?" asked Eddie.

Amber answered for Clarence, "No, silly. They were a Jewish gang. A bunch of young guys who brought booze over from Canada during Prohibition. Tianna told me all about them."

"I guess she remembers a lot of what I've been telling her," said Clarence.

"She sure does. You've made a great impression on Tianna, Grandpa Gulliver. You've been like a father to her. She's told me that many times."

Tears filled Clarence's eyes. He took a handkerchief from his pocket and wiped his face. "Thank you, Amber. I needed to hear that."

Thelma was standing in the doorway. She cleared her throat and said, "Dad, we should let these youngsters visit. I'll drive you home, and we can cook dinner together."

Clarence said his goodbyes to the two youngsters and gave Tianna a kiss on the forehead.

After they left, Amber told Eddie to pull up a seat. The two of them sat next to Tianna's bed. Amber was holding her hand when she said, "Guess who I brought with me? Yup. It's Eddie."

"OK, Eddie. Talk."

Eddie cleared his throat. He twisted around in the seat and said, "Hi."

Amber gave him a stern look and said, "You will say more than that, or I'll beat the crap out of you right here in the hospital!"

Eddie smiled and touched Tianna's hand. "Is she unconscious? She looks like she's sleeping. And did they cut her beautiful hair? And how does she pee?"

"Enough small talk, Eddie. You need to talk to her now. She can hear you, and she's tired of waiting."

With a soft voice, Eddie began, "I'm sorry this all happened to you, Tianna. We thought you would die, but now we're all happy that you're not." He turned to Amber and said, "That sounds so lame. I want to tell her how much I like her, and how I want to see her and go to the dance, and get to know her better. I think she's the greatest girl I've ever known, or sort of known. Amber, that's what I want to tell her."

"Eddie, you told her, and now she knows. I will let the two of you talk. I'll get two Cokes from the cafeteria," Amber said as she stood and walked to the door. She turned and added, "And you better not just sit there. You know if you do, Tianna will tell me. Eddie, you don't want to see me upset."

* * *

Eddie and Tianna were alone in her hospital room. The monitors connected to Tianna fascinated Eddie. He stood and checked each one out. As he was walking around without thinking, he said, "This is amazing, Tianna. You would love seeing these monitors and tubes, and medical equipment. Well, you might not like them, since they're connected to you."

Eddie turned to face her. He said, "You look like you're sleeping, but they said you can hear me. I want you to know I know why I have a hard time talking to you. It's because I fear you will tell me you hate me or something like that."

Eddie sat down again and took her hand. "The first time I saw you was two years ago, and you had a big crush on that Ricky Clawson boy. I hated him because I wanted to get to know you, and all you wanted was him. The two of you always talked and laughed. I know I sound like some kind of nut who stalks girls. It's not like that. You were just so beautiful, and I knew if we could talk, we would have a lot of common interests. We had two classes together, and I knew from Amber what you were interested in."

He stopped and thought. "You know, once in Earth Science class, we talked. You did most of the talking, but we talked. And you seemed interested in me. I wish I would have just kept that conversation going, instead of obsessing over my shyness."

"Thank you, Tianna. I feel like I heard you say you like me. That's strange. I guess Amber wasn't kidding when she said you would hear me."

"I want to tell you I've been trying to figure out who shot you. Amber's dad told her that the shooter might still want to hurt her, so I will catch him and try to protect you. If you don't mind, that is. I wouldn't want to do anything creepy. OK, nothing creepy. But

I've been asking around if anyone knows who might have a grudge against you."

Amber was at the doorway listening. "So who do you think it might be?" she asked.

"First my Coke. My mouth is dry from talking. Hey, I've been talking to Tianna. Magic! I'm cured!"

Amber handed him the fountain drink and said, "Great, now we need to figure out how to shut you up."

Eddie took a sip and said, "Clawson is still very interested in Tianna. He's attending the University of Detroit, and I hear he's keeping track of everything that Tianna's doing."

"That's creepy, but I don't think he would do anything to hurt Tianna," said Amber. "Tianna knows he still has a crush on her. They were together until he graduated. But Tianna didn't want to go with someone out of high school. It would have caused too many problems, and she's too intent on getting top grades and going to college. You know that, Eddie."

"Yes, but he's my only clue. Calvin Samson said he saw Ricky on the day of the shooting at King High School. He was driving around the parking lot early in the morning. Calvin was there for tutoring. He needs to get his grades up if he wants to play basketball this year," said Eddie.

"Eddie, we have to tell Dad this. It sounds important enough that someone should talk to Ricky and see what he was doing at school."

"So how do we tell your dad?" asked Eddie.

"Like this," said Amber as she pulled her phone from her pocket and hit dial. "Dad, I've got important information about the shooting at school last Friday. Call me back."

"Will he call back?"

"If he doesn't, I will bitch a lot when I get home," she said.

"You? Never!" laughed Eddie.

The two sat with Tianna for several hours. They talked with Thelma when she arrived to spend the evening with Tianna, and then, as they were walking out the front door of Children's Hospital, Amber's phone rang. It was her dad. "Hi, Dad. I see you got my message. Yes, Eddie might have found a lead on a suspect. I know I sound like a detective. It's Eddie. He's been acting and talking like one all afternoon. And guess what — he talked to Tianna. OK. Can I give you the details after we get home? Yes, I'll tell Eddie to stop in and talk to you. What's for dinner? Oh, no. Again? No, that's OK. Bye. I love you, Daddy."

Just as she ended the call, her mom drove up to the curb.

Alice yelled out the window, "Get in, I can't afford another ticket. This is a no stopping zone."

CHAPTER 13

After Detective Thornson finished talking to Eddie, he called his partner, Detective Lee, and told him about the early morning high school visit by Ricky Clawson.

"Did one of our guys talk to a student named Calvin Samson?" he asked

"I don't think so, but I know the kid. He's on the basketball team. He's a skilled player with a lot of potential. What does he have to do with this?"

Detective Thornson said, "Eddie told me that Calvin saw Ricky Clawson driving in the parking lot before the shooting. Ricky is a former boyfriend of Tianna's. Eddie said he still has a thing for her even though she dumped him after he graduated from King."

"I'll check it out in the morning. Aren't you coming in?" asked Jim.

"I'll be there later. The chief wants me to help with the hit-and-run downtown. I guess it was someone important, and it could have been a murder. The guy would testify in federal court next week, and the F.B.I. wants local help with the case."

Detective Lee whistled, "Hey big shot, are you headed up the ladder now?"

"I would rather not be on this case without you, Jim, but they asked for me."

"No problem, sir," Detective Lee said, and then laughed. "Have fun and let me know all the grimy details when you get back."

Eddie ended up staying for dinner after Mr. and Mrs. Thornson promised to drop him off at home on their way to see Tianna.

During dinner, Amber spent the time telling her parents about

Eddie's fixation with Tianna. Eddie looked embarrassed, so Lester tried to ease the situation by telling the story of how he won Alice's hand.

"Dad, Eddie doesn't want to hear you were a nerd when you were young."

"I wasn't a nerd. I was on the football team, and your mom will tell you I was the big man in school," Lester insisted.

"He was, Amber. Your dad was all muscle. He was just a klutz in the romance department. I had to teach him what women want from a man," she said.

"See, Eddie, Mom says because I'm a woman you should listen," Amber said.

"It's not you who should tell Eddie what Tianna wants, Amber. You're just his friend. It's your job to encourage Eddie, not to embarrass him," insisted Alice.

"Oh, I'm sorry. I didn't realize that's what I was doing. I'm sorry, Eddie, I didn't mean to embarrass you," Amber said.

"You're forgiven, and we're still friends."

After taking Eddie home, Lester and Alice dropped in at the Children's Hospital. Lester told Thelma about Ricky, and she hoped he wasn't the shooter, because his family had such a hard time, and she heard he was the only one in the family who seemed to make something out of his life.

Lester said he isn't a suspect yet. It's just odd that he was there that day.

Thelma told her friends that Dr. Kohl planned to bring Tianna out of the coma in the morning. They expected it to take longer.

She said, "Because Tianna is doing so well, Dr. Kohl sees no reason to delay. He's already reduced her medication, and by morning she should be awake."

Alice asked, "Do you want me here with you?"

"Oh, Alice, that's wonderful. We should be here by eight. If you like, I can pick you up."

"No, Thelma, I'll drive. I'll drop Amber off at school and then meet you here. Is Clarence coming too?" Alice asked.

"Yes! It would be impossible to keep him away."

Lester explained he would like to be with them, but he needs to go out with the F.B.I. on a hit-and-run case. This impressed everyone except him.

* * *

The next morning, Amber ran downstairs ready for school. When she heard her mom was going to the hospital to be with Thelma when Tianna woke up, she became upset.

"Mom, can I skip school and come with you to the hospital? I should be there for her when she wakes up. I am her best friend."

"Will you get into trouble if I say yes?" Alice asked her daughter.

"As long as you give me a slip saying I was with you, they will excuse me."

"Then you can come with me. I know it's important to you."

Amber looked around the kitchen but didn't see her dad. Alice informed her of his special assignment and said he had left very early. After a quick breakfast, mother and daughter headed to Children's Hospital.

In the car, Amber seemed very nervous. Clarence asked her why, and she replied, "What if Tianna can't walk? And what if she has amnesia or something that makes her mind go all crazy? Wouldn't that be awful?"

"Honey, don't be a worrywart. The Lord spared Tianna's life, and I am sure He will not let her down now. And if everything isn't perfect, I'm sure Tianna can overcome any handicap she might have."

"I know Tianna is very strong, but it's hard not to worry."

As they walked out of the elevator, Amber noticed that there were several nurses standing outside of Tianna's room. She felt uneasy, hoping there weren't any problems.

Alice asked a nurse what was happening. The nurse smiled and said, "Our miracle girl just woke up. She's talking to her mom and Dr. Kohl now.

Thelma yelled, "Is that Alice and Amber?"

Amber said, "Yes."

"Send them both in here. My daughter wants to speak to her best friend."

Tears filled Amber's eyes as she walked into the crowded room. She made her way to the bed, and there was Tianna, smiling her beautiful smile. Tianna put her arms out and said, "Amber, I love you, and I'm so glad you're safe and here with me."

The two girls hugged as both of them cried. The joy filled the room, and there were tears in everyone's eyes. Even Dr. Kohl had to wipe his eyes dry.

He cleared his throat and said, "I have more patients to see, girls. I sure hope I have more successes today like we've had here."

Amber stepped back, looked at her friend, and said, "Tianna, we need to work on that outfit, and you look like you've been in bed for a week, and what did they do to your beautiful hair?"

Tianna laughed. "Gee... thanks, but you know I haven't been able to see the mirror for a while, so it's not my fault."

"That's OK. We love you anyway. Do you remember Eddie being here yesterday?"

Tianna smiled. "I felt he was here. He talked, didn't he?"

"He sure did. I think he's over his shyness," Amber said.

"Girls," interrupted Alice, "we all want to talk to Tianna."

"Sorry, Mom," said Amber. "Guess we can talk later, Best Friend."

Tianna laughed. "It seems like I have been talking and listening a lot. I remember hearing everyone, including you, Grandpa. It was strange. Almost like I was in a heavy fog and I could hear you guys, but I couldn't see anyone."

"Mom," she continued, "when will I be able to go home?"

"That's up to your doctor. Before releasing you, he wants to make sure you can walk," said Thelma.

Tianna was silent for a while. She was trying to move her feet and legs. "I can feel my legs, and move my toes," she said. She tried to lift her leg, but there was nothing. "Oh. I can't lift my leg up."

Thelma saw tears welling in her daughter's eyes, and she put her arms around her and said, "Honey, we didn't expect you to live through this shooting, but you did because you are a fighter. Don't let this stop you now. You'll walk and run again. So don't you feel sorry for yourself. Understood?"

Everyone talked at once. Alice said, "Tianna, we're just so glad you're OK. We have been praying. Reverend James and the rest of the church have been praying, and I know a lot of kids at school said prayers you recover. And you did."

"Tianna, a lot of good has happened to this family, and you will walk in time," said Clarence.

"Thank you, Grandpa. I guess I am feeling a little sorry for myself. It wasn't the birthday gift I expected."

Amber picked up the iPhone from the nightstand and handed it to her. "No, but this was. Isn't it fly, Tianna?"

"Yes, it is. Thanks, Mom and Grandpa. And Mom, thanks for the audiobook you played. I love it!"

"You heard it?" asked Thelma. She had asked the nurses to leave the book playing for several hours each night after she left her daughter. Knowing Tianna heard the novel was heart-warming.

* * *

A nurse came into the room and announced, "You all have to leave for fifteen minutes while I prepare Tianna for the physical therapist."

Alice and Amber told Tianna that they would be back as soon as possible, but Thelma insisted she would stay in the room. The nurse said no, but Thelma said only Dr. Kohl could order her out of the room.

"I got my daughter back, I'm here, and I'm staying," she said.

The nurse relented when the head nurse, Sienna, entered the room and hugged Thelma.

"Is everything OK here?" she asked the nurse.

"Yes, Sienna. I asked this woman to leave while I get the patient ready for the physical therapist visit."

"There is no reason Mrs. Gulliver can't stay in the room, Larry," said Sienna.

"If you say so," replied the nurse.

Together, Sienna and Larry, the new nurse, gathered the wires and intravenous tubes and pulled them to the side. They helped Tianna sit up and asked if she could scoot to the side of the bed. She did so.

"I have very little strength in my legs," Tianna told them.

A doctor carrying a clipboard walked into the room and said, "I'm here to test Tianna Gulliver." She turned to Thelma and asked, "Are you her mother?"

"Yes, and I would like to know what the tests are for?"

"Dr. Kohl has ordered rehabilitation for her legs, and I want to determine what we will need to do. We want to get her out of bed and mobile as soon as possible," the therapist said.

She performed several tests, which included Tianna trying to perform various movements. When she finished, she prepared to leave. Tianna reached for her arm and said, "Will I be able to walk? I want to know now."

"Yes, but it will take hard work in the rehabilitation department. Because of the nerve damage, your muscle strength is low. I will request that Dr. Kohl move you to a room on the rehabilitation ward. There you will use a bed that allows you to get in and out, and you'll be close to the equipment you'll be using to strengthen your legs." The therapist turned to Thelma and Alice and said, "We can have you moved yet this morning."

Alice and Amber returned to the room when they saw the nurses leave. Amber walked over to her friend and sat in the chair. As the two were talking, a nurse entered with a breakfast tray.

Tianna laughed and said, "I forgot I asked for something to eat when I first woke up."

Alice and Thelma found chairs, and they all sat around the bed, watching Tianna eat, and discussing the future move. Amber wondered how her friend felt and what she remembered about their visits during the past days.

Before Tianna could finish eating, two nurses announced that a room was ready in the rehabilitation ward, and Tianna would move now.

Amber helped gather Tianna's personal possessions as the nurses used a portable lift to help her out of the bed and into a wheelchair. They all walked down the hall and crowded into the patient elevator.

The group walked through the halls toward Tianna's new room. Eventually, they reached Tianna's new room in the rehabilitation ward and watched as the nurses situated Tianna next to the bed with cables and lifts.

Alice and Thelma put the flowers on a table and arranged Tianna's phone next to the bed.

"Look, you have a pleasant view here," Amber said as she looked out the window. "I hope you won't be spending a lot of time looking out these windows. Even though our neighborhood isn't great, it's our home."

"I want to walk," said Tianna, "and right now I'm tired because it's been a busy morning."

A new head nurse came into the room and helped lift Tianna onto the bed. She removed the many wires and tubes connected to Tianna.

She explained, "Dr. Kohl said You are off the medications and constant monitoring. Now you'll be able to use a bedpan on your own, or the bathroom with a nurse's help." When the nurse finished, another nurse came in and announced that he would take her for another rehabilitation session.

The nurse told everyone what was happening as she wheeled Tianna out of the room. Thelma, Clarence, Alice and Amber stood in the room staring at each other, trying to decide what to do.

CHAPTER 14

The therapist took Tianna down to the rehabilitation department, where she worked on a machine that exercised her legs. Bending and stretching back and forth. She became exhausted, so the nurse brought her back to her room. She could now use the bathroom with the help of a nurse. At least she no longer had to deal with a catheter, which she found painful and irritating. *I'm afraid my life won't be what it was before Friday*, she thought, *but as Mom would say, 'It is what it is.'*

As the nurse wheeled her into the room, Tianna noticed Amber sitting in the chair waiting for her. The rehabilitation technician forbade anyone from going with her for the therapy, but it surprised her that only Amber was still waiting for her.

Tianna asked, "Where did Mom, Alice and Grandpa go?"

"Your mom took your grandfather home, and my mom is shopping. I guess it's you and me until they get back this evening."

She asked the nurse, "Can I stay in the wheelchair for a while so I can visit with my friend?"

"Yes," the nurse responded. "I'll be back later. Here's your cold water, and if you need anything else, please ring."

Amber was drinking a hot chocolate she had gotten from the waiting room and smiled. "This is nice. We're back together."

Tianna agreed as she relaxed in the chair. "It looks like your arm is better, but how are you feeling?"

"I'm great. It's you I'm worried about. I've been wondering about your memory. We thought you would have amnesia or something because all of those nano-things were messing around in your brain. Do you remember the shooting? Because, I can't get the image of your getting shot out of my mind."

Tianna looked into the distance with a very serious expression, which frightened Amber.

"What's wrong, Tianna?"

"Amber, all I've been able to think about is what happened to us. How wonderful our lives were right up to our walk to school. The park was beautiful, with the leaves turning colors, and then the gunshot. Amber, I saw a bullet hit your shoulder. After that, nothing except all of you visiting me in the hospital. I heard everything, but when I talked, my voice was silent. It was strange."

Tianna considered for a moment. She took a log sip of water and added, "But there are other things I remember, and I'm not sure how to tell you about them."

"Tianna, you're sounding way too serious. Tell me what's going on. I'm a big girl, and I can handle it."

"Amber, I remember being shot six times before last Friday. And I died each time," Tianna said as tears welled in her eyes.

"HOLY CRAP! What the hell are you talking about?" Amber said, grabbing Tianna's hands and pulling them to her. "You can't say stuff like that. They will say you are nuts."

"I know, Amber. That was my first thought. But the more I remember, the more I know it's true."

"So what are you talking about? Reincarnation? Out of body stuff?"

"I guess so. I remember living seven lives. The first one I know of was in the 1690s. And you know, they all happened here in Detroit. I don't remember my birth, or anything like that, but I remember when I was a little girl, as I was growing up, and when I got shot. I assume I died because the next memory is years later when I was in another life."

"So, this is the last life you remember?" asked Amber with a tone of skepticism in her voice.

"Don't be silly. I can't remember my next life, because it hasn't happened yet," laughed Tianna. She could see that her friend was having a hard time believing her. In fact, Tianna was also having a hard time with the situation. "It's crazy, but I remember so many details of my lives that I believe they happened. I can tell you about my first life," she asked.

"Well, even if I say no, you'll end up telling me anyway," Amber said. "Is this the one in the 1600s?" she asked.

"Yes, Amber. Get comfortable, because this may take a while. I lived for fifteen years before someone killed me. In fact, at the end of each lifetime, I died the day before I turned sixteen. It's hard to believe, but it is true."

* * *

"My name was Arianna, and I was born in the summer of 1690 in St. Ignace, in what is now northern Michigan, where Lake Huron and Lake Michigan meet. My father was the chief of our tribe of Huron Indians, and my mother's father was our clan's medicine and spiritual leader. Even though we had accepted the God of the French and attended their church here in St. Ignace, we still held many of our ancestor's beliefs."

"Grandfather and I were close. He's told me many stories about our history and our ancient beliefs. He said our ancestors are the original Huron tribes who greeted the French when they first came into the New World, but we are part of the Wyandot Tribe. We formed our tribe after the Iroquois destroyed our nation."

"Our original nation comprised many tribes with common roots, but because we were always ready to fight, we made many enemies. Our fiercest enemy was the Iroquois Confederacy. They lived south of the Saint Lawrence River, now known as Upstate New York. The Iroquois hated us, so we kept attacking them, and they vowed to destroy us. They defeated us and drove us from our homeland. The French also fought the Iroquois, and we set up our villages near their forts."

"The French helped us because we had welcomed them to the New World and taught them how to survive in our wilderness. Being skilled hunters and trappers, we became their major supplier of furs, which were valuable in their homeland. For our hard work, we could trade the furs for supplies like metal pots and pans, knives, hatchets, guns, tobacco, and alcohol from faraway places. They gave us the name Huron, which was an insult, because in their language the name described a wild beast with bristles. They called us that because our warriors spiked their hair, and we loved to decorate our clothing in wild colors and crazy designs."

"Anyway, my mother was the head of our household. We lived in a village of about thirty large families. Each family lived in a large hut built with branches and birch bark. In our society when a man marries a woman, he lives with her mother's family. My dad had to move into my mom's home. Her sisters and their husbands also lived with us, and their children. I know it's crazy, but it was nice. We always had the family there for us, which provided security when the men left home in the winter to trap for furs, hunt game, or fight wars."

"I had one older brother, Huritt. The name means *handsome*. Father gave him the name because as a child he was handsome, for a boy. I think they should have named him after a snake or rat because we didn't get along that well."

Amber interrupted, "Why didn't you like your brother?"

"He wasn't the brave warrior that my father wanted him to be. Father and I were a lot alike, and I always tried to do those things that only a brave should be doing. I enjoyed hunting, using a knife, bow and arrow, and wrestling with the other kids. My brother feared me. I could take him to the ground and rub his nose in the dirt. He wanted to help mother plant corn and tend the fields like I had to do. Father scolded me and made me help mother, and Father forced Huritt to become a man."

"Our tribe had lived in St. Ignace at the request of Antoine de la

Mothe Cadillac, the commander of Fort Michilimackinac. We called him Cadillac. Father said he was an excellent warrior and he would keep his word. We were trading partners, and we helped him protect the fort from invading Indian tribes."

"Mother hated living there. It was cold in the winter, and the land was not good for growing corn and squash. It was her job to make sure we had enough crops to survive, and Father made sure we had meat. Mother became excited when Cadillac asked us to join him at Fort Ponchartrain. It was his new fort in what they called Detroit. Mom said Detroit is French for the place where the river is narrow. She talked with the priest here, and he said our tribe would have the Lord's blessing if we joined Cadillac. This was in 1701, but our tribe did not follow the other tribes to Detroit. There was already an Ottawa village, Potawatomi Village, and a Miami village built around the small fort in Detroit."

"Our tribe moved after Mother announced she could not plant the fields because the spring was too cold and wet. After much work taking apart our village, we packed the canoes and headed south. We had to take all we could with us, except what we could replace in our new home. Mom was so happy because she heard the earth was rich, the weather was warmer, and the corn would be plentiful. I was eager to see the country and meet new people, but I think my brother feared the unknown. He kept asking if it was smart to leave what we had grown accustomed to. And Father kept saying we may have trouble with the other Indians because we would be outsiders. He and the other chiefs had attended several councils, and Father felt that the Ottawa Chief did not trust our tribe's motives."

"In June 1703, when I was thirteen years old, we built our new village. Thirty of our tribe members moved down to Detroit to be with Commander Cadillac. The move was hard, but we had moved often."

"The fort looked like Michilimackinac, only smaller. There was a tall vertical fence protecting many small log buildings. The soldiers lived in tiny log homes inside the fort, and there was a large building used as a warehouse and trading store, and the beautiful church, Saint Anne's, which was led by Father del Halle, a Franciscan priest."

"Father said Cadillac had to fight with his leaders to keep command of the fort. When we arrived, he had just gained back control. His commander gave his job to a French trading company. They managed the settlement and the purchase of furs from the Indians. When Cadillac discovered he was no longer the *big chief*, he kept fighting for his job back. Daddy said he was still there, but he didn't make all the decisions that involved money. Something Daddy said Cadillac wanted to do. Because they caught he trading company stealing, Cadillac got his job back. His King even allowed him to sell settlers land along the river. Cadillac got his share of money by making them pay rent."

Tianna stopped and asked if Amber could get her more ice water and ask the nurse to help her into the bathroom. "I hope I'm not boring you? I'm trying to help you understand what I remember. It must seem impossible, but I had the privilege of knowing Cadillac's wife and children, who were with him in Detroit."

"It's fascinating, and I can't wait to hear the rest of your story," Amber said as she walked toward the door. Amber became captivated, but she still questioned whether Tianna was reincarnated. Much of what she was telling her were stories she had told her before. Tianna had vast knowledge of the history of Detroit. Her grandfather always told her exciting stories, and this sounded to Amber like another of his tales.

The nurse came in with a large styrofoam cup of water and helped Tianna onto the toilet. While they attended to business, Amber looked at Tianna's new iPhone and noticed she was listening to the latest audiobook, *Rapture* by Lauren Kate. Amber read the first two books of the series and knew it was about two lovers who were fallen angels. Lucinda and Daniel would repeat their lives and deaths, falling in love and then dying again. She wondered if this story influenced Tianna's memories of being reincarnated.

* * *

Amber didn't tell her friend she had doubts about her fantastic story of being an Indian princess. Instead, she let Tianna continue with the story when she got back to the chair.

Tianna got comfortable again and asked, "Well, Amber, are you ready for part two of my Indian life?"

"Yes, I'm eager to learn what happened," Amber said, trying to sound encouraging.

"OK. So, I'm thirteen and we are in our new village near Fort Ponchartrain at Detroit. My father disliked the fact that some of our rival tribes also had villages at Detroit. He told Cadillac there would be problems, but Cadillac argued it would be better to have them here than outside where we didn't know what they were up to."

"My life comprised work and very little fun. When I became a woman, Father said I should plan my future. He suggested I choose one of two braves he would like me to bring into the family, but I had no interest in his old-fashioned ideas."

"Father," I said, "there are many boys, and I want to get to know all of them before I decide on one, and I don't want you picking the warrior I should spend the rest of my life with."

"He scolded me for being disrespectful, but Mother told him, "Remember when I found you? My father did not tell me who to marry; I decided. And you must admit our union was successful, and now you are our tribal chief and a great warrior."

"Father said, "Arianna must begin the search now. She is coming of age and should put the work of children aside."

"Grandfather listened, but he made no comments during their conversation. Later he asked me to walk with him. I loved talking with Grandfather. He would talk about history, the good and bad plants he uses to help our people fight illness, and the spirit world where our ancestors are."

"We walked out into the woods, and Grandfather said, "I want to teach you how to be a medicine man."

"But I am a woman, Grandfather. Are there medicine women?" I asked.

"It is unusual, but I have talked to the spirits, and they said you will be an outstanding leader. You have a gift that will help many of our people, but I must train you soon, because there are perils you will face as a woman medicine man."

"Grandfather's offer came as a surprise. I loved what he did to help our people, and I had an interest in the way he used plants, so I told him I would like to learn, but if I found I was not up to the task, I must be able to say no. He agreed and we set a time when we could study together."

"In the meantime, I had to help Mother with the corn. Along with the other women and children in our village, we supplied all the corn for the fort and other Indians. Mother was a wonderful farmer, and because of the rich soil, her harvest was huge."

"Grandfather spent many hours teaching me how to identify and use plants. He took me with him to heal the sick, and I learned how to bandage wounds and set broken bones. I loved when we went into the night and visited the spirits."

"He kept saying, "Arianna, you will have great power over the spirit world, but you must be careful. With your power, comes responsibility and much danger. I fear for you, granddaughter. I fear for you now, and forever."

"Amber, I was becoming an independent woman. At fifteen, I was interested in boys, but the one who caught my attention was a young French soldier. He came back from Montreal with Cadillac, and they treated him like a member of the Cadillac family. He was tall, dark and handsome, and he was interested in me as well."

Amber laughed. "That sounds like you now, Tianna. You always do what you want, no matter who says otherwise."

"Yes, I know. I think it is a trait I had in each of my lives."

"His real name was Aloysius Beringer, but everyone called him Louis. We became close in the winter of 1705. He asked me to marry him as soon as I turned sixteen, and I accepted. During the winter, we were always together. On weekends, we went to the skating area outside the fort. There was a small building where the French soldiers and settlers played their fiddles and sang old French songs. We ate, drank tea and hot cider, and had great fun. I had to sneak out so that Father and Mother didn't know. I told Grandfather, but he wasn't pleased, because he was afraid for me. He said I needed to study more and concentrate on learning the ways of the spirit world. Once he said, "If you take on the life of the French, you will abandon your people, and that will be a sad day for all.""

"Amber, at the time I didn't understand what he meant, but now I think I do. I didn't obey my grandfather and continued to be with Louis. We planned our future together, and I was in love, and it clouded all of my thoughts. To be honest, Amber, if he asked me to go back across the enormous lake to his home in France, I would have. I would do anything to be with him."

"Wow," said Amber. "You're always so laid back with people. I didn't know you could have those kinds of feelings. How did you handle the tensions with your father?"

"I didn't have to. Father and my brother were often away fighting his stupid wars. When they returned, I didn't see Louis as often."

"I promised Grandfather I would think hard before I decided. Louis even said he would move in with my family so I could stay with the tribe and be their medicine woman. He would do anything to make it so we could be together."

"Did you tell your mother?" asked Amber.

"Mother knew what was happening, and she understood. Amber, I loved her so much that it hurt to think about leaving our home. Mother said she would welcome Louis to her home, but I wasn't sure that was what I wanted. I wanted to fly like the birds I had always loved watching, and I wanted fresh adventures and to be more than just another Indian girl from Detroit."

* * *

"My sixteenth birthday grew nearer. In the spring of 1706, Cadillac made a trip to Quebec and Montreal. He remained in control of Fort Ponchartrain and the surrounding settlements. While Cadillac visited Montreal, Etienne Veniard de Bourgmont became temporary commander. He had gone to the fort and when Cadillac left for his trip."

"Bourgmont, an explorer, was knowledgeable about the many Indian tribes. He also was having an affair with a married woman at the Fort. He did not keep his mind on Fort business."

"Father and my brother had been home for several days, and I was trying to get up the nerve to tell him that soon after I turned sixteen, which was the next day, I wanted to marry Louis. It was a beautiful summer evening, and Mother informed me she had told Father of my plans. I feared he would be upset with me."

"Arianna," he said in a stern voice, "Mother says you will marry the Frenchman named Louis. Is this true?"

"Yes, Father," I said. "Please don't be angry. I love him so much, and he loves me. He is a good man, like you. Even though he is not an Indian, he has the spirit of one."

"Your mother told me all about him, and I talked to him yesterday. I gave him my blessing," Father said.

"I jumped into his muscular arms, hugged him, and told him I loved him and would always be a part of the family. As we were talking, several Miami Indian warriors approached Father. They told him that the Ottawa Chief Le Pesant, and his warriors were mad at both the Miami and our tribe."

"The eldest warrior said, "I understand they fear you will attack them. They mistrust your friendship with Cadillac, and they know you hate Chief Le Pesant. He feels you want to defeat him and are preparing to attack their village."

"Father laughed. "I attack only my sworn enemies. The Ottawa's are not worth my efforts. Perhaps it is you that Chief Le Pesant thinks will attack them. You dislike him more than I do."

"While they were talking, there was a sudden burst of gunfire to the south. The Miami warriors knew it was coming from their village. Father called for his braves to come prepare for a battle to help their friends."

"The only thought running through my mind was that Louis was on duty this evening and he would rush toward the fighting. I wanted to warn him, so I ran through the woods toward the Miami village. When I got there, I saw several of the Ottawa warriors shooting at the Miami braves trying to defend their families. When the Miami fought back, the Ottawa ran toward Fort Ponchartrain for protection. I followed, trying to remain out of sight. As I approached the gate of the fort, I saw a French soldier and Father del Halle standing outside the gate. The Ottawa Warriors rushed inside the fort. There was gunfire, and both the soldier and Father del Halle fell to the ground. I turned and screamed. A sharp fire burned in my stomach. My hand felt wetness coming through my clothing. Father ran up and cried out in sorrow. He bent down, tears in his eyes as he held me close to him. I could hear mother's screams as she came running to care for me, but I never told her goodbye. A heavy fog surrounded us, and I could feel myself being pulled toward bright lights. Then there was nothing as I rose to heaven to be with Jesus. My memories end when I left Earth."

CHAPTER 15

Tianna stopped talking, and Amber could see she her eyes filling with tears. She moved close and put her arms around her friend. "I'm sorry, Tianna. It's a beautiful story, but how do you know it's real, and not just your imagination?"

"Trust me, Amber, it's real. I remember every vivid detail now. There are no memories between my lives here on Earth, but my memories of those lives are very complete. I'm not sure why I now have these memories, but I do."

Tianna sighed, thought for a moment and then added, "The story isn't what is making me sad, Amber. It's knowing on Friday it all could have happened again. I could have died, and so could have you. It's frightening and sad, because I don't know why this is happening. I keep asking myself, who is trying to kill me, and since I didn't die this time, will they try again?"

Amber stood and walked to the window. She looked into the distance and said, "I don't know. My dad said they definitely tried to kill you. Tianna, it's getting late, and our moms will be here soon. Will you tell me about your other lives?"

"Yes, can you stop by tomorrow after school?" Tianna asked.

"It's a date, and I'll see if I can convince our moms to let us talk by ourselves again," said Amber.

The nurse walked in and told Tianna that she needed to get rest. She helped her into bed using an electric lift. The nurse took her blood pressure, temperature, and oxygen level.

"You're doing great, Tianna," she said. "The therapist wants you to come down after dinner for another session. They say you will be here until at least next Sunday."

Tianna fluffed her pillow and set the bed into a sitting position. "I wish I could go home now," she said.

"I know honey, it's always nicer to be home," the nurse said.

"Girls, we're back," said Thelma as she and Alice walked through the door. "Did you have a pleasant talk?"

"Yes, Mom. Can Amber and I visit alone again tomorrow after school? We've been talking a lot about some personal things."

"Yes, but only until six o'clock. Then, your grandfather and I will be here. The preacher and some of the church members will want to visit with you. They promised not to stay long. I hope you don't mind," said Thelma.

"That's fine. I hope I don't get tired out. They worked me out today, but I think my legs are stronger. Look, I can lift them a little," Tianna said. She turned and saw that Amber was not listening. She was looking out the window as if in a trance.

Thelma was unpacking items from a duffel bag. "Honey, Alice and I picked up things you'll want here. We got makeup, shampoo, your toothbrush and toothpaste, and some new perfume. I also brought your robe. They may want you to use their things, but if they let you use this robe, do it."

"That's for sure," said Alice. "And we got you some paper and pencils; so if you want to write to anyone, you can."

"Mom, if I want to write, I'll use my new iPhone. But thanks. I might want to draw something."

Alice hugged Tianna and told Amber that she was ready to go home.

"I'm all set, Mom," Amber said. She walked over to Tianna and smiled. "I'll be back after school, and we can finish that story you were telling me. Should I say anything to Eddie?"

"Yes, tell him I will go to the dance with him, provided I'm out of here before Thanksgiving."

"Lord, Honey, you'll be out of here by Sunday. When is this dance?" asked Thelma.

Tianna laughed. "It's the day after Thanksgiving, Friday evening at the high school."

"She'll be there. And I'm sure she'll be able to dance, too," Thelma said.

Amber hugged Tianna and said goodbye. She and Alice walked out as the handsome young physical therapist was coming in.

"Be nice to your cute therapist, Tianna," yelled Amber.

* * *

On the way home, Amber was silent. She was deep in thought about the story Tianna had told and the thought of someone still trying to kill her.

"Honey, what's wrong?" asked Alice.

"Nothing, I'm just a little blue today. Mom, do you think Dad's right about the killer still wanting to hurt Tianna?" Amber asked.

"I don't know, Honey, but if it's bothering you, ask your dad tonight," said Alice. "Did Tianna say something that upset you?"

"We talked about what happened, and I told her what Dad said. Both of us are a little upset because we can't think of anyone who would want to hurt her," Amber said. She wanted to tell her mother the fantastic story Tianna told her about her previous life as an Indian. But she promised Tianna, and friends don't break their promises.

It was almost time for dinner, so Alice called for takeout and then stopped at the Lucky Dragon Chinese Restaurant on Jefferson. "You must come in with me, Amber. It will probably take the two of us to get our food back to the car."

In a few minutes, they were pulling into the driveway. Lester was outside raking leaves. Amber yelled, "Guess what we're having for dinner?"

"Chinese from Lucky Dragon?" he said, laughing.

"Not fair, Dad. Mom must have told you."

"She did. I'm hungry; so let me help you get that into the

house."

In the kitchen, Alice set the containers on the counter and pulled out plates and bowls. Lester washed up and helped get food and drinks to the table. When they each had a full plate, and a bowl of egg drop soup, Lester bowed his head and said, "Lord, you have given us this food as a blessing. We thank you for that, and we thank you for giving us back our friend, Tianna. Bless us all, and keep us safe, Lord. Amen."

"So, Amber, how was your visit with the miracle girl today?" asked Lester.

"It was great. She's recovered fast, and they said she could walk after some therapy," Amber said. "Dad, we talked about what you told me about the shooter. That someone wanted to kill Tianna. Do you think they will try again?"

"I don't know. We plan on catching whoever did this. In fact, my partner, Jim Lee, and the crime investigator, Jason Arborsen, are coming over this evening. We're working this case on our own time, and Jason has more information to share. Do you want to join us?"

"Dad, I would love to. You know how much I love a good mystery, and I would make a brilliant detective," said Amber.

Alice laughed at her daughter. "Since when? You've wanted nothing to do with your dad's job."

"Well, this is the first time that his job has something to do with me," said Amber.

* * *

The Thornsons were just finishing up dinner when the doorbell rang. Amber was the first to the door as usual.

"Hi! Dad said you would be here," she said. Then she noticed that Clarence Gulliver was standing behind them. "Grandpa Gulliver, I didn't know you were coming. There's nothing wrong at the hospital, is there?"

"Heavens no, child. These men think I might have information to share. God knows what it is."

Lester came forward to hang up their coats. He seated them at the table where Alice had already placed a coffee thermos and four cups.

"Have a seat, guys. We could play poker tonight if you like, but that might distract us from our case," said Lester.

Jim laughed. "Poker would be a great idea. I could use extra cash."

"And what makes you think you'd be the winner?" asked Lester.

"Because I'm a better poker player than you are," said Jim.

"Well, that's true," Lester said. "Jason, did you tell Clarence why you asked him over tonight?"

Clarence interrupted, "No. He didn't, Lester. So, perhaps that's where you should start, and if you had wanted to play poker, I would have brought over my Social Security check. As it is, I only have five bucks on me."

"No, we wouldn't want to take your money. We need information, and you are the history professor."

"OK. What do you need?" asked Clarence.

Lester sat down and made himself a cup of coffee. As he stirred his cup, he turned to Jason, who had placed a packet of papers and his laptop on the table. "So, Jason, you want to take it from here?"

"Sure. As you know, I've been looking into the other murder, in 1967. The fifteen-year-old girl, who lived in the Brewster-Douglass apartments and died during the riots.. Her name was Amanda Carson, and I have information that...."

Before he could finish, Clarence interrupted him. "I knew Amanda Carson. She lived on the same floor as my family. God, I still remember when she died. Is that why you asked me here?"

Amber was standing in the kitchen doorway. She looked shocked and confused at what she heard. "What's this about another shooting? Is it the same guy?"

"Amber, come here and sit down. You wanted to know what was happening with the investigation, so join us and listen as we go over the evidence. If you have questions, you can ask them later," instructed Lester.

"OK, but I already have a dozen questions," said Amber.

"We'll get to them, but right now we need to cover some of these new findings," said Lester.

Jason picked up his folder and pulled a copy of a Free Press article from 1967. "Clarence, you were in Europe when Amanda got shot in 1967. I understand you heard about the shooting and cut your trip short. Why did you rush back to Detroit?"

Clarence began, "I was a good friend. We used to sit in the hallway and talk for hours. Amanda was an amazing young woman with so much potential. She was kind, smart, and caring. Her family had it rough, but they were getting by. When I heard about her death, I felt I had to come home to be with her family. It was the right thing to do, and I had my studies in Europe completed. After my class on European history, I stayed a few weeks for some personal time."

Jason turned to Lester and Lee and said, "The police report claimed Amanda's death resulted from a random sniper attack. From my records and the articles in The Free Press, this is wrong. At the time of the shooting, there had been no other sniper shootings in this area. She died on Sunday afternoon while walking on Woodward Avenue and Winder Street. Her mother said she was coming from J.L. Hudson. She walked downtown from the projects after hearing about the riots that started in the 12th Street area. When she got to Hudson's, she was told her mom had already left for home. They were getting ready to close the Piccadilly Circus Cafeteria, and her mom, who was a cook, left to go home. At the corner of Winder Street, a police car stopped, and the officers told her to go home. She turned on Winder the police heard a gunshot. The officers reported that the young girl had died instantly."

Clarence agreed with Jason's version of the events. "That's the story I heard. Some of Amanda's friends said they thought she was trying to get in touch with her boyfriend, Ronald Woods. He was a few years older than Amanda. I met him many times. He was smart, ambitious, and in his second year at Wayne State University. That summer he was attending classes and working in the library full time. I don't know what happened to him. They said he wasn't at the funeral, and I never heard of him again."

"I'll get to that later," Jason said.

"The police found the gun used in the shooting behind a car parked in a lot on Wilder. Again, it was the same gun used to shoot both Amber and Tianna. The police identified it, but couldn't find any matches to the prints on it. Remember, there were no computer systems available then to match fingerprints with other departments around the country. It was a slow process to compare books of fingerprints to other known prints. At the time of Amanda's killing, the police had a riot going on, and they didn't have the time to spend looking for one shooter."

Lester got up from the table and walked to the counter. "Any of you guys want a Coke instead of more coffee?" he asked.

Amber was the only one who wanted a Diet Coke, but she offered to get it herself. Standing next to her dad, she whispered, "Dad, isn't it amazing that Tianna's grandfather knew Amanda? The odds of that happening must be astronomical. And why were they both shot one day before their sixteenth birthday?"

"Amber, Clarence is not a suspect in these investigations," Lester said.

"I know, but it's just too strange to ignore, isn't it?" Amber asked.

"Yes, and you would be a good detective. You definitely have the insight needed," Lester said as he brought the coffeepot back to the table to refill the thermos.

Jason was sorting out his paperwork and pulled up an article on his computer.

When Lester returned to the table, he told Jason to continue.

"I dug deeper into the disappearance of Ronald Woods. The Free Press said his brother found him dead in his apartment on August 15, 1967, from suicide. His wrists were slit, and he was in his bathtub. Ronald's brother broke into the apartment when he couldn't reach him. His body had decomposed, so the police took fingerprints and dental molds to confirm his identity."

Clarence whistled, "That's amazing. He must have really loved her... kind of like Romeo and Juliet."

Amber was confused and asked why they were like Romeo and Juliet.

Clarence replied, "Haven't you read the play by Shakespeare? It's a tragic story about young lovers."

"Oh, the two lovers who killed themselves by mistake," said Amber. "I get it now, Grandpa Gulliver."

After Jason said that the fingerprints on the gun were Ronald Woods', Lester asked Jason if there was any doubt whether he was the killer.

"Well, if he were alive today, it would be a hard case to prove. We only have the fingerprints, and being in love with someone is not a motive."

The last subject to be discussed was Tianna's old boyfriend, Ricky Clawson. Jim Lee said, "I talked to Calvin Samson about his seeing Ricky the morning of the shooting at King High. He is positive that it was Ricky. The two of them used to practice basketball together. He knows Ricky has a crush on Tianna, and he is attending college to make something out of himself. Ricky told Calvin that the only way he could have a girl like Tianna would be if he were a successful man."

Jim continued, "I tried to contact Ricky, but no one has any idea where he is. His mom hasn't seen him since last Friday, and he hasn't been to any of his classes. I've been calling his cell phone, and his mom said she would call me if he came home. Any further attempts would involve a search warrant, and we would need more reason to get one."

Lester sighed, "Well, Amber, what do you think?"

Amber laughed. "I think it's all crazy." She wanted to tell her dad that Tianna had told her about being killed six times over the last three hundred years, but that would really be crazy. She just added, "I think you guys need to find Ricky. Perhaps you can see if there were any other fifteen-year-old girls killed in Detroit. I'd look over the total history of Detroit. Perhaps it's one of those paranormal things. Could there be a curse of some kind taking place in Detroit?"

CHAPTER 16

Amber's mother dropped her off at school early Wednesday morning. Amber was tired because she couldn't get to sleep. She kept thinking about what Tianna had told her and also what she had learned from her father's detective team.

"How am I going to keep from going insane? I need to tell this to someone," she whispered to herself when she reached her locker.

Eddie found her at the locker and asked questions about Tianna's condition. "Is she awake yet? Did she know I was in the hospital talking to her? Does she want to go to the dance, provided she's out of the hospital?"

"Eddie, stop with all these questions. Let me answer them one at a time; yes, to all of them," she said. "I'll see her again this afternoon. I'm eager to see her, but there is so much going on with stuff that it's driving me crazy. Dad's team is finding some strange evidence about the shooting, and they're looking into a 1967 shooting that involved the same gun. I wish I could tell you more. God, I wish I could tell you."

"So tell me. You're aware I can keep a secret, if that's what you're worried about," Eddie said.

"I don't know what Tianna would think if I told you."

Eddie questioned, "Why don't you call her and ask?"

Throughout the day, Amber wanted to call Tianna, but she waited until lunch when she was sure Tianna would be in her room.

The phone rang twice and then Tianna said, "Hi, Friend. What's up?"

"Hi, how's your day going? I'd tell you what I'm eating, but I wouldn't want to make you sick."

"Well, I'm having pizza, some breadsticks, and a great root beer float. And they are fantastic."

"Nice, I guess I need to be hospitalized to get an enjoyable meal. Say, I've got a lot to tell you and ask you about the investigation. I was with Dad and his men last night, and I got the lowdown on some stuff. But the big question is... can I bring Eddie this afternoon? He wants to know what's going on."

There was a silence on the cell phone, then Tianna said, "Do you think we can trust him not to tell anyone until we say he can?"

"Yes, I know we can. He's always upfront with me, and I know he wants to help."

"Then bring him, but please don't tell anyone else," Tianna warned. "You have told no one else, have you?"

"No. It was hard not to tell Dad last night, but I didn't," said Amber.

During English class, Amber and Eddie sat together and talked about going to the hospital after school. Eddie asked Mr. Ewald if he could use the restroom, and while there he called his mother for permission, which she gave him. In fact, his mother was glad he was talking to Tianna. She knew of his shyness with girls he liked and had been trying to encourage him.

Mr. Ewald's assignment for the day was to write a story about a friend who needed your help. The paper was to be at least three double spaced typed sheets. Amber got a laptop from the cabinet and worked on hers while Eddie wrote ideas down on a piece of paper.

Mr. Ewald came over to their table and pulled up a chair.

"Amber, I wanted to ask you how Tianna was doing. Her mom told me Monday night she was awake, but she didn't have time for details."

"She's doing super well, Mr. Ewald," said Amber. "I was with her yesterday after school, and Eddie and I are going again today. She's getting help with her walking, and she hopes to walk enough to go to the dance with Eddie, here."

Eddie was grinning from ear to ear. "Ya, with me," he said with pride.

"Lucky man, Eddie. Just remember to treat her like a queen," said Mr. Ewald.

Amber chuckled, "More like a princess. An Indian princess."

* * *

Amber and Eddie jumped into Alice's car in the school parking lot. As they drove down Lafayatte Ave., Alice asked Amber what she thought about her father's detective meeting last evening.

"It was interesting, Mom. They dug up stuff that would make a crazy mystery book, but I think they found more questions than answers."

"That's what your dad said. And Eddie, I hear you're talking now?"

"Yes, it's a miracle of modern science. Or something like that. I needed to get my confidence up. Amber said Tianna was glad I could ask her to the dance after Thanksgiving. Now, I need to learn how to dance," Eddie said.

Amber and Alice laughed. Eddie wasn't sure if he should laugh with them, or be embarrassed. He laughed.

"Amber, you can teach this young man how to dance, can't you?" Alice asked.

"Yes, Eddie. I'll teach you how to dance. But you better not step on my feet."

Alice pulled the car up to the curb at Children's Hospital. As the two teenagers jumped out, Alice reminded them to be ready at six o'clock.

"Don't worry, Mom, we'll be right here."

Amber raced Eddie to the front door... winning by an arm. When the two got off the elevator on Tianna's floor, they saw Tianna's mom, Thelma, saying her goodbyes.

She walked up to Amber and said, "Tianna's in a good mood because her therapy is going well." Thelma smiled at Eddie and said. "Eddie, I hope you have a pleasant conversation today with Tianna. She told me You were here when she was still in a coma." She turned, smiled and started down the hallway. When she passed the head nurse, she said, "Karen, I'll be back this evening."

Amber and Eddie walked into Tianna's room. Amber hugged her friend, and Eddie stood and watched.

"Well, Eddie, why don't you come over here and give me a hug, too," said Tianna.

He did and said, "It's great you're so much better, Tianna. And I'm glad you let me come with Amber."

"Great," said Tianna. "Now, let's get down to business. Tell me what your dad found."

"First I have questions, Tianna. Other than at King High School last Friday, when was the last time you got shot?" asked Amber.

"That would be in July 1967," said Tianna. "But why are you asking now?"

"And your name was?"

"OK. My name was Amanda Carson, and I lived in the Brewster-Douglass apartments on the seventh floor."

"Damn, I thought I would trip you up. Did you know Clarence then?"

"You know I did. We used to talk a lot. He was in college, and he was super nice. I haven't told Grandpa yet, but I can't wait to tell him," Tianna said.

Eddie was standing with a blank look on his face. "Will one of you tell me what the hell you're talking about?" he asked.

Both Tianna and Amber laughed. Amber told Eddie to sit down, and she would give him the skinny on what's happening so far. As she told Eddie, he questioned the whole story.

"Are you sure your memories are of actual reincarnation, and not just imaginations from when you were unconscious?" he asked.

"Positive. I think that's why Amber tried to trick me. So when did you find out about Amanda?" she asked.

"Last night, Dad and his partner were over at our house with your grandfather. They investigated Amanda Carson's killing in 1967. It seems the same gun used in our shooting last Friday is the same gun used in 1967, and then your grandpa told them he knew you back then. It was so unreal, Tianna. I wanted to tell them what I knew so badly, but I didn't."

"Good. Now, Eddie and Amber, are you ready for the story of my second life?"

"Yes," they said in unison.

"This may take a while, so if you need to use the bathroom, do it now."

Eddie looked at Amber. She shook her head, and he said, "We're ready to listen, Tianna."

* * *

"When my first life ended, Fort Pontchartrain was a French fort. France and England were not on friendly terms with each other. The two nations seemed to always be at war. They were more like Indian clans than they realized."

"My second birth was on July 31, 1748. My father traveled from Montreal and came to Detroit in 1745. I think he was trying to get away from his family because he had nothing good to say about them. The French wanted more people to settle in Detroit. So, they made it easy for him to purchase land with the little money he had earned in Montreal. He fell in love with the Detroit wilderness as soon as he arrived, and he became great friends with his neighbors, the Ottawa."

"Over time, Dad built a small home on his property and started an orchard, bought chickens, cows and other animals from the French authorities. He met Mother, an Ottawa Indian, when she and her sisters helped him clear the back section of his land. Dad and Mom fell in love, and he asked her father for her hand. Because the Ottawas like the French, and my father was a good man, he won approval to marry. They were married at Saint Anne's Church by the priest and settled down on his farm."

"Daddy always said Mom was beautiful in her traditional Ottawa wedding dress. I arrived the year after they married. Mother named me Shawnna because it was a name from her ancestors. My little brother, Joseph, was born the next year, and my little sister, Agatha, when I was three. Mom and Dad were very busy with the three of us youngsters."

"During this time, there was a lot of turmoil in Detroit. The Hurons fought alongside the British in the war against the French. They became upset when the French stopped selling brandy to them. The British were more than willing to sell them alcohol as long as they fought for them against the French and their allied Indian tribes. Mother's tribe, the Ottawa, were loyal to the French."

"Fort Pontchartrain fluctuated between being a forsaken outpost to a booming settlement with many soldiers. Sometimes few soldiers were present, and their supplies always ran out. Mom and Dad had to help feed the soldiers, without. When the British fought for control of France's territory in the Americas, more troops came to Detroit along with supplies. Daddy said the war brought some good to the area. The French also gave incentives for people to move here and start farms."

"When I was four years old, illness and famine swept over Detroit. The famine resulted from a sudden early freeze the year before that destroyed the crops. Father said the illness that killed many people was smallpox, a deadly disease that came over with the European people. I saw a lot of death that winter, and I remember the sorrow that filled our home when my little brother became ill. He suffered terribly and died in my father's arms. Mother cried for days, and Father grew silent and didn't want to play with me and my sister. I was only four, but I had to help take care of my sister and help with the chores around the farm."

"Mom overcame her grief in a few weeks, but Father never recovered. He died when I was eight. My mother said sadness took him to the spirit world. Losing his only son sucked the life out of him. I always wished I could have become a boy, so he would smile again and live longer."

Amber felt Tianna's sorrow and said, "Tianna, it wasn't your fault that your dad couldn't live with his grief. Today, they would call it depression. It's an illness, not a weakness."

"I know, but it still hurts. Mother married again the following summer. He was a nice man, and also a Frenchman. Mom said he married her because he could marry into a family and gain a farm to call his own. He made her happy and treated us well. It would have been impossible for her to keep the farm by herself, and I think she loved him."

"In 1760, when I was twelve, the British took over the fort in Detroit. They won the war with France, and the treaty gave them all the forts in Michigan. The new British commander of the fort was Major Robert Rogers. My step-father grew upset, as did the Ottawas and their leader, Chief Pontiac."

"My step-father spent most of his time away from Detroit. He told Mother he had business dealings in Montreal and spent most of the summer there. We missed him, but it almost seemed easier when he wasn't there. When he was home, he and Mother would argue, and my sister and I felt like we were the reason for their troubles. Mother said it was the British who made him so angry. She said he hated the British so much that he could not stand to be near them. He went back to France to see his family, and she didn't know if he would return."

"I spent most of my spare time with the Ottawa people, who often camped near our home. They were amazing, and I loved their lifestyle. My mother didn't mind. She said it was half of my heritage, and she wanted me to learn everything I could about her people."

"One day she told me, *Shawnna, you have within you the spirit of our people. I believe you will become an important link between the worlds of then and now.*"

"I wasn't sure what she meant, but I now realize Mother knew more about me than I did."

"One day, while I was visiting the Ottawa camp, Mother and my sister were helping our cousins clean and preserve deerskins. I went for a walk, and as I walked through the still woods, I kept hearing someone behind me. I stopped and hid so I could see who it was. When I saw the young warrior trying to keep from being seen or heard, I jumped in front of him, and he fell on his back. I frightened him, and he turned as white as a Redcoat."

"Laughing, I said, *What kind of warrior are you? You're so noisy, the dead spirit of my father could have heard you.*"

"He said he wasn't trying to follow me, but I knew better."

"We sat for a while, arguing about how to walk without being heard. I showed him. My skills amazed him."

"You are good for a girl," he said.

"A girl? You make me sound like being a girl is a bad thing. You're the one who acts like a girl. Perhaps you should stay with the old women when Chief Pontiac goes to war. If you go with him, everyone will know he's coming."

"I'm not old enough to go into battle yet. Soon, though. Father says I will make a great brave because I have his blood. He is one of the strongest warriors in our tribe."

"I learned his name was Achak, which means spirit, and he became my best friend. When the Ottawas moved their village north, to be away from the British, Achak asked if he could stay with me and my mother to help her on the farm. There were several other Ottawa Indians who were staying, and Chief Pontiac gave his approval. Pontiac and Mother were friends, and Achak would learn much from Mother, and he could help us keep the farm in operation."

"Achak stayed at our farm, but he would not stay inside our home."

"Mother spoke to Achak, saying, "There is room for you to sleep inside our home. We have a soft bed for you. So, why don't you want to become a member of our family?""

Achak replied, "I am a warrior. I will stay on the outside of your home and watch for intruders. My chief has given me much responsibility to protect you, Shawnna, and her sister, Agatha.""

"I knew it would be useless to keep trying to convince him to change his mind. Like Mother, he was stubborn."

"Achak and I would talk, walk through the wilderness, and visit for hours. Together we worked in the fields, hunted for small animals, and helped mother with the farm animals. We also took produce to the store at the fort to trade for items that Mother needed. I was falling in love with him, and I knew he loved me as well. It felt like the spirits predetermined our love."

"Whenever Chief Pontiac and his warriors came back to Detroit, they would set up camp either on mother's or our neighbor's farm. The French farmers became divided in their opinion of the British. Some of them accepted British rule over the fort and the Detroit settlement, but my step-father and mother hated them and did everything they could to help the Ottawa. Mother wanted Chief Pontiac to fight for the removal of the Redcoats from the Indian Nation, and my step-father again left Detroit. He was trying to get help from France."

"Pontiac met with the chiefs and warriors of the Ottawa, Chippewa, Huron, and Potawatomi tribes. He convinced almost sixty other chiefs to help him wage war against Fort Détroit and the other British forts in the surrounding areas. They came up with a plan to get the British to let them into the forts, using trickery. Once they were inside, they would begin a full scale attack from inside and outside the fort."

* * *

"The date of the Indian attack on all Midwestern British forts would be May 8, 1763. I was fifteen and Achak was seventeen. His father told him he would not be among the fifty warriors who would go to the fort with Chief Pontiac that day. Chief Pontiac had sawed-off shotguns hidden under blankets he told the fort guards were a special gift for the commander. The plan was to get inside and then attack. The warriors outside would storm through the open gate and join the battle."

"Pontiac didn't know someone, perhaps a farmer or Indian who was in league with the British, had informed the commander of the plan. The commander didn't let the warriors into the fort."

"The Indians who were invading the other forts were much more successful than Pontiac. Indians took over all the other British forts, except Fort Detroit and Fort Pitt. Since Pontiac didn't overthrow the fort, he attacked it from outside. The war was on, and it would be bloody."

"Pontiac vowed, *You will not have food, weapons or ammunition delivered to your fort until you surrender.* He would keep up the siege but could not rouse them out of the fort."

"Every day the fighting continued. Some farmers tried to get food into the fort, but when Pontiac saw that, he captured and killed them to show everyone how serious he was. After he killed someone, they scalped them and staked their bloody body to the outside of the fort. He wanted to scare the soldiers to make them surrender quicker."

"During June 1763, a British Captain, James Dalyell, sailed down the river to the fort. Pontiac could not stop large ships from reaching the fort by the river, and supplies were coming into the fort."

"On the 21st of July, Mother and I spent the night at the Ottawa encampment, a few miles north of the fort. We were there because the next day would be my birthday, and Mother wanted to take food to our friends to prepare for a celebration. One farmer, who the British thought was on their side, told Pontiac that Captain Dalyell would attack his village before dawn. Pontiac took all of his warriors south to the mouth of the creek running through his encampment and set a trap for the British Redcoats."

"Achak and I talked during the early morning hours before the battle."

"Shawnna," he said, "I know you fear for me, but I am a better warrior than I was when we first met. I want you to promise you will not come near the fighting."

"Achak knew me too well. I wanted to be there to protect him. I loved him and would die for him if needed."

"I won't follow you, Achak, but when this war is over, promise you will marry me so I can be the mother of many children with you."

"We hugged, and he joined his father and the warriors. Mother and I sat with the other women and children, hidden from the view of the British. We were not afraid, as we had been in fights like this before. This time, however, it was the British who wanted to kill us, not another Indian tribe."

* * *

"I listened throughout the early morning. In the distance, and heard gunfire, and I could smell smoke and burning flesh. We were afraid to come out into the morning light. We didn't know if our braves were safe, but if they were not, we were sure the British would kill us."

"As the sun painted the morning sky with light, I heard the scream of a young brave, and knew it was Achak. Jumping into the clearing. I wanted to run, but I had to keep my promise, no matter what happened. I walked forward, straining to hear or see anything I could, and suddenly I felt something explode in my chest. For a moment, my eyes became blurred. Like a tree fallen by beavers, I fell face forward, crashing into the leaves on the forest floor, smelling the musty earth where my ancestors are now buried, and where my grieving mother would place my lifeless body. My spirit lifted above my body, and I felt myself floating over the forest. I could see the small creek, flowing red with the blood of my people and the British soldiers."

CHAPTER 17

Eddie jumped up and said, "That's the most powerful story I've ever heard. Damn, Tianna! You were with the Indians during Pontiac's raid on Fort Détroit! You were there! Holy Jesus, that's unreal."

Tianna laughed. "Eddie, I like your enthusiasm. You can keep talking because I like what you're saying."

"Well, I liked the story too," said Amber, "but I still wonder if it's a dream or a genuine memory from the past."

"Amber, I will figure out how to prove to you it's not a dream," said Tianna.

Eddie walked to the window ledge, turned back toward the two girls and in a low voice said, "Are you going to tell anyone else about this?"

"I don't know, Eddie."

"Well, I think you need to be careful. I mean, I've heard of people who wound up in mental hospitals and had all kinds of electroshock treatments, and potent drugs, because they told stories like that."

"A little dramatic there, Eddie, but you have a point," said Amber. "I already told Tianna not to tell anyone or they'll think she's nuts."

Tianna looked sad for a moment. "Amber, you don't believe me, do you?"

"Hey, I do," said Eddie.

"Tianna, it's not that I don't believe you think you lived before. It's just so hard to imagine it happening. The more you tell us about your lives, the more I realize you couldn't just be making it up as you go. It's too real, and I want to believe you." Amber's eyes filled with tears.. She gave Tianna an enormous hug, and said, "Don't be mad at me. You know you're the serious one, and I always say the crazy stuff. I love you, Tianna, and I would never hurt you."

"It's OK, Amber. It feels good just to tell you and Eddie about my previous life. Speaking about it helps me too. And soon, I'll figure out how to prove it's all true. Every day, I'm getting stronger and more aware of the past. I'm sure I can show you it's all real."

Eddie asked if the girls wanted him to get a drink for them. Tianna told him to go to the waiting room and get coffee, or he could get three ice waters at the nurses' station. As he walked out the door, she watched him. "You know, Amber, he's even cuter than I remember. Did you see him walk? I wonder if he can dance?"

"Don't worry, Tianna. If you can get on that dance floor, he'll be ready to sweep you off your feet. I promise."

Eddie came back into the room with three large Styrofoam cups of ice water. "Here you go. Now, do we have time to hear the next one?"

Amber checked her phone for the time and said, "We have two hours before our moms get here. Is that enough time?"

"Yes, provided there are no interruptions," said Tianna.

"This time, I returned in 1802. I was born to Joseph Andrew Collingwood and his wife, Mary Elizabeth. My mother died giving birth, and because he wanted a boy to carry on his name, he named me Josephina. I always wished Mother had lived long enough for me to know her. Father said she was born in Detroit and was a mixture of French and Indian. She lived on the farm a half mile from where Father grew up."

"When I was a young girl, Father would tell me, *Josie, your mother was the most beautiful woman in all of Detroit. She was kind, smart, and a joy to be with. I will miss her forever, but I have you to always remind me how wonderful she was. I believe you will be as beautiful and wise as she was.*"

"My father was an exciting and energetic man. He was always busy making money. I learned from Grandfather that as a youngster, Father would buy and raise chickens so he could sell the eggs and then, when the chickens got old, he sold them as boiling hens. He worked on his parents' farm and made money for himself and his family. When he raised enough of his own money, he bought baby pigs and cattle, and raised them until he could sell them for even more money. When he was sixteen, he had enough money to rent a small building in Detroit where he sold his produce and the produce from other local farms. He kept buying and selling until he was a wealthy man."

"The store in Detroit was wooden, like all the other buildings, and Father had built several small rooms on the second floor. When he was working, he would stay above the store. Sometimes he was away from us for many weeks. I stayed on the farm that Father purchased from the farmer who lived next door to his parents' house. There was a beautiful old French farmhouse on it. Father's eldest sister, Ann Marie, stayed with me. She became the housekeeper, babysitter, and my best friend. Ann Marie's husband died when the ship he was sailing on sank in a severe storm on Lake Huron. Neither Father nor his sister wanted to remarry, so sharing a home satisfied both of their needs."

"It was wonderful being an only child. Every Christmas, all the gifts were for me, and since Father owned his own store, I could ask for anything. Well, almost anything. Once I asked for a little sister, and I learned the facts of life. Father Christmas does not bring little girls a baby sister, and my father was not intending to do it himself."

"Detroit was a small village in 1805, with many wooden homes and businesses. When it rained, which was often, the dirt streets turned to mud. Horses and buggies were the primary form of getting around, so Father had a stable behind his store where he kept horses and buggies he used for his business. The business had four workers in the store: two salespeople, and two men who stocked the shelves. Father sold everything from food to clothing. He said it was a general store, which meant that he sold generally just about everything. At least, that's what I thought it meant."

"At the time of the great fire of 1805, the new United States of America separated Michigan from the rest of the Northwest Territory and called it the Michigan Territory. Washington named Detroit as its capital. I was four when the fire started. It was on the far side of town. We could smell its smoke before we saw the fire. Father and his employees knew the fire would reach his business; so they loaded everything from the store onto the wagon and took it outside of town. The store was close enough to our farm that Father could take the merchandise there, and the men put everything in a barn. It took about four hours to empty the store, and then he helped other families move out their belongings. Around the village, there were piles of things that people were trying to save from the fire. Father said the old wooden buildings in Detroit burned up like kindling. When the fire ended, there was only one building left standing, and you could see all the fireplace chimneys. Everyone was sad, but I still had a home to sleep in that night. Many people had to sleep on the ground guarding their belongings."

"A few days after the fire, my father and his men bought wood and other supplies from nearby towns. They purchased building supplies and brought them to the farm. He announced he would give credit for much of the material, so his friends and neighbors could rebuild."

"Before the villagers rebuilt, they held meetings to decide how to layout the new village. The area was now part of the new Michigan, and the leaders of Detroit wanted to make sure designed the village in a manner befitting of a great city. There were many ideas, but the territorial governor, William Hull, and Judge Augustus Woodward designed Detroit as a planned community, like the larger cities around the world. Woodward drew up a city map based on the design of Washington, D.C., the new capital of the great United States. Since he drew up the design, he named one street after himself, Woodward Ave. The villagers didn't mind because they liked the design and they also liked Judge Woodward."

"Once they marked the streets and drew the property lines, the reconstruction began. It was amazing. I watched as men, women and children helped rebuild the homes and businesses destroyed less than a year before. And the buildings were larger and nicer because they were new, and of a modern design. Because Father had purchased land on both sides of his business, he built his general store larger than any other store on Woodward. He wanted to have the largest store in the new city, and for a while he did."

"As the city grew, so did the area outside the village. There were small towns popping up everywhere. New farmers were coming into the area, and roads were being built to connect the villages. Father kept buying land and selling it to the new settlers. The people he lent money to were paying him back, and he reinvested that money into new ventures. Everything was going great, but his life was his business."

"During the War of 1812, Britain again took over the fort at Detroit, and they also captured the fort on Mackinac Island. There wasn't much change in our lives, and the Americans took control of Detroit again in 1813 after the battle of 1812. Father continued his business dealings, even during hard times."

"It got to where I would only see him on weekends. My aunt was raising me as best she could. She knew I missed being with Father, but she kept telling me, *Josephina, your father is a very important man. I know he loves you very much, but you will always have to share him with the city he also loves.*"

"That was a hard lesson to learn because my father spoiled me. I always got my way, and it upset me that Father didn't do more with me. I was now thirteen and becoming a woman. My aunt was like my mother, but she wasn't, and I felt alone."

"I didn't have friends, as they felt I was too well-to-do for them, so I spent most of my time reading and writing. I wrote dark poetry about life, and I wrote angry letters to my father, which I never sent him. One beautiful summer day, as I was sitting on the farmhouse porch reading one of my aunt's romantic books, a boy from the farm across the way stopped in and asked if we needed any help. He was my age, very nice looking, and soft-spoken. I told him to wait a moment as I ran into the house. I talked fast and worked hard to convince my aunt to give him a job because I wanted a friend… a boyfriend. My aunt laughed at me, but she told him to come by every day for three hours in the afternoon. She would pay him to help clean and trim the orchard and garden."

"Travis Monroe became my friend that summer, and I would go out into the orchard while he was working to help him do his job. I had never done work before, and I discovered I loved having dirty hands. I loved to garden, watch the plants grow, and enjoy the feeling of accomplishment when I completed the job. And by the end of summer, love filled my heart for my new world and for Travis."

* * *

"Travis and I spent hours together. We planned our future, and I discovered he was very much like my father. He saved every penny he earned and wanted to own his own business. A month before my sixteenth birthday, he asked me to marry him. He said he would buy me a ring, but I told him I had enough rings. We would use his money to build a business, like Father did."

"Amber, he made me so happy, but I couldn't tell Father. Work consumed all his time, and now he only came back to the farm on special occasions. He lived in the apartment above one of his businesses. Father had enough money, but he couldn't stand to be with me. When we were together, he was distant and always solemn."

"Aunt Anna said, *Josie, you look so much like your mother that your father can only think of her when he sees you. I know it's wrong, but you have to understand.*"

"I couldn't understand why my father didn't want to love and be with his only child. It made me angry."

"A day before my birthday, my aunt took me into Detroit to see James Madison, the President of the United States, On Wednesday, August 13, 1817, Father and many other important business people who had been meeting with the president were to be speaking to the city. As they spoke about how the city rose from the ashes, and how important the city was to the United States, we were all very proud. We loved our city, and we loved our country."

"After the speech, we toured Detroit's business district. Father was so proud of his general store and real estate holdings. He now owned a bank and helped many other business owners. They scheduled a dance for the evening, and I asked Father if I could go."

"You? No... you're much too young to be going to such an important dance like that," he said. "Perhaps after you turn sixteen."

"But Father, I will be sixteen tomorrow and soon I will marry Travis."

"Father burst out laughing. *You will not marry that farm boy, Josephina Collingwood. You are my daughter, and he is not of a high enough standard for you. I want you to marry someone of my choosing. Someone who has money, education, and upbringing.*"

"Father, I love Travis because he is the man you must have been when you were young. And since when did you become an aristocrat? You were only a farm boy who worked your way up to become a business owner. You started out just like my Travis."

"Josephina, I will never allow you to marry that boy, and that is my last word."

"When he said that, I screamed at him, slapped his face, and yelled, *I hate you, Father, and I am going away forever.* I ran to the stable behind the general store and hitched up a horse and buggy. Travis and I planned to meet later that afternoon at the bend next to the river near his father's farm, so I could tell him what Father said, but I would talk him into leaving with me today. I would not spend another day under my father's control."

"I was riding much too fast over the rough road when the buggy hit a rut and almost tipped over. I stopped and stood up to see if Travis was at the river bend. Suddenly, something knocked me over the edge of the buggy, and I tumbled down the ravine, and into the river. I was lying on my back, looking through the leaves toward the sky. I wanted to get up, but I couldn't move. My eyes stayed open as I felt myself lifting out of my body. Floating above the trees, I turned and looked down, and I could see that my face was bloody and the water surrounding my head was red. I was dead, lying in the river while the horse and buggy headed toward home. I knew my father and Travis would think I left them unless they found my body before the wild animals did. My third life was over, and again I never reached my sixteenth birthday. As I floated toward the spirit world, I wondered why?"

Amber had tears in her eyes. "Tianna, I don't know how much more of this I can take. I saw you get shot once, and now I'm reliving your deaths. We need to stop now."

"I'm sorry, Amber. I don't want to make you sad, but I need to find out why this is happening."

Eddie stood and said. "Yes, and we also need to find out who the killers are. There must be a reason you're being kept from turning sixteen." He sat down again and thought. "Why didn't you die this time? What happened this time?"

"Dr. Carter's little nanoparticles?" asked Amber.

"Perhaps that's why. Dr. Carter said I would die if the treatment didn't work. God bless modern medicine," laughed Tianna.

CHAPTER 18

Amber heard her mother's voice coming from the hall. She jumped up and walked to the open door of Tianna's room. She looked down toward the nurses' station and noticed her mom with Tianna's mother. They were talking to the nurses.

"Tianna, our moms are here. Is there anything you want Eddie and me to do for you before we go?"

"Well, you could do my physical therapy for me. That would be a great help," she said.

"No, I'm being serious. If you need anything, let me know. I will be back after school again tomorrow, if that's OK? Eddie, do you want to come back with me?"

Eddie smiled his big smile and said, "If Tianna will have me back."

"Are you kidding, Eddie?" said Tianna. "You're always welcome. Besides, I have more stories to tell the two of you."

Alice and Thelma were standing in the doorway. Thelma walked into the room and asked, "So what stories are you telling these two?"

"Hi, Mom. I've been giving them history lessons. And how are you and Mrs. Thornson?"

"Oh, we're fine," said Alice. "Amber, Eddie, are you two ready to go? Your father will be home soon, so we should get going."

"Can we drop Eddie off at his place?" asked Amber. She then added, "It's on our way… sort of."

"No problem, Honey. Tianna, it's great hearing you're doing better, but how is the physical therapy going?"

"Great, I can stand on my own… with help. My therapist says I should walk in two days," Tianna said with pride.

"Wonderful. We will be back tomorrow," she said as she approached Thelma. "I'll talk to you later, and you and Carson have a good time. Be sure to call me when you get home; I want all the details."

"Hell no, Alice," declared Thelma. "I don't kiss and tell."

Alice laughed and started for the door, with Amber and Eddie behind her. After they left, Tianna asked her mother, "Mr. Ewald? You're seeing my English teacher tonight? When did this all come about, Mom?"

"Don't get all worked up, Tianna. He was here to see you when you were still unconscious, and we sort of hit it off. He asked me out to dinner after I leave here tonight. I like him, and he seems to like me. So, Honey, is that OK with you?"

"Yes, Mom. I like him too. In fact, sometimes in class, I daydream about how you two would make a good couple. He sure is a looker, isn't he?"

"Hell, yes! Almost as good-looking as your dad was. Not that I'm trying to replace your dad," added Thelma.

"I understand, but you've been a single woman long enough. You need to be with men your age, and I'm sure Grandpa won't mind."

"Mind, he pushed me into accepting Carson's invitation. I hesitated, and your grandfather told me to get off my butt and take a chance."

"Yup, Grandpa sure knows how to use the words, doesn't he," laughed Tianna. "I hope it works out for you, Mom."

After spending an hour, Tianna suggested her mom should head for home. "You'll want to be ready for Mr. Ewald, and I'm tired. I talked so much today my mind is in overdrive. I want to relax a little."

Thelma agreed and kissed her daughter goodbye. "I love you, Honey, and I'll tell you everything when I see you tomorrow after your physical therapy sessions."

"Every detail, Mom," said Tianna.

After her mother left, Tianna asked the nurse if there was anything she could take to help her sleep. The nurse talked to Dr. Kohl, and he suggested warm milk, but no medications and no caffeine. Happily, Tianna slept through the night without waking once. The Doctor's remedy worked.

* * *

"Hello sunshine," came the cheerful voice of her physical therapist, Jordon. "Are you ready for a good workout this morning?"

"I guess. At least I had a good night's rest."

"Great! Let's see you get off the bed."

"I can't. You know I can't," insisted Tianna.

"No, I don't. So show me you can't. But you have to try."

Tianna pulled at her legs. With great effort, they moved to the edge of the bed, and she turned and dropped them down the side, pushing herself toward the floor. Jordon was ready to catch her if she fell, but she landed on her feet. He pulled the wheelchair around so she could sit under her own power. A huge grin filled her face, and she laughed.

"Oh, my God. I did it, didn't I?"

"Sure did, and after today you'll be able to stand and get back in bed by yourself. Now, let's get down to the department. We've got work to do and muscles to stretch."

When Tianna got back to her room, she saw her grandfather sitting in the chair, reading a book on his iPad. She wheeled herself into the room, up to him. "Hi, Grandpa," she said.

"Lord, you startled me," he said. "They told me you were getting your legs adjusted. How are they doing this morning?"

"Great! I got out of bed on my own, and I could stand for two minutes with no one holding me. Grandpa, I think I'll be able to go home soon."

"Wonderful. The house is so empty without you. No loud music, no neighborhood kids traipsing through the kitchen. It's just God awful boring."

"Good. I'm glad you missed me. So what are you reading today?"

"I'm reading a book about the Underground Railroad in Detroit. It's interesting," he said, handing the iPad to her.

Tianna wanted to share the life she lived during the 1850s, but she didn't know what he would think.

"It sounds interesting. Perhaps when you're done, I can read the book," she said.

Tianna decided she would have to wait to tell her grandfather about her previous lives until she sorted it out for herself. The memories are becoming even more vivid, and she now realizes that when she recalls a memory, she is there reliving the moment as the person she was. It has become very hard on her because the trauma of her deaths are as real now as they were when she first died.

"Grandpa, do you believe in reincarnation?" she asked.

"I don't know, Honey. Why do you ask?"

"Amber and I have talked about it several times. Sometimes, I feel like I've done things before. You know, I think they call it déjà vu. Isn't that what they call it?"

"Yes. I think we all get those feelings. I'm not sure why we have déjà vu. Maybe we've lived before, but more likely maybe we had a dream or experience in the past. We remember those dreams because it reminds us of the present event. God only knows for sure, Honey," Clarence said.

Clarence reminded Tianna that she had schoolwork to finish. Tianna's teachers sent over homework she could do so she wouldn't get behind. She had already caught up on most of the work, but some math problems would be a challenge.

"Do you want to do my math, Grandpa?"

"No! I was not an excellent math student, so you would be better off without my help. History, English, and Social Studies are my better areas."

Tianna laughed and buzzed for the nurse. When she responded, Tianna asked if there was a place she could go to do her homework. The nurse smiled and said there were classrooms and tutors who could help. Together, they gathered Tianna's books and wheeled her down the hall. Clarence walked with them, and while Tianna worked with the tutor, he continued reading.

By noon, Tianna had finished with her schoolwork and got ready to return to her room for lunch. Clarence decided he would catch the bus and return home since he was also hungry and had things that needed fixing around the yard.

"You're doing so well, Tianna. I understand your friends will be here at three today, and Thelma is coming tonight. So, I'm on my way out. I love you, Honey."

"Love you too, Grandpa. And remember, I have an iPhone, so call me."

"I'll do that."

* * *

During the afternoon, Tianna listened to her audiobook, had another workout session with Jordon, her physical therapist, and then slept until two o'clock. After that, she had the most wonderful opportunity to have a shower. When she got out of the water, a nurse's aide worked on her hair. Tianna put lipstick on and used some perfume her mom bought for her.

"There you go, Tianna," said the aide. "You look beautiful. You can hardly see that they cut your hair in the back, and the scars will disappear soon."

The doctors removed the last bandages after lunch, and she was now feeling whole again, and could walk several steps on her own at therapy. Jordon told her she would go home by the weekend, and then go daily for therapy, perhaps after school.

Tianna asked the aide, "Samantha, do you think my hair would look better cut short? If it would, then I wouldn't need to hide where they cut it off for the surgery."

"Honey, I would never cut that beautiful long black hair. We could give it a little trim…. but short? I wouldn't."

As they finished up with Tianna's makeup, Amber and Eddie walked through the door. Eddie whistled and said, "Wow, you're beautiful, Tianna. Did they take you to a spa today?"

Tianna laughed and said, "Sort of, Eddie. I got my bandages removed and spent an hour with Samantha here."

"Great job, Samantha," said Amber. "Isn't her hair beautiful to work with? I wished my frizzy top was as smooth as Tianna's hair."

"Honey, your hair looks fine," said Samantha. "Tianna, I'll be back tomorrow, so you guys have a pleasant visit."

While Amber and Tianna talked about makeup, perfume, and hair length, Eddie looked over Tianna's homework and made two changes to her math worksheet.

"Hey smarty," yelled Amber, "what makes you think your answer is better than Tianna's?"

"Because I was in class today when the teacher gave the answers."

"Great," said Tianna, "you can check all the math problems. I tried to talk Grandpa into helping me, but he was clueless."

"Where are we in your stories?" asked Amber.

"Are you ready to continue? I feel stronger, but every time I go back to a previous life, I feel like I'm dying again. It's not as easy as it sounds. I relive the experiences, and not just remember them."

"If it hurts too much, then don't," said Eddie.

"I wanted to tell the story, and I wanted the two of you to know why I get emotional. The pain is real, but I want to share everything with my two best friends."

Amber and Eddie pulled up a chair next to Tianna's wheelchair. Tianna began, "I was reborn in 1835, into a colored family in Detroit. Mom's father was once a slave in Alabama. Grandpa's owner gave him his surname, Smith, and a first name of Aaron. His owner died having no family left, and his last will and testament asked that Grandpa and the other slaves were to be given their freedom. Grandpa was a preacher of sorts. He didn't have a formal education, but he could read and write, something his former master taught him. In reading the Bible, he taught the Lord's message to his friends and neighbors. In 1800 he moved north and married grandmother who was half colored and half Indian. Grandma lived in an Indian village south of Detroit. She met Grandpa at a prayer meeting where he was preaching about the words of Christ. When he saw a beautiful colored woman standing in front of him, he knew she would be his wife. Together they moved up to Detroit, where no one knew she was half Indian."

"Grandma found a job as a maid for a white family, and Grandpa worked as a gardener at the same estate. Every Sunday, he would invite their colored friends over and give Bible lessons. There were not a lot of colored families in Detroit, and none of the churches would accept colored members. They had to organize their own religious services. In 1812, Mother was born. She was the second child and was a beautiful girl named Rebecca."

"My father, Alexander Davis, was a free man from Buffalo, New York. A white man trained him as a blacksmith's assistant in Buffalo, and he heard there were many opportunities for free blacks in the fast-growing city of Detroit."

"The Erie Canal opened in 1825 and connected New York City and Buffalo. It then connected Lake Erie and made it possible to take a ship from the east coast to the Great Lakes. Father knew Detroit would become a great city, and he had friends who had already settled there. They considered Detroit a good place for coloreds, even though there were also some slaves there. Years earlier, white Detroiters had bought and sold as slaves both colored and Indians. Still, it was a fast-growing city with many opportunities."

"Dad left his home in 1829, when he was eighteen, and sailed across Lake Erie and up the Detroit River. He found his friends waiting for him, and they had already arranged living quarters and a part-time job in a blacksmith shop. On the second day of his new life in Detroit, he met my mother, Rebecca Smith. His friends invited him to a prayer meeting one Sunday morning, and Grandfather was reading from the Bible, and singing hymns. It was a joyous event, especially when he met Mom. They fell in love, married and for many years they lived with Mom's parents. I was born in 1835 and given the name Carol Ann Davis."

CHAPTER 19

The most important lesson I learned as I grew up is that freedom is the most precious gift that God can give us. We are truly blessed to have our freedom. I had to learn this lesson from others because I was born free and never tasted the pain of slavery. Grandpa would tell stories about what it was like being a slave, and I would cry when he told of the atrocities inflicted on his family. His master was better than most, but he still treated his slaves as less than human beings who were there only for the service of the master. I have a hard time understanding how a person could think of themselves as the master. Only God is the master who we look up to, and I know white Men Are Not Gods.

When I was eleven years old, I met many people of color who were slaves and former slaves. We all lived in a closely knit neighborhood on the lower East Side of Detroit, and we vowed to help our brothers who also sought freedom. Because of this desire, we worked with both white and colored groups of Quaker, Baptist and Methodist congregations and individuals who believed no one should suffer as a slave. Momma called them abolitionists. The group organized into the Underground Railroad to help slaves escape to freedom.

It was the path that runaway slaves took to reach Canada. Each step of the way, guides, or conductors, were there to provide them with shelter and guide them to the next station. Detroit was the last station where slaves crossed the Detroit River to freedom. We were there to provide them passage to Canada, a free country where slavery was illegal. If a slave made his way to Canada, he was a free man. And in time, that person could return to the United States as a free man, even if he lived in Detroit again.

Deadly Sixteen

Detroit was very important in the Underground Railroad because you could swim across the Detroit River and reach Canada. I wouldn't try it though. Dad says there is an undercurrent that can pull even an excellent swimmer down. He is always careful when he takes former slaves across. He uses small boats, and sometimes in the winter, when the river freezes over, runaway slaves have walked across. But that can be dangerous because of the thin ice.

I enjoyed having a grandfather who was a preacher. We all knew he wasn't a real preacher, but he knew the Lord's word better than any preacher around. There were many colored families that considered him their preacher.

My education came from family and neighbors. Those who could read, write, or do math, taught the children. Youngsters would come over to their house at a preset time. Grandpa, Dad, and Mom spent a lot of time teaching us. Dad was the best teacher because he taught math and science. He read a lot of practical books on how to make things. As a blacksmith, he had to know about everything, because people would come in and ask him to make items for them. If he said he didn't know how, they would leave and tell their friends he wasn't a good blacksmith. So, Dad always said he could do it, and then he found a book that told him how. Or he experimented until he found the solution. As I got older, I realized Dad was smart. Not just smart for a colored man, but smarter than anyone, colored or white.

I liked when my mother taught reading and writing. She would bring exciting novels that her employer loaned her. There were many old romance, adventure, and mystery books. All the kids would have to take turns reading out loud. But everyone enjoyed it when they asked me to read. I liked to change my voice to match the characters in the book. Mom told me I should become an actress on the stage because I read dramatically. Perhaps she meant I could be a show off, which I admit, is true.

When Grandpa taught reading, we had to read the Bible, and Lord knows that's hard to do. Some words made little sense, especially to the children who came from the South. They spoke with a strange drawl, and even I had trouble figuring out what those kids were saying. They would drag their words out and clip them short. Dad and Mom worked hard to help the southern folk learn how to talk and act like northerners. Dad said it was important not to act like Southern slaves if you wanted the respect of northern white employers. We helped new settlers find places to live and jobs they could do. We gave them clothing that didn't look like it belonged to poor southern people.

"In 1847, during the summer of my twelfth birthday, a family from Ohio made their way north. They were Mr. Edward Freeman, his wife Abigail, and their son Nathaniel. They moved north because there were new jobs becoming available in Detroit, and also because Ohio was getting stricter with people of color. Michigan's constitution said there could be no slavery in the state. Mr. Freeman feared they would have trouble staying free in Ohio, since his wife was a runaway slave and the laws said if the owner came and found her, she had to return with her owner."

"I was twelve and Nathaniel was fourteen. He was a very handsome colored boy over six feet tall with beautiful curly black hair, and he couldn't have weighed more than a hundred eighty pounds. Unlike most of the boys I knew, he already had to shave, and his muscles were very pronounced. Mom said he resembled my dad when he was young. It's hard to imagine Dad ever being as young and handsome as Nathaniel."

"Our church found the Freeman family a home to rent and a job. Mr. Freeman was an experienced carpenter, so he found a job at a factory building carriages and wagons. Dad said he was lucky because he had so much experience working in Cleveland. After the family had settled in, Mom invited them to our house for a picnic after church. There were several families who attended, including the Freemans. Everyone lived in the same neighborhood, so they walked to our house carrying platters of food. We set up tables in the backyard, and the women worked in the kitchen preparing the meal."

"I saw Nathaniel standing alone in the yard. He was looking at our garden. I approached him and said, *Do you like our garden, Nathaniel?*"

"Sure do. I miss the garden we had in Cleveland, and I spent a lot of time helping Mom with it."

"His comment surprised me, and I said, *Gee, I wouldn't have expected you to be into gardening.*"

"Why not?"

"Well, you don't look like the gardening kind of guy. I don't know... I mean... you know, you look like you would be into more manly things than the garden."

"Manly things?"

"You're going to let me hang out on this limb without helping me down, aren't you?" I asked.

"He burst into huge laughter and grinned from ear to ear. *Yes, but we can start over if you like.*"

"Please do, I feel like a fool now," I said.

"Hi, my name is Nathaniel, and I love your garden. Oh, and I think you're cute, too," he said, grinning.

* * *

"At that moment, I realized I was falling in love with Nathaniel Freeman. He was two years older than I, muscular and tall. I loved that he could do physical labor and still had a gentle side. He was the type of man that my father was. Strong, yet tender-hearted with a great sense of humor."

"That first summer we did everything together. I was a tomboy, so we avoided girly things, but we tended the small garden in the backyard and raised chickens for eggs and meat. We liked to play games such as jump rope, marbles, pickup sticks, and hopscotch. And, mom made us a cloth ball we threw around. Even though I had two homemade dolls, I never let him see them. I was becoming a woman, and I wanted Nathaniel to see me as one."

"Mom and Grandma worked at the Brandt estate on Woodward Avenue. Mr. and Mrs. Brandt employed them and worked in their wonderful three story castle. The home had a tall spire on one corner, and the room's walls were solid wood panels, polished until they were a deep shiny mahogany. Mrs. Elizabeth Brandt hosted many beautiful parties, and I often worked in the kitchen. When I was twelve, Mrs. Brandt asked if I would help serve the guests small treats from a beautiful silver platter."

"I told Mrs. Brandt that I would have to ask my mom. I ran up to her and asked, *What will happen if I drop something on one of her guests, or, Lord forbid, spill the entire platter on the floor?*"

"Then I will clean it up, and you will be embarrassed in front of all the guests. Don't worry, you are as graceful as a tall ship sailing down the Detroit River. You won't have an accident."

"If I do, I'm blaming you for talking me into it," I insisted.

"I loved Mrs. Brandt's parties. Her guests dressed in the most beautiful gowns. It was summer, and the women and girls wore huge flowing skirts with the smallest waists I have ever seen. Mom said they wore some kind of garment that made them skinny. The men wore suits of fine wool, fancy vests with watch chains and long pants with shiny shoes. They also wore tall black hats, which they took off when they walked through the doorway. Some of them forgot to remove their hats, and they hit the top door jamb and fell to the floor. I could hardly hold myself from laughing at them."

"I so wished I could own beautiful clothing like those women wore, so I told myself that when I got older, I would get a job that paid as much as Mr. Brandt's job. He was a doctor, and I was sure I could help people by being a doctor, too."

"Nathaniel was also working. Dad took him in as an apprentice at his blacksmith shop. He said that Nathaniel could learn many skills working with him. I didn't have any brothers, and Dad sometimes called him his adopted son. I don't know if he told Nathaniel or his parents that, but he told me."

"While I was growing up, my family helped smuggle runaway slaves into Canada. Nathaniel and I could not go with them when they were being taken across the river, but we helped take care of the former slaves while they were in our home, or at the church. Even though I was never a slave, I learned firsthand what it was like. I heard stories about the brutality of the masters. I heard women talk about how their babies had been sold to another master and ripped out of their arms, and how masters would physically abuse them, just for their enjoyment."

"One Sunday after church, the preacher came up to Mom and asked her and Dad to take two men and a woman into our home for two nights. The three of them were runaway slaves from South Carolina. Their master was cruel, and these three were the only members of their family who could get away. When they came into our home, Mother asked the two men to change into new clothing she had for them. They took off their shirts, and I gasped with shock. Their backs were cut with a thousand crisscrossing scars."

"Oh my God, what happened?" I asked.

"Massah, he did that. I've been gettin' whooped since I were a boy," the old man said.

"Ain't you ever been whipped?" the mother asked.

"No, never," I answered. "Does it hurt?"

"Did when he done it," he said. "Don't hurt now, tho."

"Why did he whip you? Did you do something wrong?"

"Ya. I be a slave. That's what I done wrong."

"Go on, Pa. You know why he whooped you," she said.

"Cause I'm a fighter. I fight back, and he hits me som' more, then I get madder, and he hits me even harder," he said, laughing.

"The stories of how these people survived and kept searching and asking the Lord for their freedom made me appreciate my freedom. I thanked God that night for everything I have, which is what these poor souls are still seeking."

"Mom and Dad continued to help the runaway slaves at our church, The Second Baptist. We also helped people like Mr. Finney, who owned the Finney Hotel in downtown Detroit. My folks helped George de Baptiste, a free colored man who was a business owner and owner of the T. Whitney, a steamship he purchased. These abolitionists helped thousands of runaway slaves reach Canada and freedom."

"On the day before I was to turn sixteen, Dad came home from his blacksmith shop and said, *Mr. Finney has ten runaway slaves hidden in a barn, and they need to get across the river tonight.*"

"Mom was cooking dinner, and she had bread in the oven. She frowned and asked, *Why so many, and why tonight?*"

"Because there are several slave hunters at his hotel. They know the slaves they are looking for are in town, and they won't stop 'till they catch them."

"I asked how they would get them across the river if the hunters are there, and Dad said, *We have to draw their attention to the wrong place. Mr. Baptiste can't take them because some hunters are standing guard at his steamship.*"

"Dad asked Mom if it would be OK if we all dressed up in old clothing and pretended to be runaway slaves."

"What will happen when they find out we're not slaves? Will they hurt us?" she asked with a frightened tone in her voice.

"I hope not, but what else can we do?"

"I'm willing to go. And I could ask Nathaniel to come with us," I suggested.

"He'll be going with another group of people. They are going in the opposite direction. The plan is to have four groups of us moving along the river shore. When the slave hunters follow us, then the real runaway slaves will cross the river in a rowboat. Mr. Finney has it all planned. He said that the hunters have been drinking all day, so they shouldn't be much of a match for us, but we have to be ready by eleven o'clock tonight."

"The sun had another hour to set, so we made our plans. After we ate supper, Mom brought out old clothing she had saved from past runaway slaves. She knew they might be useful, and tonight they would be. I put on a simple dress and an old coat and scarf. Dad wore old tan pants and a shirt that with rips and stains. He also had an old torn coat and a straw cap. When we went down to the meeting place, there were two other families dressed in similar clothes. We looked the part of runaway slaves, and I could see how this plan would work."

"Dad made noises to get anyone watching to notice us. We started down the riverbank as if we were looking for the boat to come and get us. We walked slowly and kept looking out over the river. One woman had her baby with her, and the little girl kept crying. She would cover her up and hold her tight to keep anyone from hearing. We wanted them to know there was a baby with us as one runaway had a baby with her."

"Suddenly there was yelling, *Stop there, you niggers!*"

"Three men with guns ran out at us. They were yelling and screaming. One man fell flat on his face because he was so drunk. Dad laughed and told me we could outrun these idiots if we were actual slaves."

"Don' shoot. We are just lookin' at the river. Ain't it pretty?" Mom said.

"We know you are runnin' away. We got you now. Where's the rest of your group?"

Dad laughed, and a slave hunter hit him in the face. With a big grin, Dad said, "You just hit a citizen of Detroit, Michigan, Mister. I'm the blacksmith and a friend of Judge Woodward. You know him. He loves to throw slave hunters into jail. Mom, don't you think we should turn these hoodlums over to Judge Woodward. I bet he'd throw their sorry asses in jail."

"Citizen my ass, you are my runaway slaves, and we got the papers to send you back to South Carolina," the slave hunter said.

"Dad pulled out his own paperwork that showed we were all residents of Detroit. The men became irritated, and swore at us, and warned us to stop messing around with them. *We got every right to hunt these niggers.* They kept saying that over and over as they walked back toward downtown."

"As we walked home, we sang *Steal Away To Jesus*, the spiritual song that many runaway slaves and conductors sang while traveling from one station to the next."

Amber and Eddie, it's such a touching song, and it goes like this: and Tianna sang....

Steal away, steal away, steal away to Jesus! Steal away, steal away home, I ain't got long to stay here!

My Lord calls me; He calls me by the thunder; The trumpet within-a my soul, I ain't got long to stay here.

Steal away, steal away, steal away to Jesus! Steal away, steal away home, I ain't got long to stay here!

Green trees are bending, Poor sinner stands a-trembling; The trumpet within-a my soul, I ain't got long to stay here.

Steal away, steal away, steal away to Jesus! Steal away, steal away home, I ain't got long to stay here!

Tomb stones are bursting, poor sinner stands a-trembling; The trumpet within-a my soul, I ain't got long to stay here.

Steal away, steal away, steal away to Jesus! Steal away, steal away home, I ain't got long to stay here!

My Lord calls me; He calls me by the lightning, The trumpet within-a my soul, I ain't got long to stay here.

Steal away, steal away, steal away to Jesus! Steal away, steal away home, I ain't got long to stay here!

"As we approached our house that night, I finished the last refrain. There was a gunshot, and I felt a pain in the back of my head."

"Dad screamed and grabbed me and I slipped to the ground. Mom and Dad were holding me and crying. My spirit left my lifeless body, and in my mind I could hear singing. *Green trees are bending, Poor sinner stands a-trembling; The trumpet within-a my soul, I ain't got long to stay here. Steal away, steal away, steal away to Jesus! Steal away, steal away home, I ain't got long to stay here!"*

"From above the green trees, I could see my family and neighbors bending over my body. On the river were several tall ships sailing by. The large rowboat with the runaway slaves was on the Canadian side of the river. A group of people of color helped them out of the boat and hugged them. They were being welcomed into their new land. I was crying. Not for my pain and loss, but because I was so happy they found their freedom."

CHAPTER 20

Eddie exclaimed, "Wow! That was beautiful. I can't believe you lived during that period of history. I've read some about the Underground Railroad, but God, you've lived it."

Tianna was ready to speak when she noticed that Dr. Kohl and the head nurse were standing at the door of her room. Amber noticed the look on Tianna's face and followed her eyes to the door.

"Dr. Kohl," she said. "Did you hear the tall tale that Tianna was telling us?"

Eddie chimed in, "Yes, she is a skilled storyteller. I think she gets it from her grandfather. He's been telling us stories about Detroit, too."

"Amber, we know it wasn't just a story," Dr. Kohl said. "The nurses have been listening to your stories, Tianna. I need to know what this is about. Do you think you have memories from a previous life?"

"Wow!" said Eddie again.

"Well, Tianna, I need to know," insisted Dr. Kohl.

"If I say yes, you'll think I'm nuts. I know I'm not crazy. I know what I feel and remember," said Tianna.

"Tianna, you had a serious brain injury on Friday, and over the weekend you had millions of nanobots running around inside your brain. You are the first person to have the experimental procedure we used, and I do not know what the ramifications are. It's important that we know everything that is going on in your head. If we altered your memories, if you can't sleep, or if you see pink elephants... we need to know."

Dr. Kohl walked into the room. Eddie stood and offered his seat next of Tianna. The only sounds in the room were the beeping of the monitors in the other rooms down the hall.

Tianna spoke. "When I awoke from the coma, I realized I remembered my past lives. As I let the images play in my mind, the details became clearer. The only people I've told are my friends here. And now you know."

Dr. Kohl had a grave look on his face. He thumbed through the papers on his clipboard and said, "I don't know what to say. I'm not a believer in reincarnation, yet there are millions of people who believe."

"I know it sounds crazy, Dr. Kohl. You know that this isn't something I wanted to happen. I would have preferred not hearing about my former lives."

Dr. Kohl turned to Eddie and Amber. He asked, "You've heard the stories of her former lives. What do the two of you think? Do you believe they are actual memories?"

Eddie said, "I believe she lived in the past. Her stories are just too realistic to be imagined."

"Amber?" asked Dr. Kohl.

Amber kept her head lowered, and she looked like she didn't want to answer the question. She shifted herself in the chair and looked at Tianna. "I believe Tianna lived in the past."

Tianna laughed. "Amber, you don't have to tell Dr. Kohl that for my benefit. I know you think I remember the stories Grandpa told me."

"That's what I thought until you told me you were Amanda Carson and you died in 1967. Dad told me that your grandfather Clarence admitted he knew Amanda. I asked you about it, and you said it was true." Amber turned to Dr. Kohl. "Tianna told me she knew her grandfather when she was Amanda, long before I told her what Dad said."

As the group was talking, Alice and Thelma stepped into the room. Thelma looked surprised that Dr. Kohl was there and asked, "Is there a problem, Dr. Kohl?"

"We have discovered that Tianna is now experiencing memories she feels are of former lives she has lived. The nurses heard her tell Amber and Eddie about them, and they notified me. We're just trying to determine what is happening."

"Good Lord, Tianna, why didn't you tell me?"

"Because I knew you and everyone else would think I was going crazy. I was afraid you would all react just like you are now," said Tianna, almost in tears.

Thelma hugged Tianna and said, "Honey, I don't think you're crazy. I love you, and I want the best for you."

"Even if it means you have to put me in a mental hospital and give me shock treatments and psychotic drugs?"

"Where is this coming from, Tianna?" asked Dr. Kohl.

Eddie interrupted, "Isn't that what they do to people they think are crazy?"

Dr. Kohl stood and faced Eddie. "No, Eddie. Not anymore. There are treatments for mental problems, just like there are treatments for physical illnesses. And besides, we don't even know if Tianna has any mental problems. Hell, for all we know, she is reincarnated."

Dr. Kohl sensed Thelma was upset. "Mrs. Gulliver, I don't think there is any problem that will interfere with Tianna's recovery. Her mental state is good. I will set up some tests to see if we can better understand why she is having these memories."

"I was hoping she would come home soon," Thelma said. She had tears in her eyes and looked sad. "I want my daughter back the way she was."

"Mom, don't cry. I feel great; my legs are getting stronger, and these memories are from the past. They are just memories. I'm living in the present while trying to understand the past," Tianna said to comfort her mother. "Dr. Kohl, what tests do you want to do? You name it, I'm ready."

"I'm ordering an M.R.I. scan to show your memory areas and patterns. We will also do a psychological exam to rule out all problems,"

Dr. Kohl said. "Don't worry about them. You're not displaying any emotional problems. I want to figure out where these fresh memories are coming from. The nanobot repairs may have caused you to mix memories of things you've learned with memories of your own life. There was a lot of cellular repair done in your brain, so anything is possible."

Tianna clenched the arms of her wheelchair and said, "Could the nanobots have helped me remember my previous lives? I know these memories of my past lives are real, and I am sure I will prove it."

"Fair enough," said Dr. Kohl. "I'm not saying they aren't real, but I want more information."

The Doctor stood and walked out of the room. As he left, Tianna's physical therapist came in and announced that it was time for her next session.

"The work never stops, does it?" complained Tianna.

"If it gets you out of this place, honey, it's worth it," insisted her mother.

"I know, Mom. Amber... Eddie... will you be back tomorrow?"

"Mom, is it OK?" Amber asked. She had a pleading look on her face that Alice could never refuse.

"Yes. Take the bus, and I'll pick you up at six."

Tianna hugged everyone before she left for her session. Her mom told her she would stay in the room and wait for her. "Your grandfather is coming this evening, and so is Carson, your English teacher."

"Sounds like fun. Can I tell him about my previous lives?" Tianna said with a chuckle. "He might want to write a book about them."

* * *

The physical therapy session went well, except that her favorite male therapist, Clinton, wasn't there. She was stuck with Sandra, a fifty-year-old therapist who was all business.

"Tianna," she said, "you need to work harder. Here, get on the bars, and I want to see you walk without help. If you feel you'll fall, grab the rails. But I know you can do this, and so do you."

"Yes, I did it," Tianna yelled when she reached the end of the walk. "Does this mean I'm done with therapy?"

"No, but when Dr. Kohl sees these results, he might let you go home and attend therapy as an outpatient. You've done well."

After the hour of therapy, Sandra wheeled Tianna back to her room. Clarence, her mom, and Carson Ewald were in the room. So was her meal. A hot dinner was sitting on her roll-away table, but the thought of having to eat in front of three people was not a fun concept.

"Don't worry, Honey. We're going down to the cafeteria. We will be back in half an hour, so you can enjoy your dinner in peace," her mom said.

Mr. Carson smiled and said, "I'm glad you're doing so well, and yes, Tianna, I want to hear everything about your reincarnation memories."

"Thanks, I'll see you later."

Tianna put her headphones on and listened to the last chapter of her novel. As she ate, she considered the day's events. Everyone now knows about her reincarnation, and neither the doctor nor her family and friends are calling her crazy, but deep down she feels she must convince herself she isn't going insane. With her mind filled with doubt, she asked herself, *Why me? Why would someone want to kill me? Could I still be in a coma? No, this is real!*

It didn't take long for her to finish dinner, and with the help of an aide, she took a quick shower and fixed her hair. She styled her hair to cover up the shaved patch and the scars from the bullet and surgery.

Tianna was coming out of the bathroom when her three guests returned from the cafeteria. The nurse's aide helped her get to the wheelchair, and then she left for her next patient.

"Thank you, Carol," said Tianna. "I'll see you in the morning."

"If you're still here. I would guess you'll be going home soon."

"That would be nice. Even though I love all of you nurses, I sure miss home and school."

Thelma walked up to her daughter and directed Carson and Clarence to pull up a chair. "Honey, I take it you did well at your physical therapy session?" she asked.

"Yes, Mom. The therapist had me walking on my own. She said I could go home and do therapy as an outpatient."

"That's wonderful," said Clarence. "We miss you so much. The house just isn't home without you. It's so empty and quiet."

Knowing her three guests wanted to know about the memories she shared with Amber and Eddie, Tianna broke the ice. "I guess I should tell you about the memories. I'm glad you don't think I'm going crazy, but I believe I am reincarnated."

Thelma smiled and said, "Yes, we would like to hear your stories."

"OK, I'll tell you the same way I told Eddie and Amber. From the first life I recall to the last. I would suggest that you get comfortable as this will take a while. In my first life, my name was Arianna, and I was born in the summer of 1690 in St. Ignace, in what is now northern Michigan, where Lake Huron and Lake Michigan meet. My father was the chief of our tribe of Huron Indians, and my mother's father was our clan's medicine and spiritual leader. Even though we had accepted the God of the French and attended their church in St. Ignace, we still held many of our ancestral beliefs."

By nine o'clock in the evening, Tianna reached the last story. She described her death in 1850. "Dad screamed and grabbed me. I slipped to the ground while Mom and Dad held me and cried. My spirit left my lifeless body, and in my mind, I could hear singing. *Green trees are bending, Poor sinner stands a-trembling; The trumpet within-a my soul, I ain't got long to stay here. Steal away, steal away, steal away to Jesus! Steal away, steal away home, I ain't got long to stay here!*"

From above the green trees, I could see my family and neighbors bending over my lifeless body. On the river were several tall ships sailing by, and the large rowboat with the runaway slaves was at the Canadian side of the river. A group of people of color helped them out of the boat and hugged them. They were being welcomed into their new land. I was crying. Not for my pain and loss, but because I was so happy they reached freedom.

Tianna looked at her guests and felt saddened because they all had tears running down their faces. "Hey, I'm sorry I made you guys sad, but I wanted you to know who I was in the past. There are still two lives I need to tell... my life starting in 1910 when I lived above my grandfather's deli on Hastings Street and I died in 1925. In my last life, I was born in 1952, and I died during the riots of 1967. My name was Amanda Carson, and yes, Grandpa, I loved talking to you when we lived in the Brewster-Douglass Apartments."

Clarence was a little surprised, but not shocked. "You heard the news reports, or did Amber tell you? I'm enjoying your historical stories, Tianna, but I question if they are memories of your past, or stories you've heard and think they are memories."

Tianna had a disappointed look on her face. "Grandpa, do you remember when Amanda told you about the goldfish she ate as a challenge in Clifford's apartment? I told you I could feel it swimming inside my stomach, and I had to throw up.... all over Clifford. He got mad and told me never to come there again."

"Damn, that's true. What about the time *you* went to see Diana Ross in the parking lot? She was walking through the apartment where she used to live," Clarence asked.

"It was in the fall of 1965, and *we* saw Diana Ross, Mary Wilson and Florence Ballard. We couldn't get close enough to talk to them, but they waved at us."

"They waved to the entire crowd. Not just us. I kept telling you, *They're big shots now; they don't wave at little people like us.*"

"Clarence, I could tell they waved at you. You were a handsome man back then. And you were one of my best friends, and you were my mentor. You made me want to get an education and be someone special. Now you are my grandfather. But you are still my friend and mentor."

The two reached for each other and hugged.

"Wow! I need time to let this sink in, Tianna, or should I say Amanda?" said Clarence as he hugged her.

"Tianna, your stories of reincarnation are amazing, but Thelma, I have to get ready for school in the morning, so we need to get going," said Carson.

Thelma agreed and told Tianna, "Dr. Kohl said he's doing tests tomorrow. I can't get here until around six again, so your grandfather is coming down to be here with you. If either of you needs me, call me at work. I love you, honey." As She left. Thelma reminded everyone to keep Tianna's reincarnation stories to themselves. "You know, we don't want this information to get into the newspapers. It would be a zoo if it did."

They agreed, hugged and kept saying goodbye until they were out the door. Tianna wheeled herself to the bathroom and walked herself to the toilet.

When she finished getting ready for bed, she called Amber. On the first ring, Amber picked up and said, "Hi, how did it go with your mom and grandfather?"

"Mr. Ewald was here too. It went fine. Everyone says they kind of believe my story, but I can tell they still think I'm a little crazy. I got Grandpa though. He questioned my being Amanda Carson, but as we talked about things we did and said, I could see he believed me. One down, and the rest of the world to go."

"Not one down, Grandpa makes four. You, Eddie, your grandfather and I are believers in your reincarnation. Now we need to figure out why you keep getting killed."

"True, Amber… very true. I hope you will be here again tomorrow after school. And if you are, please bring Eddie. I think I like him a lot," added Tianna.

"Tianna, we'll be there. Now do the homework I brought you and then get rest."

"I finished my homework, but I need rest. Oh, I have to tell you something important. I walked to the toilet a few minutes ago."

Amber smiled and said, "So?"

"So? So I *WALKED!*"

"Great, I'm very proud of you. You're a big girl now, Tianna," Amber said, trying to keep from laughing out loud. "You know I'm kidding. Congratulations. I want you back here in one piece, 'cause we've got a lot of things to do before the big dance."

"Yes, like teach Eddie how to dance," Tianna said. "I love you, Amber. Goodnight."

CHAPTER 21

The nurse woke Tianna before dawn and told her she needed to order breakfast now because she would have several M.R.I. tests. "I guess they want to see what's happening in that beautiful head of yours."

"Well, they might find a lot of cobwebs if they do the test too early. I'm still tired."

"Let's get you out of bed and into the shower. That should wake you," suggested the nurse.

During her shower, the kitchen delivered her breakfast. She avoided getting her hair wet so she wouldn't have to style it. She ate, listened to the news on television, and then waited for the nurse to take her for the test. Just as a nurse walked in to announce he was taking her for the M.R.I., Clarence entered her room.

"You're up early," he said.

"Hi Grandpa. I have to go for tests," she said. "Why don't you come with me? You might have to stay in the waiting room, but I'll know you're close at hand."

"I'd love to," said Clarence as he walked alongside Tianna's wheelchair. "Your mom might be here a little later. I'll tell the nurse where to send her when she gets here," he said, reaching the elevators.

"I thought she was working today."

"She went to the office early so she could get her work done. Dr. Kohl asked her to be here by ten this morning to go over the results of the tests."

Tianna sighed, "I don't know how they can show whether I imagined or remembered my previous lives."

"Neither do I, but then I'm not a doctor."

"Grandpa, you are a doctor. You have a doctorate in history education."

Clarence chuckled as the elevator doors opened and the trio entered for their ride down to the Imaging Department.

"Yes, Tianna, I stand corrected. I am a doctor. My former patients were all college kids. The only disease I treated was rampant apathy."

When they reached the department, the nurse told Clarence to find a seat in the waiting room. Tianna went into a room with the huge M.R.I. machine. Dr. Kohl, Dr. Clark, and three assistants were standing at the machine's control panel. They were going over files and talking about Tianna's reincarnation stories.

Dr. Clark approached Tianna and smiled. He said, "I understand you have been having memories that appear to be recollections of previous lives you've lived. What we want to do is look at where these memories are coming from. This M.R.I. will scan your brain while we ask questions. When you remember, we can see what area of your brain is being used. The normal memory area is the frontal lobe of your brain."

"How will you see my memories?" Tianna asked.

"That's the fun part," replied Dr. Clark. "Under normal conditions, takes a day to process the images, but we've set up a link to a supercomputer at the University of Michigan. We will use a technique that allows us to see a three-dimensional picture of your head. This image will show what part of the brain is active when you recall the memory."

"We have to get started," said Dr. Kohl. "We only have the use of the supercomputer for a short period."

With an assistant's help, Tianna laid down on the bed of the M.R.I. with her head inside the round scanner. Dr. Clark sat next to the machine and said, "We will ask you a question, but we don't want a verbal answer. Just think of the answer. As soon as I have the image back from the computer, I will ask the next question. You cannot move your head. It has to remain still. The processor can adjust for slight movements only."

Tianna responded, "OK, I'm ready."

As Tianna lay on the flat table, Dr. Kohl, sitting on the other side of Tianna, started the questions. "Tianna, please think about the day before you got shot. What were you doing before, during and after school?"

Dr. Clark asked the second question: "Tianna, think about the first life you remember having. I understand it was during the early days at Fort Detroit."

The doctors asked a dozen questions. They alternated between memories of her life now and those of her previous lives. Dr. Kohl helped her off the M.R.I. table. She walked to the wheelchair and sat. Dr. Kohl commented on how far she had come, and then turned to Dr. Clark and asked, "Well, Dr. Clark, do we have the results back from Ann Arbor?"

Dr. Clark and his assistant watched their laptops and, on a larger monitor, an image of Tianna's brain appeared. It was multicolored with areas of green, red, yellow, and blue. The image amazed Tianna, so she asked, "What do the colors represent?"

Edward, the taller assistant, smiled and said, "They represent areas that are active, partly active, or not active at all. The active areas are colored red, and the inactive area is green. The other colors show degrees of activity not relative to our study."

Dr. Clark said, "Edward here is the memory expert. He is a researcher at the University of Michigan and will walk us through the results. OK, Ed, you can begin."

Edward was studying the images, and he asked Dr. Kohl and Dr. Clark to come closer. The three talked softy. Tianna tried to hear what they were saying, but could only pick up a few sentences. It appeared there was an anomaly in the images. She heard Edward say, "I've seen nothing like this before."

Dr. Kohl asked Dr. Clark, "Could your nanoparticles have caused this memory formation?"

"I don't see how. They created nothing new; they only repaired the neural connections."

As Tianna listened, her mother walked into the room. She stood next to Tianna and asked, "Did they do the test yet?"

"Yes," Tianna said, "but there seems to be some kind of glitch. They're talking among themselves. I hope it's not bad news."

Thelma walked toward the doctors and asked, "Dr. Kohl, it there a problem?"

"Mrs. Gulliver, no, there isn't a problem." He walked over to Tianna and pushed her wheelchair closer to the large monitor. "We found that Tianna's memories are coming from an area where memories are not stored. As you can see in this first image, when we asked her a question about a recent memory, her frontal lobe showed red, as it should. This red area shows where the memory is coming from. Then, I asked her to remember her first life experience, and her cerebellum lit up."

"So what does this mean?" asked Thelma.

Edward answered, "It means that Tianna's memories of her past lives are not memories of historical events she has learned from reading or from her grandfather. They originated in an area of the brain used only for regulating coordination, posture, and balance."

"The cerebellum, known as the *little brain*," added Dr. Kohl. "We believe it developed before the cerebrum."

"Also, when she remembered these previous life experiences, there was activity in her brain stem. This is the part of the brain that develops first in the embryo stage," said Edward as he pointed to a red area on the screen.

Clarence was standing behind Tianna and asked, "Doctors, we need to know if Tianna is OK, and when can she go home?"

"We're sorry. We get so wrapped up in these medical mysteries we forget the basics," said Dr. Kohl. "Yes, Tianna is fine. We don't know why she has memories of a previous life, but they did not originate from recent memories of the Detroit historical events you told her. Why the memories are there is a mystery that we may never solve."

Thelma then asked, "OK, but when can she go home?"

"As soon as I can get the discharge papers ready. I will arrange outpatient physical therapy. To start, I'll schedule a therapist to come into your home. After one week, we will determine what more you need. I want to see Tianna in two weeks for a follow up," Dr. Kohl said.

Clarence, Tianna, and Thelma hugged and thanked Dr. Kohl. Even though she was eager to get her life back to normal, in the back of Tianna's mind was the realization that normal would never be the same as it was before she turned sixteen. She knows she will walk and run again, her hair will grow back, and she might even go to the dance with Eddie. However, the memories will never go away, and in her heart is a foreboding that there is more danger to come. The knowledge she gained from her Indian grandfather in Fort Pontchartrain keeps rushing back to her. He introduced her to the spirit world and warned that she would face danger. She now understands what that danger is. Her ability to walk in the spirit world is growing every day, and the masters of the spirit world will try to stop her. Fear made her shiver.

"Honey, are you cold? Let's get you back to the room so we can go home," said Thelma.

"Thanks Mom. I'll be OK. I need to call Amber as soon as possible."

* * *

Thelma and Clarence gathered Tianna's belongings. Her room had become a typical teenager's hangout. She had a poster on the wall, a photograph of her family on the nightstand, and a bathroom stocked with personal care products. Clarence started with two plants. He considered asking the nurse if he could use a wheelchair, but Tianna told him that if he didn't ask, they wouldn't say no. He found a chair in the hallway and brought it back to Tianna's room. She helped gather plants, stuffed toys and other gifts from her family and friends. They stacked them on the seat of the chair, and he wheeled them down to the car.

"Clarence, I can take them to the car," insisted Thelma.

"I need the exercise, and besides, you will be busy signing a bunch of paperwork. Just give me the keys so I can open the trunk."

She put the keys in his hand and kissed his cheek. "Thank you." She turned and looked at Tianna. "It will be so nice having our little girl home at last."

Clarence didn't answer. He was already out the door heading for the elevator. The nurse came in and asked if she could help them move.

"No, two trips to the car is all that's needed," said Thelma.

Another nurse came into the room. She was holding a clipboard and asked Thelma and Tianna to sit and go over the discharge information. She gave instructions for physical therapy, medication, and advised them of a follow-up appointment with Dr. Kohl in two weeks. "Remember, if you have any problems or questions, call the number listed here," said the nurse.

They finished in half an hour, and another nurse told Thelma to bring the car to the front entrance while she used the wheelchair to take Tianna down to meet her.

Thelma checked the room to make sure she missed nothing and then she headed down the hall. Tianna told the nurse she would rather walk with the crutches she had been using since her last therapy session.

The nurse said, "No" and explained that the hospital rule required that each patient exit in a wheelchair. Tianna, the nurse, and Clarence started toward the elevator. As they waited for the elevator, Tianna considered how much her life had changed in the past week. Leaving the hospital made her feel good, but she would miss the many friends she had made there. She thought about keeping in touch, but realized that it would never happen. *It's strange,* she thought. *So many people helped me survive being shot. If medicine hadn't advanced to this point, I would have died again, and I would have had to wait another lifetime to reach sixteen.*

CHAPTER 22

Thelma opened the back door of the car and helped Tianna. "Honey, are you sure you don't want the front seat?" she asked.

"No, this is fine. Grandpa can sit in the front," she said, pushing gifts from her hospital room aside to make room. "Can we stop for a burger and fries? I'm starving."

"Honey, I thought you didn't like fast food?" asked Clarence.

"I didn't have lunch yet, and I'm hungry and want to get home."

"Don't worry, Tianna. We have plenty of food you can heat. I'll make you a bowl of soup and a sandwich."

As the car sped through the familiar streets of Detroit, Tianna realized she had a new perception of her hometown. Each street and building holds memories from her past, and many of them have changed. Streets have alternative names, while others have vanished. The Interstate I-75 freeway has buried the Hastings Street home where she lived in the 1920s. The loss made her sad, but she knew she would have to deal with these feelings each day, so she struggled to get her emotions under control. *I can't let my past disrupt my present,* she considered.

When they drove past the former site of the housing projects, she asked, "Grandpa, do you miss seeing the Brewster-Douglass Housing Projects since they tore them down?"

"It depends on my mood. Sometimes I drove by the neglected buildings filled with the joy of remembering the great times I had. I loved our talks when you were Amanda. Other times I got angry thinking of how they pushed us around and forced us into segregated neighborhoods. That's when I'm glad the buildings disappeared. Like I said, my feelings are mixed."

DEADLY SIXTEEN

The car pulled into the driveway and stopped. Tianna pushed her door open and twisted herself until her feet were on the cement. She grabbed her crutches, and in one swift movement, she was standing. She walked toward the front porch, and her mind was so set on getting into the house she didn't hear her mother talking to her.

"Tianna, slow down. I don't want you falling, and besides I have to unlock the door."

"Sorry, Mom. I'll wait on the porch for you guys. It feels so great to be home."

She worked her way up the steps and sat down in the patio chair on the porch. Taking her cell phone out, she checked the time and decided that she could call Amber. It would be the lunch hour, so Amber would be free to answer the phone.

"Hey, I'm sitting on our porch getting sun. I want you and Eddie to stop by after school. We need to talk, and I want to tell you guys about the last two lives I lived. I'm sure you'll enjoy hearing about them. I remember loving them until I died... that is."

"Great news, Tianna. How did your memory test go?" Amber asked.

"Good... I guess. Dr. Kohl said I'm not crazy, and the memories are real and not made up. I'm worried, though. I think I discovered who is trying to kill me, and they won't stop."

"Damn, that sounds serious. Should we ask my dad for help?"

"I'm not sure he can since they're not from here. I believe they are from the spirit world."

"Now, you're sounding crazy. I'll see you this afternoon, and you better have a better answer than that. OK?"

"See you, Amber," Tianna said as her mom and grandfather finished loading her belongings into the house.

"Well, are you coming in, or staying on the porch?" asked Clarence.

Tianna stood and worked her way into the house. She walked to the kitchen table, where her mom was busy making lunch. "Mom,

Amber and Eddie are stopping by after school. I'm telling them about the last two life experiences I had. Would you and Grandpa like to listen too?"

Clarence said, "I do! It will be nice listening to you talking about Detroit as someone who has lived in the past."

"I want to listen to your stories, but I want to tell you I find them troubling. It's hard for me to accept that you lived in the past. The notion of reincarnation feels wrong."

"I understand what you mean, Mom. I still have to struggle with the idea," Tianna said with a heavy heart. She knew her mother had doubts, but hoped she would come to understand.

After lunch, Tianna had a visit from the physical therapist assigned to her case. The woman went over the schedule, and after they completed the paperwork, Tianna exercised for over an hour. She grew tired, and when the therapist left, she took a nap on the couch in the living room. Her grandfather and mother stayed in the kitchen and promised to wake her when her friends arrived.

* * *

Three old men wearing long black robes walked through the wall and into the living room. The room filled with a thick fog as the figures approached Tianna. She sat up wanting to scream, but she couldn't. There was no sound. Even the air was silent. The tallest man said, "Tianna, you have broken our most sacred rules. We told you not to cross the line between the living and the realm of the spirits. We will stop you... you will not continue to break our rules."

Tianna wanted to cry, but there were no tears. The oldest man, with high cheekbones and long black hair, said, "You have reached sixteen, but your time is short. Stop trying to revisit your past. Stop or....."

Tianna's mom called to her, "Tianna, Amber and Eddie are here to see you."

Tianna opened her eyes and realized she was dreaming, but the vision was genuine enough to send shivers down her spine. She reached for her crutches and stood. "I'm coming, Mom," she said as she walked to the kitchen. She was nervous, and it was a feeling she wasn't used to. Courageous by nature, her dream put doubt in her mind. She questioned her plans. *Should I heed their warning, or should I keep searching for more answers?*

As soon as she entered the kitchen, Amber rushed forward and gave her friend a hug that almost knocked Tianna down. "Tianna, it's so good to see you here. Not that you didn't look good in the hospital, you look great here at home," she said.

"It feels good to be home. Amber, we have to talk. Mom, is it OK if I have a few words with Amber before we start the storytelling?"

"Sure, just let me know when you want us," Thelma said.

"What about me, Tianna?" asked Eddie.

"Come on with us, Eddie. Your opinion is important, too."

The three teenagers went into the living room. Tianna sat in a rocking chair, and Eddie and Amber settled on the couch. "So, Tianna," Amber said, "what's so important?"

"Three old people dressed in black robes visited me. They are from the spirit world and warned me against trying to relive my past. They said I could die if I do."

In a low voice, Eddie said, "That sounds serious. Did your mom and grandfather see them?"

"No, it was a vision. Only I could see them because I was asleep."

"So, you're all worked up because you had a dream?" Amber asked with a tinge of sarcasm in her voice.

Eddie turned to Amber and said, "You shouldn't get upset with Tianna. If she feels the dream was a message from the spirit world, then it was."

"Eddie, I'm sorry, but this is getting strange. I'm not comfortable with spirits and visions and past lives. I want my best friend back like she was," Amber said as tears ran down her cheeks. "Tianna, can't you let it go? I fear for you, and I hope nothing else happens."

Tianna tried to stand, but slipped back into the rocking chair. "I'll be glad when my legs work like they used to."

"See, even you want things to go back like they were," Amber said.

"I wish they could, but they won't. Amber, I've crossed into my future. My grandfather, the shaman, warned me about this day. I can't avoid what will happen, so the best I can do is make sure I survive. And you know I'm not the type to give up. I need to know what the spirits fear. I need to investigate my past and learn as much as I can. But I need your help. I want you and Eddie to help me find out who the killers were and why they killed me. Perhaps then I can stop the next one."

Eddie stood and offered his hand to Tianna. "I will do anything I can to help you," he said.

Tianna took his hand and put a hand out to Amber. "Please ... Amber. I need your help too."

Amber took Tianna's hand. Tianna stood with their help, and they all hugged. Eddie commented they were like the Three Musketeers, and Amber laughed. "I hope we don't have to fight like the Musketeers, Eddie."

"Don't worry, I'll protect my two favorite damsels," he said, bowing.

"Mom, Grandpa, are you ready to hear about how I almost became a member of the Purple Gang?"

CHAPTER 23

Tianna's remembrance was about to begin. Amber brought her a large glass of Coke. Tianna sat in her grandfather's oversized leather chair so everyone could see her. Her mother and grandfather were sitting on the couch, and Eddie and Amber shared another large easy chair. Just as they were ready to begin, the doorbell rang. Thelma went to the door and welcomed Amber's parents, Alice and Lester.

"We were just ready to listen to Tianna's tale about her life during the 1920s," said Thelma.

"That's why we're here," said Lester. "Amber told us all about Tianna's previous lives, and we would like to hear more. I hope it's not a problem? I came home early so I could hear her story."

"Come on in, I was hoping you two would show up," yelled Tianna from the living room.

After hugs and greetings, Tianna was ready to remember. "I want you to know when I go back and remember my previous lives, I feel I am in the past. It's a strange feeling, unlike remembering what I did yesterday or last month. I can picture the events in my mind as if I am there. Perhaps I can explain it better later, after I tell you about my life on Hastings Street during the 1920s."

Tianna began.... "In 1910, I came into the family of Jacob and Bethani Weinberg. My parents named me Sarah after my father's great grandmother. We lived in a second-floor apartment across the hall from Dad's parents, Grandfather Josef Weinberg and Grandma Iris. My grandparents immigrated to America from Germany. They suffered persecution in their homeland because they were of the Jewish faith, and they left for a better life in America. In the early nineteen hundreds, many Jewish immigrants settled in Detroit. Most of these families made their homes in the Hastings Street area. German immigrants built the homes and businesses during the eighteen hundreds. Those builders moved north as more blacks and Jews migrated to Detroit to find work in the booming manufacturing businesses. The German builders and business owners knew it was an excellent investment to rent or sell their old homes and business locations to the immigrants. Some say the Hastings area was an awful place to live because the homes and businesses were old, and there were blacks and Jewish people crowded into a tiny area, but it was my home."

"My mother's father, George Bauer, came to Detroit in 1860. He was a German farmer, and he purchased farmland north of Detroit. He met and married a woman who was part German, Indian, and French. Grandfather Bauer died when he got tangled in the reins of a horse and then dragged for over a mile. Grandma Elizabeth kept the farm going with help from her two brothers and her children. She died of complications of influenza during the outbreak of 1918. I remember the visits we made to the farm when I was young, and her funeral in the old Lutheran Church will be forever in my mind. Mom loved talking about Grandma's great sense of humor and quick wit. I think my mother must have inherited that wit and humor from her mom."

"Grandfather ran a deli, and most of his customers were Jewish families who wanted kosher groceries. Dad attended Eastern High School, and after he graduated, he went to study at Detroit Medical College. He wanted to become a doctor, but after one year, he joined the army. He got assigned to Fort Wayne on the security detail. While stationed at Fort Wayne, he met my mother working at a restaurant near the fort, and Dad fell in love with her. Because of his experience as a military police officer, Dad joined the Detroit Police when he left the Army. Mom and Dad got married in 1909, and nine months later I was born. Mom insisted they had waited until after the wedding to conceive me! I could have been a late delivery."

"Mom was very proud of my dad and his choice of occupation, but

Grandfather felt he took a job below his standing. Grandfather was a business owner, and he couldn't understand why his son didn't want to become a doctor, lawyer, or at least an entrepreneur like himself. Dad was not the entrepreneur type. He needed direction. At home, Mom decided, and at work it was his superiors. I'm not saying Dad was dumb, but he had a hard time deciding."

"It was the Roaring Twenties. World War I was over, and Detroit was growing like crazy. Ford was paying high wages, and it seemed like everyone was trying to start an auto company. Detroit was an ideal manufacturing location. Being on the Great Lakes, businesses could ship all around the world by water, and overland by railroad to Chicago and further west."

"Thousands of immigrants heard Detroit was the new paradise, and they were all trying to find homes and jobs in Detroit. There were not enough homes for the immigrants; so many people had to share crowded homes with other families. Many Detroiters, including my dad, thought the Hastings Street area was becoming too overcrowded and dangerous."

"Dad," my father would say, "you and Mom have to get out of this area. The Purple Gang members are making this place too dangerous. Just yesterday we found two dead men. They think they were rival bootleggers. You know how bad it is. You hear what your customers are saying. Why don't you move north, to a nice white area, where it's safe?"

"Son, your mother and I will never move from here. If you want to move, move. I'm here until you put me in the Lafayette Street Cemetery," Grandpa always said.

"Neither Grandpa nor Grandma wanted anything to do with moving. They had made their life in the Deli and they felt like they were too old to change. My mother agreed with them. She loved the wildlife in the Hastings community and said she would miss it if she had to be a lonely housewife out in the countryside."

"I spent most of my time in our apartment, the alley in the backyard, and playing downstairs in the deli. Grandma and Mom took turns watching me. They both worked at the deli alongside Grandpa. I loved the smell and sight of the deli. The long counter with the fresh cheese and meats fascinated me. I remember I could stand and look into the glass cases. I didn't understand what the names meant, but I loved cheese and would ask to try every kind. On the shelves along the walls, there were rows of canned and dry goods and all kinds of bread from the bakers at the Eastern Market. Grandpa had barrels of kosher pickles, bulk nuts and sometimes oysters covered with ice in the center of the store. From the ceiling, Grandpa hung smoked sausages of all kinds with strings of garlic and dried peppers. I loved the counter where Grandpa kept the penny candy in large glass jars. If I helped him pick up stuff that dropped on the floor, he gave me one piece of candy. That's how I learned to work for Grandpa, but Dad kept telling me I couldn't work for candy all my life."

"Grandpa also sold tobacco, and before Prohibition he sold wine and liquor behind the counter. Since it was illegal to sell alcohol, Grandpa had to send his customers downstairs, where he had what he called a Jewish meeting place. Mom said it was Grandpa's way of saying he built a speakeasy in the basement so he could sell illegal booze to all of his customers who still drank. I couldn't go downstairs until I was older. Mom said she didn't trust the sleazy customers who hung out there."

"Crowds of people walked up and down Hastings Street, but I could not go out alone until I was five. Then I couldn't go further than the next corner. I enjoyed walking up and down the sidewalk. The street was dusty in the summer, muddy in the spring, and we could smell automobile fumes and horse droppings year round. There were several colored men who cleaned up the streets during the day. Grandpa said it was important to keep the place looking nice because no one wants to walk through trash to buy their dinner."

"There were other children my age who walked the streets, both Jewish and colored. We all lived together there on Hastings Street.

Grandpa said it was wrong to think of people of color as less than human, like many Christians did. He said, *They are my best customers now, so why would I treat them like that? I treat them like friends, and they know I would never cheat them.*"

"Dad had a different view. As a police officer, he had to help keep them away from downtown Detroit and other white only areas. Colored people had to live and shop in their own areas. I think Dad felt bad about the way he treated them. I mean, he grew up with colored friends, and now he had to be mean to them. Perhaps that's why he wanted to move north. He kept talking about the business districts on 12th and Dexter streets. He said it was where many Jewish business people were building new homes and retail stores. There were no colored people there, and the locals welcomed the Jews into the community."

"In a lot of ways, we were like the colored people. We had to be careful where we moved. You couldn't tell if a white person was Jewish or not, but some people hated Jews, and when they found out that a Jewish family moved into their neighborhood, they would treat them terribly. I couldn't understand why people hated other people because of their color or religion. Aren't we all alike? Didn't God make all of us? It was a question I kept asking myself and others. I can't say I ever got a suitable answer."

* * *

"I attended a school for Jewish children until I finished sixth grade. I didn't like the school because my black friends couldn't attend because they were not Jewish. They attended a public elementary school. German and Polish Jews who had recently immigrated to Detroit made my school overcrowded. A lot of the new students couldn't even speak English. I kept asking Mom and Dad to let me go to the public school, but they refused. I struggled along until I was ready to enter middle school."

"There was a new school that was a short way from our home. It was the Sidney D. Miller Intermediate School. The school was on DuBois Street, and a lot of the other students in my neighborhood were planning to attend school there. Dad wanted me to go to another private Jewish school, but I was a stubborn eleven-year-old and I didn't want to go to another Jewish school. In my angry tone I yelled, *If you try to make me go to that school, I'll stay home, or better yet, I'll work the streets like those women you keep arresting!*"

"Mom was so furious that she almost slapped me, but she controlled her anger. Mom and I had an unusual relationship. We spent a lot of time together and were more like sisters than mother and daughter. Besides, she knew I might tell Dad we were smuggling booze across the river from Windsor. Being a police officer, Dad could arrest and jail us, but I doubt he would. I mean, he never arrested his own dad for running a speakeasy in the basement, so why would he bother with us?"

"Mom said it was our little secret. It was 1922, at the height of Prohibition. Grandpa purchased most of his alcohol from the Purple Gang, but his customers kept asking for a better quality. Grandpa said the Purple Gang, a group of nasty Jewish boys who controlled almost all the illegal alcohol sales, took the good whiskey from Canada and cut it with homemade cheap booze. That way they could sell more and make more money. Grandpa asked Mom to help him get the better booze from Windsor, and Mom, a woman who loves an adventure, agreed to smuggle bottles across the river. Dad always called her his favorite flapper girl because she was a little crazy and loved to dance and party. I don't think he would have gotten angry if he had known what she was doing, but Mom insisted we didn't tell him. Because he was a police officer, she feared it would put him in a difficult position. I'm sure she didn't want him to say no, because she would then have to go against his wishes."

"Every two weeks, Mom and I, along with one neighborhood toddler, would take the ferry across the Detroit River into Canada.

We took Dad's Ford down to the dock and parked. Then Mom put the little kid in a custom-built baby buggy, and we walked over the ramp onto the boat. As we left the docks, I enjoyed looking at the skyscrapers looming over downtown Detroit. Mom said, "All the business people in Detroit are trying to outdo their neighbors. They're making tons of money and are spending it like a bunch of crazed men on an all-night binge."

"I wasn't sure what she meant, but there sure were a lot of tall buildings, and I could tell that many of them were unfinished. "

"When we reached Windsor, a man picked us up and drove us to an old building near the riverfront. We got out and went into an office where Mom paid the man, and he gave her ten bottles of the good whiskey. Mom looked at each bottle, took a sip to make sure it wasn't cut. When she was sure it was the good stuff, she put them in the bottom of the baby buggy, while I held the little kid we were babysitting for the day. He was only three, and I told Mom he smelled funny. Ignoring me, she took him and placed him back into the buggy. The driver drove us back to the dock, where we had a snack and waited over an hour for the next trip back to Detroit."

"Mom, what would happen if someone found out we were doing this?" I asked.

"Don't think about that. They would never suspect a mother with two children, so don't worry," she insisted.

"She was right. When we walked by the customs men, they didn't even ask us questions. They looked at Mom closely since she wore a dress that was short and she was beautiful. She caught the eye of most men."

"Grandpa wanted Mom to make this trip every week, but she would only go twice a month. In the winter, she refused to drive across the frozen river like some other rumrunners did. I don't think I would have gone with her if she did. I heard that a lot of those drivers ended up at the bottom of the river, and if the Purple Gang saw you driving across, they would take your smuggled cargo and dump you in the river, or shoot you dead."

Dad said, "Those gangsters are a scourge on the city, but they must have friends in high places, because they never seem to get caught."

CHAPTER 24

During my time at Miller Intermediate School, I met my best girlfriend. Esther was a beautiful colored girl who was my age. She lived three blocks from our apartment. At school, she was caring and funny. She made me feel good about myself and my life. Her father was a laborer at Fisher Body, and her mother was a housewife. There were eight children in the family. Esther was the second oldest, so she helped her mother with the kids. I met Esther in choir class. We both enjoyed singing and loved listening to the latest big bands playing our favorite dance music. The Fox Trot was all the rage, and we knew every dance move. Mom had a vast selection of records, and she would let us listen to them. She was the one who taught us most of the dances. Mom and Dad went to the dance halls at least two times a week. I wanted them to take Esther and me, but she never did.

During my last year at Miller, I met Joshuah Bernstein. Joshuah was also Jewish, and his family lived toward the north of East Grand Blvd., on Smith Street. His dad was a dentist, and he only had three sisters, two younger and one older. Joshuah's family lived over a mile from Grandpa's Deli, but he was always hanging around Hastings Street. He loved music and enjoyed the jazz and blues that were happening there. We met while Esther and I were standing outside a club one evening, listening to a group of black singers. They were singing Black Bottom Blues. I loved the sound, and Joshuah surprised me when he came up and asked if he could listen with us. We were all too young to go into the club, but there was no law against sitting on the sidewalk, so we spent an hour listening and talking about music.

Joshuah was the keenest boy I'd ever met. He was polite, well dressed, and he didn't smell like a boy. He wore Hudson's best men's cologne, was over five feet tall, and he had a fantastic build. Unlike a lot of boys, Joshuah loved to dress up and look smart. He wore long dress pants, a white shirt, and a sport coat and tie. He said he got handed down suits from his cousins. I later learned that his cousins were Abe, Joe, Raymond and Izzy Bernstein. Dad told me they were the leaders of the Purple Gang and were killers. When I asked Joshuah about them, he said they were from the bad side of the family, and he only saw them at the family reunions, weddings, and funerals, and vowed that he was not into the gang thing. Joshuah wanted to be a bandleader and write and play jazz and blues. I believed him with all my heart, and I lied to Dad about him being my boyfriend. Dad didn't want me to associate with anyone related to the Bernsteins. I think he thought I would go bad or something.

"When it came time for high school, we all went to Eastern High School. One thing I hated about school was how the kids picked on everyone. Because Joshuah and I were Jewish, other students often called us names. Dad said it was that way everywhere in Detroit. On the radio, there was this preacher who talked about how the Jews did this, or did that. Even Hudson's Department Store wouldn't hire Jews for its stores. At least blacks could work there cleaning after hours or in the kitchen. There was a group of men who went around trying to run the Jews and blacks from Detroit. Known as the KKK, the group later became Detroit's Black Legion. Dad said they were as bad as the Purple Gang, perhaps even worse."

"But I still loved Detroit. It was a time when it seemed everything was happening. New cars, new music, new buildings, lots of jobs and money, and women finally got the vote."

"As Mom often said, *It's time to party and let loose.*"

"And party we did. Even though it was illegal to drink. Hastings Street was one big party. Grandpa's Jewish club in the basement was doing a good business. It was a relaxing atmosphere, like someone's kitchen. I guess it was a club. The only customers Grandpa and Grandma would invite were their best customers and friends. But

Grandpa had to be careful. The Purple Gang members would come in to make sure they were getting their cut of the profits. Grandpa called them the Underworld IRS. He had to pay their taxes to stay in business and alive. Mom and I continued to smuggle booze across the river, but not as often. She ordered barrels of oysters filled with whiskey instead of oysters. Grandpa's Deli became known for its oysters, which I hated, but many black customers loved. Mom said if we kept going over with a baby buggy, they would wonder how she had so many babies, but only took two with her."

"I was becoming a music star. Well, not really, but that's how I felt. Esther, Joshuah and I formed a band while we were in high school. Joshuah and eight of his friends played the music, and Esther and I sang. Our group performed at school dances, and one club on Hastings Street asked us to perform two times.. We could only perform during the daytime because we were underage. But we drew sizeable crowds of both teenagers and adults. Dad thought our group was silly, and he wanted me to consider a suitable career like being a secretary or telephone operator. I told him I would, but only if I lost my voice. Mom laughed when I said that."

She said, "Sarah, you will never lose your voice. Someday, people from around the world will know you because you are someone important."

* * *

"By 1926, I was in the tenth grade at Eastern Detroit High School, and our band was doing well, but my dad was pushing for us to move out of our apartment on Hastings Street. Mom and Dad were fighting all the time. He wanted her to act like a good Jewish wife. He kept insisting she stop trying to look like a young girl and wear what Mom called, "old women's clothing." I took Mom's side and told Dad I wouldn't move. If I had to, I would live with Grandpa or move in with my friends. He wouldn't hear of it and said, "You will do as you're told, or I'll send you to a reform school for wayward girls."

"I tried to listen to Dad's side and understand why he was so angry. He was always talking about the killings that took place on the streets of Detroit, the women of the evening who were everywhere along Hastings Street, and the thousands of blacks moving into our neighborhood. I think Dad was afraid. I think he worried about our safety and about the way his world was out of his control. His job now involved trying to stop the rumrunners from smuggling booze across the river. He knew of Mom's rum running for Grandpa, and it bothered him because he had to look the other way with his own family. I wanted to sing and dance, be with my friends, and play in our band. I was almost sixteen and had the crazy dream of becoming a famous singer or silent film actress."

"In 1926, I was looking forward to my sixteenth birthday, which fell on Saturday, December 22nd. Mom decided we would have a big party at the Graystone Dance Hall. She and Dad spend a couple of nights a week there, but the owners wanted too much money for a Saturday afternoon party. Dad thought it might have been because of our Jewish name, but Mom said it was because she told the man that there would be both colored and white friends at the party. After looking around for another place, they settled on having the party at a local restaurant. As Mom searched for a restaurant to have my birthday party, she soon realized what I had always known. It was no fun having a birthday so close to Christmas. We were Jewish, but everyone else, it seemed, was having Christmas parties. We ended up reserving a room at the Ivanhoe Café on the corner of Joseph Campau and Frederik."

"When Mom told Dad and his parents about her decision, Dad yelled, "The Polish Yacht Club? We're not Polish! Why the hell would we want to celebrate our daughter's birth in a Polish bar?"

"Because that's the only place I could find. We can't use the basement, because everyone would see all the booze down there. We can't rent a dance hall because your daughter has a colored girl as her best friend. And we can't skip this party because, damn it, Sarah is turning sixteen, and she deserves to have her first birthday party."

Dad smiled. "Well, in that case, Ivanhoe's Café sounds like a wonderful spot for a party."

"I jumped into Daddy's arms and hugged him. "Thank you, Dad. I promise we won't cause any trouble. After the birthday dinner, we will go to a movie at the Capital Theatre."

"And what movie is playing?" asked Dad.

"*The Black Pirate*," said Mom. "It's about pirates, and it stars that dreamy Douglas Fairbanks and Billie Dove."

"Well, at least I'll like the movie," said Dad.

"Grandpa said he didn't want to see any stupid movies. He would keep the store open so Grandma could go. "You know, Ma, she likes those crazy movies."

"I sure do," Grandma said. that dreamboat, Douglas Fairbanks. Why can't you be young and sexy like him?" she asked Grandpa, pinching his cheek.

"Because I'm not young. I'm an old Jewish man who is getting tired."

"Dad reminded Grandpa, "That's why you should sell this place and move north. Even if you went to Oakland Ave. That's where Sarah's boyfriend lives. It's a friendly area, with less crime, and fewer blacks."

"Damn it, Son. It's not the colored that bothers us. It's those damn gangsters. If you would do your job and put them behind bars, we'd all be better off."

"Dad scowled, turned around, and walked out of the room. We could hear the door slam as he started down the stairs and out to the street. Mom didn't bat an eyelash. She knew Dad. And she knew he meant well. But his parents will never leave Hastings Street, and neither will she."

"The Friday before my birthday party, Mom and I went shopping at Hudson's and Crowley's. Mom drove down Gratiot Avenue and found a parking spot near Hudson's. We got there before the store opened, so we could be first in line at the doors. Our first stop was Crowley's. When the doors opened, we headed downstairs to the Bargain Center and the cafeteria. Mom needed her cup of coffee, and I wanted a root beer float for breakfast. The ice cream was so good, and Mom said she had never made coffee as good as they serve here. We planned to spend the day shopping and sightseeing around downtown. Unlike Christians, we had already celebrated Hanukkah for eight days, starting on December first and ending on the eighth. For Hanukkah, Mom got me my personal record player and some records. She also bought me a necklace and a long winter coat for school."

"As we sipped our drinks, Mom said, "Sarah, tomorrow you will turn sixteen. I wish I could have given you a more fitting coming out party, like rich society people do, but at least I can let you buy your own birthday gifts. She opened her purse and reached down to the bottom, searching for something. When her hand came out, she had two brand new fifty-dollar bills. "This is for your birthday. I want you to spend it all today. Buy clothing, jewelry, makeup, perfume, or anything else you may want."

"I couldn't believe her. "Are you joking with me, Mom? That's so much money. I know how hard you and Dad have to work to save that much. Are you sure you want to do this?"

"I'm sure. We've saved enough money, dear. So don't worry about that. With Dad's wages, the money Grandpa pays me, and the money I've made buying stocks and bonds, we have money. Not millions, but we have enough."

"Then why aren't you moving out of Grandpa's apartment? If you can afford to, why don't you buy an enormous home like Joshuah's dad owns?"

"Because your grandfather and grandmother need us. We could go live on our own, but we're family. I don't want to leave my family behind. Do you understand what I mean?" she asked.

"Yes, Mom. I love you more today than I've ever loved you. Thank you for the money and thank you for being both my mother and friend."

"It was difficult trying to decide what I would buy with the money Mom gave me, but after two hours of shopping, I bought gifts for my friends. I found a dress, hat, and shoes I knew Esther would love. As we walked through Hudson's, I checked the directory and found the music department on the thirteenth floor. I knew Joshuah wanted a new trumpet, so I took the elevator up to the department and asked the salesperson what kind the big band leaders would use. He sold me the same one that the Graystone House Band was using. It was beautiful and took almost one of my fifty-dollar bills. But it was worth every penny, and I couldn't wait to give it to Joshuah. Yes, I know what you're thinking. Why would I give my friends gifts on my birthday? It should be obvious enough."

* * *

"It was mid-afternoon when Mom and I got home from our shopping trip. I have to admit I bought a ton of things, but Mom filled the back seat of the car, and she had some larger items that were being delivered. When I asked her what Dad would say, she reminded me it was her money to spend."

"I was eager to give my friends their gifts, so I took Esther's gifts and walked down to her home. She was on the enclosed porch with her grandmother when I got there."

"Hello Sarah," she said. "What's in the bags?"

"They're your birthday gifts."

"My birthday isn't for another two months. You're a little early, aren't you?"

"I told her about Mom's gift and my decision to give her and Joshuah a gift. She was delighted to get a present. I knew her family was having a struggle to keep all the children in clothing, so I helped my friend. Everything fit, and Esther gave us a fashion show by walking up and down the sidewalk showing off her new look. Her grandmother commented on the short skirt, but she didn't criticize her granddaughter."

"Esther took me aside and said, "Sarah, I only got you a small gift. This makes me feel sad I couldn't give you more for your birthday."

"Esther, every day you give me more than money can buy. You give me encouragement, advice, and hope. I wanted to thank you for being my best friend."

"We hugged, and I reminded Esther that we would meet at Grandpa's Deli at seven. She said she was coming with her new boy-friend. He was a football player at Eastern, good looking, and also into music. He had a voice that made us swoon."

"Is he going to join our band?" I asked.

"No, he's singing with four other guys. They sing old gospel songs without music. I heard them sing, and it gave me goosebumps. They have great harmony."

"I can't wait, Esther, so I'll see you at seven," I said as I started down the sidewalk toward Hastings Street."

"Black children played in the snow-covered street, and I could see Christmas trees in the windows of many homes. I love Christmas decorations and kept thinking as a Jew, I was missing the Christmas fun. But we have our celebrations, and I can still enjoy the decorations."

"After dinner, Dad and Mom went to the Graystone Ballroom to dance. I sat in the front room with the curtains pulled back, waiting for my friends. We will stop at one of the teen hangouts on St. Antoine Street for a Coke, and then we will see if we can get into Graystone. We won't, but at least we can stand at the back door and listen to the music. It would be so romantic to slow dance with Joshuah in the alley, with light snow falling around us. Wow, that would make a splendid setting for a movie or stage production. I must write that down and compose a song about it."

"Sorry, I'm getting distracted from the story. Esther and her boyfriend arrived first. About fifteen minutes later, Joshuah drove up in his beautiful midnight blue 1925 Chrysler Sedan. I jumped in the front seat, and Esther and Burton cuddled in the back seat. The car was enormous and expensive. Joshuah's father bought it for a graduation present. He won't graduate for six months, but his dad thought he should have it now."

"We drove up and down Hastings several times and then stopped at the St. Antoine Cafe. There were a lot of other teens there. A three-piece band was playing the latest jazz music. Joshuah kept complaining about how bad they were. He said we should perform on the stage. Our group had more members, and we found it hard to get everyone together for a small performance. I suggested we make our group smaller, like the band here, but that only upset Joshuah."

"Esther and Burton were having fun dancing, but Joshuah didn't want to. He seemed to be very distant tonight, not himself at all. Around eight o'clock, a tall older man, dressed in a long black coat, came into the cafe looking for Joshuah. He lifted Joshuah out of his seat and whispered in his ear. I wasn't sure what he was telling him, but I knew it was making Joshuah upset. He told me to stay in the cafe, and then he followed the man out the back door to the alley."

"Burton saw what was happening and came back to the table with Esther."

"Does he need my help?" he asked.

"I'm not sure. He told me to wait here and not follow him. Those guys look like they might be Purple Gang members, don't they?" I said.

Esther said, "Well, whoever he is, he didn't look like a nice guy. But you know Joshuah; he'll handle himself with no trouble. Your man's got style, Sarah, don't worry about him."

"I can't stand this. I'll be right back. You two can dance another number, but don't follow. I need to see what's happening," I said.

"I then ran into the kitchen and pulled the back door open. It was dark, and there was a strong smell of spoiled food coming from the alley. At first I couldn't see anyone, then I noticed the group of men standing next to a black Ford. I started toward the men and yelled out Joshuah's name."

"All four of the men turned, and I saw a flash of light. I didn't see the bullet, but I felt something crush into my face, pushing me to the ground. The snow felt cool on my back. I knew I was dead because I could see myself lying on the cold ground. As my spirit lifted higher, I saw Esther and Burton running out of the kitchen toward my lifeless body. The four men scrambled and ran to Joshuah's car. They sped off as a group of onlookers ran into the alley. I could hear a band playing Paul Whiteman's *I'll Build a Stairway to Paradise.* A child was crying, a man was yelling at his children, police officers chased a man down Hastings Street, and gunshots rang in the distance. I looked down and could see the tall buildings towering over my city and, on the frozen Detroit River, a stream of old trucks carrying liquor to fuel the party. During my death, I felt like I was returning home, not leaving home. A burst of joy filled my spirit, but as my spirit lifted toward the bright glow of the heavens, I felt sorrow because I had failed again to reach my sixteenth birthday."

CHAPTER 25

Tianna's living room was silent as her family and friends stared at her in awe. Lester was the first to speak. "Amber told us how moving your stories of the previous lives were, but I had to hear it to understand. Tianna, I need to tell you something. Jason and the guys downtown have found the records of Sarah Weinberg and Joshuah Bernstein's deaths. As you told us, you died in an alley behind the St. Antoine Cafe, and Joshuah died in the parking lot of the Cafe, when someone stole his car. The police did not consider the deaths gang related, but in those days they often overlooked crimes like this."

"Wow!" exclaimed Eddie. "This is getting deep. You have one more life to tell us about. Do you want to wait another day?"

"No!" exclaimed Grandpa Gulliver. "We want to tell the story of Amanda Carson now. Tianna, you know this is our story."

"Yes, Grandpa. You were a huge part of my life when I was Amanda," said Tianna. "But I want to do a little walking, and I need to use the bathroom. Let's take a twenty-minute break, and when we get back, Grandpa and I will tell you about the 1967 Riots."

Everyone talked at the same time. Thelma got Tianna's crutches and helped her out of the chair. As Tianna worked her way to the bathroom, Amber joined her. The two were laughing as they went into the bathroom together.

Eddie and Lester exchanged information about the search for Ricky Clawson. Eddie said, "Word at school is that he's staying with his brother and some of his gang friends. I guess the police want his brother for rape and he's hiding?"

"Yes, he is. Do you have any idea where they might stay?" asked Lester.

"One of the Kingsmen, the gang at King High School, said Ricky is hiding out in an abandoned house near the intersection of McDugall St. and East Grand Blvd. I don't know whose house it is. Another guy thought Ricky was staying somewhere near Woodward and Englewood Street," Eddie added.

"I'll check into it. Perhaps someone has seen them there. We'll get a picture of Ricky out and ask people in the area tomorrow."

Alice came up as Lester was talking. When she saw him finish talking to Eddie, she asked, "Do you believe Tianna's story?"

"If it's a coincidence, then it's the biggest coincidence I've ever seen. She would never have known about Sarah Weinberg on her own. It took days to find any info about the killing, and I told no one about it. Yes, her story is far-fetched, but what could it be besides reincarnation?"

"I don't know," sighed Alice. "It's just so much to take in at one time. I wish we could put everything back like it was a few weeks ago."

"Alice, it never will be like the past again. I see people every day who wish they could have a loved one back, the way they were. Children shot, husbands sent to jail, daughters raped and abused. Life can suck, but then we have a miracle like Tianna to show us there is hope."

"I love you, Lester," Alice said as she gave him a hug and kiss. "Don't you ever change on me. OK?"

"I promise, and I love you too."

Tianna and Amber returned to the living room through the kitchen. Thelma had a spread of assorted sweets and snacks, and everyone was standing around the table talking and eating. Tianna grabbed a paper plate and filled it with cookies and potato chips. She carried it back into the living room, and Amber carried a large Coke for her. Sitting in her chair, she watched her friends as they milled around enjoying each other's company. Being loved by the best people in the world filled Tianna's heart with joy.

"I'm ready to start. Grandpa, why don't you pull your chair up here so we can do this together?" Tianna said.

Lester grabbed the oak rocking chair and moved it next to Tianna. "Here you go, Clarence."

"Thank you. I feel like a movie star, ready to do my first screen test," Clarence said. "Tianna, you can start, since I didn't get to know you until you were twelve."

* * *

"In 1952, I came into the world as the first child of Della and Robert Walden. They rushed Mom to the Thomas Memorial Hospital, on Garfield and St. Antoine. I had no inclination to meet the world in the right direction, and I wanted my feet to touch the ground first and the woman who was helping Mom with the birth at home, did not want to lose me, like she had lost other children in my condition. So, she instructed Dad to bring the car around to the front door. She called the hospital to make sure a surgeon was on hand, and they rushed me to my delivery. Mom said I spent a few days in the hospital, and she enjoyed her stay because it was a colored hospital and all the doctors and nurses were Negro. She didn't feel like a second class patient, but it didn't matter to me. I wanted constant feeding and diaper changing. I guess I was an excellent baby."

"Mom and Dad lived in an older apartment located over a music store on Hastings Street. In the year of my birth, Dad's father, William Walden, purchased a two story brick building that had been the home of a former Jewish deli. The owner was a Jewish woman who had been renting it to a plumbing and heating company, but she wanted to sell the building before it fell down. She had lost her daughter in 1925, and her husband, who was a police officer, died during a raid on bootleggers in 1930."

"The woman's father-in-law and mother-in-law lost interest in running the deli when they lost their son, and Mrs. Weinberg moved into a large home on Dexter with her new husband. He was the lawyer who helped her in-laws find a black renter for the business. In the year Grandpa opened a music and record store, the building became vacant. It was the ideal location, and there were two pleasant apartments above the store that Grandpa thought Mom and Dad could use. Grandpa owned a beautiful two story home on Farnsworth, near St. Antoine, and he told Mom and Dad that if they lived above the store, they could have both apartments, rent free. If they wanted to use both for their home, they could, or they might want to rent one out for the extra income. Dad rented the second apartment to his best friend, Adam Good, his wife Carol, and their daughter Diane."

Amber interrupted Tianna's story. "Oh, my God! Are you telling us you lived in the same apartment you lived in during the 1920s?"

Tianna laughed and said, "Yes, Amber. I lived in the same place for two lifetimes. It's a crazy coincidence, but that's what makes life interesting."

Grandpa Clarence said, "Let's let Amanda Carson continue with her story. I'm eager to get to my part in her life."

"Thank you, Grandpa. Mom and Dad brought me home to the apartment over Grandfather William's music store. Grandpa, as I called him, was a jazz musician. He came to Detroit from New York in 1919 because he heard you could make good money in Detroit. The musicians were creating the latest jazz and blues style music there. He had talked to several Detroit musicians who had made their way to Harlem, where he lived, and when they heard Grandpa play, they suggested he move here."

"Grandpa got a job in an auto factory, where he worked during the day, and at night he played music. He met Grandma while he was playing in a big band. She was from Detroit and was a popular backup singer. Grandma was a stunning woman with Indian and African blood, but she didn't like the limelight, so she never wanted to be the star. She wanted a small part of the music scene. My grandpa wanted stardom. His ego was bigger than all of Detroit, and people considered his trumpet playing the finest, only Grandpa's job almost cost him his life. He worked in the foundry, and one day he became overcome with blazing hot smoke and almost died. After the accident, he discovered he couldn't hold the air he needed to play the trumpet, and it almost killed his will to live, but Grandma helped him learn to play other instruments. He was musical and learned to play drums, bass and lead guitar, ukuleles, and the piano. This made him an important member of any band because he could fill in for almost any musician when they couldn't play. Through the forties he was on many records, playing backup to some of the best singers, and he made enough money to buy his own home."

"Dad was born in 1934 during the Great Depression. The depression was a time of extreme poverty for colored families. Grandpa was lucky because he kept his factory job and could play with a band. Even during the depths of the Depression, music and movies were important to people. It was a way to forget how bad the times were."

"Even before America entered World War II, Detroit became involved in the war effort, making arms for Great Britain. Grandpa's auto factory, Packard Motor Company, made airplane engines for the military, and after Pearl Harbor there were plenty of jobs in Detroit. Thousands of immigrants poured into the area looking for work. More immigrants arrived in Detroit than at any other time in history. The factory wanted Grandpa to work long hours, but he wanted to spend more time with the band, playing the blues. He hated the factory job."

"The colored men got the worst jobs available even though they were members of the United Auto Workers Union. If a job was dangerous, dirty, and hard to do, then they told a colored man it was his new job. The best jobs went to the white men, who refused to work next to a colored man. The unions talked about how they were not racist and were in favor of working hand in hand with the Negroes, but in reality they were as racist as a southern police officer. They lied about it to everyone except those that they discriminated against.

After the war, Grandpa quit his job at the factory and devoted all of his time to his music."

"I was an enormous surprise to Mom and Dad. Mom was only seventeen when she and Dad had to get married. Dad graduated at the top of his class at Miller High School, on DuBois Street. He got accepted into Wayne College and was studying to be a lawyer. Having seen how the U.A.W. and auto companies had treated his dad and other black men, Dad decided he would become a professional man. He would never allow himself to be a pawn of the white man. He met Mom at a party near her home in the 12th Street neighborhood and fell in love with her. They dated every weekend. He became dumbfounded when she told him she was pregnant. All of her high school friends told her she should get an abortion, but Mom couldn't give me up, and Dad knew he would be the world's best dad, but how could he support a family and go to college?"

"And that takes us back to the apartment on Hastings Street. I started my life there, but I remember little about my early years. I know I played with Diane, my next-door neighbor. Grandma and Grandpa took lots of photographs of us little kids playing in the music store and back alley. We could not go onto Hastings Street, but we snuck out a few times, just to see what was so special about it. It was old, dirty, and it smelled terrible. I heard Mom talk about how it got wild at night. Thousands of people would come down every night to listen to the latest jazz and blues performers sing in the nightclubs. I would lie in my bed and listen as the sound filled the night air. It was better than listening to a record player because I knew it was real."

"Because Dad and Mom had to make money, Dad took a job at Dodge Main and Mom found a job as a cleaning woman at Hudsons. She worked evenings after the store closed. Hudsons didn't want people of color to be visible during store hours because it upset the white customers. Dad hated his job, but he had to pay the bills. He kept taking classes at Wayne State University, but could only complete a few classes each year. He would joke about becoming a lawyer after he retired from the factory job. If the factory job didn't kill him first."

"Grandpa Bill loved running his music store. He was there every day, with two young musician employees who helped him, and on the weekend he would play with a band. His store always had the latest records and record players. Sometimes famous people would stop in to see him and buy records or equipment. I didn't know who they were, but Mom and Dad always tried to be there to meet them. I enjoyed music, but when I was young, I didn't think it was something to get all excited about, and I couldn't understand why my family seemed to think Detroit's music was the most important thing in the world. At least that's how I felt before I became a teenager."

CHAPTER 26

"Hastings Street was an old part of Detroit, but it was *our* business district. Grandpa was so proud of the fact that he was a successful business owner and that his store allowed him to own a beautiful home. He hired and paid his help good wages, and he paid taxes to Detroit and his country. Every time the mayor talked about urban renewal, Grandpa became angry. The city of Detroit labeled our community an eyesore, and we embarrassed the mayor. Instead of coming up with a plan to replace some old buildings and help the business and homeowners fix up their property, the mayor wanted to push the people of color out. It sickened Grandpa to know that someday he would lose his business to the mayor and his rich friends."

"The destruction started to the south of us as the city condemned the Black Bottom slums. When the dust settled, there was nothing but acres of dirt where the homes of black families used to be. A few years later, there was nothing but grass growing in the large empty field. Many years after they destroyed the area, someone built a large apartment building and smaller apartments. It upset Dad when he learned the homes were all going to be too expensive for us to live there. They were creating more homes for rich blacks and white people. As my dad said, "They tear down our home so they can make more homes for whites. I guess they expect the poor black families to fend for themselves, like we've always had to." The mayor didn't plan on building more homes that poor colored families could afford to live in; they wanted to get rid of our old houses and us."

"Grandpa talked about how he felt cheated. When he purchased the building on Hastings Street in 1951, he had heard rumors of changes coming. The business district was losing businesses as well-to-do blacks moved to other areas of the city. But he didn't realize that by 1958, he would have to move out of his building. He closed his business with a going out of business sale. Mom, Dad, and I helped him remove those items he wanted to keep before they tore it down. I was only six years old, but I remember helping in the music's basement store. Dad said it was a speakeasy during Prohibition, but I wasn't sure what that meant. There were a lot of boxes down there, and we went through them all to see if any were good enough to keep or sell. I found a large picture album, and I sat on the floor looking through it. It was old, but there were pictures of our apartment and the store when it was a deli. There were many pictures of a young girl who must have been my age, and I felt like I knew her. At least I thought I knew her. The pictures gave me the strangest feeling. It was like they were from my dreams. Distant memories of things I had seen. When I told Mom, she said it was my imagination, but somehow I knew the memories were real."

"Mom and Dad found an apartment in the new Brewster-Douglass Projects, and we moved all our belongings into our new home. I remember being fascinated by the elevators we used to move our furniture up to the sixth floor. We had two beautiful bedrooms, so I had my room."

Clarence interrupted Tianna's story. "I grew up in the neighborhood where Amanda's grandfather lived. After the city tore down Hastings Street to build the freeway, they tore down our neighborhood. This made room for more hospital space, apartments for the people who worked there, and The Art Center. The city wanted to remove every trace of the black slums. Even in the areas where the homes were very nice and well kept. My father was a lawyer, and our home was a two story Tudor house. It was beautiful, but he was a black man, and they also designated us as part of the Hastings Street Slum Area."

Clarence continued, "I was attending Miller High School, and in

1960 they forced us to move. Dad, being a lawyer, tried to fight the eviction, but when he failed, he decided we would stay in the area. So, we also moved into the Brewster-Douglass Apartments. We were on the sixth floor, a few doors down from Amanda's parents. I met Amanda the day we moved in. She was standing in the hallway watching every move I made."

Tianna laughed. "Grandpa, remember I was an eleven-year-old girl, and you were the best-looking guy I had ever seen. Yes, I had a crush on you!"

"That sounds strange, so everyone please remember, Tianna wasn't my granddaughter then," Clarence continued. "We became good friends. As the song said, *Times they are a changing*. There were protests everywhere. Our black community loved President Kennedy, our new president, and we hoped Rev. King would help move civil rights into the consciousness of the nation. I wanted to be a part of the marches and protests, but I was just a high school student, so my friends and I would sit around and talk about them. Amanda loved to join our conversations, and she delighted all of my friends. She had a deep-rooted understanding of the struggles that blacks had endured in Detroit. It was amazing; this young girl added so much to our conversations. And in our own way, we pushed for equal rights in our city by being involved in the conversation."

"Thank you, Grandpa," Tianna said. "I will always remember the great times we had back then."

"Living in the projects was very nice. Like Clarence said, we were a community. We spent a lot of time visiting our neighbors, who became our friends. The buildings were safe, and the crime was low. Dad was still working at the factory and studying part time. The added expense of the apartment made it hard to make ends meet, so we had to all do our jobs. Mom was still working at Hudson's, but now she was in the kitchen as a cook. She took classes at Wayne State University after she completed her high school degree. Hudson's hired a few black workers who were visible. The store had opened branch stores in the suburbs, where the whites had now moved. About this time, Hudson's even announced that a black girl named Diana Ross would become a busboy for them. She was cleaning tables. Hudson's was so proud of how non-discriminatory they were. After a hundred years in business, they finally allowed a black person to be seen cleaning the tables of white customers. Wasn't it wonderful that a high school girl named Diana Ross could now work at Hudson's as a servant?"

"To help make money, I would go over to Mom's parents' home in the 12th Street district and help them clean house. I also found several jobs as a babysitter. I would stay at Grandma's house when I babysat for someone. It was while I was there that I met Ronald Woods. He was two years older than I, but he was smart. We dated several times during the summer of 1965, but he went to a different school. During the school year, we could only date on weekends. He was great, and I was falling in love with him. Ronald and I would talk about our dreams for the future, and we both wanted to go to college and become professionals. We could see that an education was the only way we could be free, and we knew that blacks with an education seemed to be happier. They lived in nicer homes and drove impressive cars."

"Ronald's older brother wore nice clothing and drove a new car, but he was a drug dealer who never completed high school. Ron and his mom hated what his brother was doing. Even though he was making tons of money, he was doing it at the expense of his black brothers. Drugs were an escape from reality for many people, and Ronald promised he would never get involved in either selling or using them. I enjoyed going to the 12th Street area. It reminded me of Hastings Street because a lot of the people from Hastings moved there. Still, I have to admit, I felt safer in our project's apartment than I did at Ronald's home. I told him that if we ever got married, I wanted to find a nice, safe place to live in Detroit. Ronald laughed and told me that would happen only if I became a Motown singer or a Hollywood movie star."

Clarence injected, "I had a talk with Ronald one time when he was visiting you at the projects. I liked him, and I felt he was a great match for you. As you said, he was smart and grounded. I could tell he would make something of his life."

"That's why I find it hard to accept that he was the shooter," said Tianna.

Lester said, "All the evidence points to him, but it's not conclusive."

"Anyway, I want to continue. There was a lot of rumbling going on in the Black neighborhoods. There had been riots in other cities and a huge riot in California, the Watts Riot. We watched it on television and talked about how it could happen in Detroit since we had the same problems here. Our city leaders kept talking about how Detroit differed from Los Angeles. We had employment, not segregated, and blacks loved the city and got along with the police."

Clarence laughed. "The city fathers did not understand. They were a bunch of white men, and the black Uncle Toms, who never understood the problems faced by poor black residents."

"Those were my dad's feelings, too. He finished college, but he still had to work at the auto factory. He said the factory was more segregated than ever. There was a lot of unemployment, especially in the black community. Blacks had given up hope, but I wouldn't let myself fall into that trap. I knew I could be more because I saw Mom and Dad work their butts off and attend college hoping to find a better life for themselves and me. I would not let them down, and my best friend, Clarence Gulliver, kept me encouraged. We would talk about opportunity when everyone else talked about the lack of opportunity. Our conversations revolved around hope when others talked about despair. We looked to the future with dreams of a better life. I learned from Clarence what many blacks learned from Dr. Martin Luther King. We *can* dream, and we *can* make our dreams a reality."

"As my sixteenth birthday approached, Mom planned a party at the Brewster Civic Center. She had rented space for a party, and we planned on having a picnic, with all of my friends. Clarence was studying in Europe, but he had already sent me a present, which I opened while we talked long-distance on the phone. He gave me an Eiffel Tower lucky charm and a photography book of European sights. Clarence was so proud that he had completed his class on European history. He told me about the places he was visiting and the people he met. He said he felt so free being in Europe."

"Like I told you, Amanda," Clarence said, "the people in Europe accepted me as a man from America, and being black was just a part of who I was. Here in Detroit, people saw me as Black, and I was someone who they would rather not know any more about. But, Amanda, continue with your story. I fear you are reaching the end."

"Yes, it was the day before my birthday. It was hot in Detroit, and Mom had all the arrangements made for the party. My birthday was on Monday, but Mom and Dad wanted to celebrate on Sunday. Mom had to go into work early Sunday morning to prepare the soups and specials for the Sunday crowd at Hudson's. She told us she would be back by noon. The party would start later in the afternoon, and the guests were to arrive by two."

"Dad was still at work because he had to work the night shift on Saturday. I got out of bed and turned the radio on. I listened to WJLB, but instead of music, they were talking about a riot in the 12th Street area. I called Mom's parents, and they told me about the fires they could see over the treetops. There wasn't anything happening in their area, but they were staying in the house with the doors locked until the riot was over. Dad's parents were on another vacation, so I couldn't call them. Every summer, they would go with friends to enjoy the music scene in New York City."

"When I called my boyfriend, there wasn't an answer. Ronald didn't have one of the new answering machines, so I couldn't leave a message. I sat around listening to the news until Dad got home. He was dead tired and said he could see the smoke, but he had no problems getting home. He went into the bedroom to nap so he could be up for my party. As I listened to the news, I got worried. They talked about the busses not running in some areas, and the police were not letting people into other sections of the city. The phone rang, and it was Ronald. He said he had been out on the streets, but he was not looting any of the stores. His brother and a lot of his friends were stealing, but he promised me he wouldn't."

"When I told him that Mom was still working at Hudson's, he suggested I go meet her at Hudson's and then walk home with her. He would meet me there and then come and help with the party. I didn't wake Dad to tell him where I was going; instead, I left a message on the table. I had made the walk many times to Hudson's. It was just over a mile and would only take me about twenty minutes. Wearing my favorite shorts and a tank top, I followed Winder Street and then headed south on Woodward Avenue. It was hot, and the sun was blazing on me. I could smell the smoke from the riot to the North and there was the constant sound of police sirens blaring. When I got to Woodward, I saw several police cars along the road. It seemed like the police were everywhere, which made me nervous. When I reached Hudson's, I went to the Piccadilly Circus Cafeteria on the mezzanine. The store was almost empty, and I had to ask for help. An older white woman came out, and I told her I was looking for my mother, Della Walden."

"Oh, honey," she said, "Your mom left half an hour ago. We let everyone go early because of the riot up in the 12th Street slums. You should have stayed home. It's so dangerous out there. I'm going home as soon as I can get my paperwork done."

"I left Hudson's and headed north on Woodward. I was upset that Mom had to walk home alone, but there wasn't anything I could do about it, and wanted to get home safely. When I reached Winder, a police car with two white officers stopped and yelled at me, "Hey, what are you doing?"

"I was at Hudson's picking up my mom, but she had already left."

"Well, get your ass home, young girl. Don't you know there's trouble up north of here? If you're not careful, you'll get hurt."

"I thanked them and started down Winder. I walked past a parking lot and thought I saw Ronald. I stopped to look, and suddenly I was falling backward. I knew I was dead before I hit the sidewalk. My spirit lifted from my lifeless body. I could see myself staring toward the heavens; my eyes were still open. As my spirit lifted, I could see smoke rising from the 12th Street neighborhood. I looked toward the Projects, and I saw Mom and Dad running down Winder, toward me. In the parking lot, I saw Ronald on his knees with his head in his hands. He was crying, and I knew he must have seen me die. Sorrow again filled my spirit. Sorrow for Mom, Dad, and Ronald. Sorrow because I wouldn't see my friend Clarence again. Sorrow that my city was in turmoil and my people were in danger. I saw the light of heaven and felt myself drawn toward it. My sorrow turned to joy as I entered the light."

CHAPTER 27

Clarence stood and walked toward Tianna. "You are alive, you are sixteen, and we love you. No matter what your past was, you have a wonderful future. Tianna, I loved you as my friend, Amanda. And today I love you as my granddaughter."

Tianna could see that all of her family and friends had tears in their eyes. Even Lester, the strong Detroit detective, was wiping tears off his cheeks. "Yes, I am alive," she said. "And I need to use the bathroom. So, hand me my crutches. No! I will see if I can make it on my own."

She stood and walked toward the bathroom. When she reached the door, she turned and smiled.

"Way to go. You are a miracle," said Amber.

Lester and Alice stood. Alice turned to Amber and said, "As soon as Tianna returns, we need to get home for dinner. Do you want to walk home with us?"

"Yes, let me say goodbye first," Amber said.

Lester and Alice spoke to Thelma and Clarence and made plans to go to church on Sunday together. Lester commented, "You know, everyone at church wants to see their miracle girl."

"We'll be there," said Clarence. "I think all of their prayers helped Tianna survive this."

"Amen," said Lester.

When Tianna walked out of the bathroom, everyone broke into a standing ovation.

"Don't expect me to bow," she said. "I'm getting steadier on my feet, but I think I would fall on my face if I tried to bow."

"Don't bow," said Thelma. "Your friends and family are going home now."

After saying goodbye, Eddie was the last to leave. "Tianna, I want to make sure you still will go with me to the dance. It looks like you're walking better. We don't have to dance if you don't want to."

"Yes, Eddie! I want to dance with you! But I was wondering, can you come here tomorrow afternoon? Mom and Grandpa are going away for a few hours, and Amber and I need you to help us with an experiment."

"Nothing kinky, I hope," replied Eddie.

"No! I want to see if we can discover who killed me in my past lives. I think I can take you and Amber back in time with me."

"That will be awesome. I wouldn't miss it for anything," said Eddie.

Tianna told Eddie to meet at her house at twelve-thirty. That way, as soon as her mom and grandfather leave, they can start. Eddie agreed and left for home. As Tianna watched him walk away, she thought she saw three hooded men standing in the shadows next door. She looked again and decided it was just the shadows. Shaken, she shut the door and crawled under a blanket on the couch. She put her earbuds in and started her audiobook. *I will not let them control my life.* She whispered, *I'm sixteen, I'm alive, and damn it, I'm staying alive this time.*

* * *

The young boy was lying face down on the ground with a bullet hole in his back. Even though the shooter was sitting in the police car bragging about what a good shot she was, Detective Thornson knew better than to take anything in a homicide investigation for granted, The coroner pronounced the boy dead, and Jason Arborsen, the crime scene investigator, took photographs of the body before moving it to the morgue.

Lester's phone rang. "Let me get this, Jason," he said, pulling the phone from his pocket. "Detective Thornson here."

"Detective, this is Sargent Timmons, from the Thirteenth Precinct. We have a Ricky Clawson asking to talk with you. The problem is he's got a gun and is threatening to shoot himself. He's in an abandoned house on Englewood Street, off Woodward Ave. Our negotiator has been talking to him for two hours, and he's messed up. We don't think he's on drugs. He's just extremely upset. Do you want to talk to him?"

"Give me the house number, and I'll be there in a few minutes," Detective Thornson said. He jotted the number down and turned to see his partner, Jim Lee, staring at him.

Detective Lee paused his interview of a witness and asked, "Well, what is it now?"

"They found Ricky Clawson, and he's asking for me, but he's got a gun and wants to kill himself. Sound familiar?"

"Yes, it's like the guy in '67 who shot Amanda Carson. Need me with you?"

"No, someone has to stay here. I'll run over there; you mop us this shooting investigation. At least we know who shot this guy."

Detective Lee laughed. "Yes. I have to admit that drug dealer's an expert shooter. She's one dealer who won't let you get away without paying for your drugs."

Lester laughed, "A broke substance abuser and a crazed woman dealer. That's a terrible combination."

The crime scene was a residential area just south of Eight Mile, near the State Fairgrounds. Lester checked his GPS and headed east on Eight Mile. He turned south on Woodward and then east at Englewood Street. He didn't need to check for house numbers, because there were three police cars, and an emergency services vehicle parked in the street and driveway. Lester pulled over, and the officer on the street waved him on.

"Looking good, Lester," said the officer. "How's your little girl and her friend?"

"It's a miracle, Tony. They're both almost healed. We're thinking this kid might be the shooter because he was Tianna's boyfriend until this year," said Lester as he continued toward the front door.

Lester surveyed the neighborhood. The house was a small, abandoned brick home. It looked like many other abandoned homes on the street. Plywood covered most of the windows, but someone had removed the front door, and the house was open for anyone to crash in. Sargent Timmons, a short man with fuzzy white hair, greeted Lester on the crumbling concrete porch.

The two men walked into what was once the living room. The room was littered with trash and stained mattresses reeking of a strong odor of urine mixed with the smell of weed and rotting food. "Let me fill you in, Lester," Sargent Timmons said. "Harry, come here. This is Detective Lester Thornson, from Downtown Homicide. He's one of our finest, and a nice man too."

A young officer walked over to the two men and said, "Hello, Sir. I'm Harry Carver. I'm with special services, specializing in hostage negotiations. This is an odd situation. The kid has a gun pointed at his head. He's been crying, and he keeps asking, *Why did I kill her?* He doesn't appear to be drunk or on drugs."

"Do you think he's suffering from a psychotic episode?" asked Detective Thornson.

"Nothing I could pinpoint, other than perhaps being bipolar. But he doesn't appear to be having personality swings. He's just upset because he shot someone. He thinks he killed her. Do you know who he might have killed, Sir?"

"Yes, my daughter's friend, Tianna Gulliver."

"The girl from last Friday's King High School shooting?" asked Harry.

"The same," said Lester

"But I heard she survived the shooting. It was all over the news. Some kind of miracle cure from Ann Arbor... wasn't it?" asked Sargent Timmons.

"Yes," said Lester. "I don't think Ricky has heard the news. Harry, go tell him I'm here to talk with him, but don't tell him anything else."

"Got it, Sir," said Harry. The junior agent walked into the hallway, being careful not to get anything on his polished shoes. Lester could hear him talk, and then he heard Ricky cry out, "Mr. Thornson, I need your help, please," Ricky cried.

Lester walked into the hallway toward Ricky while Harry stepped away from the door. With care, Lester stepped into the room and kneeled down. "Ricky, there's something you need to know," he started.

"No, I want you to tell Tianna's mom how sorry I am. I didn't mean to hurt her. I don't remember shooting her, but I saw her die, and I had the gun. So, I killed her. Oh, God! Why did I kill her? I loved her. Mr. Thornson, I loved her more than life itself. I've always loved her. Why did I kill her?"

"Ricky, Tianna is alive. I was over at her house yesterday, and she is fine. She's walking around on her own, and she's going to the school dance in a few weeks. YOU DIDN'T KILL HER. Do you understand, Ricky? YOU DIDN'T KILL HER!"

"But I saw her die. I saw the bullet hit her in the head. I'll never forget seeing that. The moment it blew a hole in her head, I realized what I had done. Oh God, why did I kill her?" Ricky lamented.

"Ricky, do you want to tell Tianna how sorry you are?"

"I can't, she's dead," cried Ricky. "I killed her."

Lester took out his phone. Ricky watched him and became irritated. He pushed his gun closer to his mouth. "It's my phone, Ricky. I'm just going to call for help." Lester pushed the screen several times and said, "Tianna, we found Ricky. He's messed up and thinks you're dead. Can you talk to him? I know it's hard, but we need your help," said Detective Thornson.

He handed the phone to Ricky. "Someone wants to talk to you. Please talk to her, Ricky."

Ricky stretched his hand out and took the phone from Lester. He listened, and his eyes grew huge. "Tianna, is this you? Oh God. You're alive? But I killed you, Tianna." Ricky listened and cried. His gun fell to the ground, and Lester leaned in and picked it up. He stood and took Ricky into his arms and lifted him while he was still talking with Tianna. Ricky hugged him and began a deep, uncontrollably sobbing in Lester's arms.

Special Agent Harry Carver wiped his face and said, "That was something, Sir. I know now why you're considered Detroit Homicide's best detective."

The two men helped Ricky out of the house and into Sargent Timmons' patrol car. Lester told Tianna that Ricky would be at the Central District Station at 7310 Woodward Ave. for observation and questioning. "The prosecutor will decide what charges he will face," he said. "Thank you, Tianna. I think you saved Ricky's life today."

CHAPTER 28

Tianna put her iPhone down and sat silently for a moment. Knowing the police found Ricky pleased her, but it upset her when Lester said Ricky confessed to shooting her. *Why would he want to shoot me?* She asked herself. *What would possess him to do something so violent? Ricky would never hurt me.*

"Honey, your grandfather and I are on our way to his appointment. Are you sure you don't want to tag along?" asked Thelma from the kitchen.

"No. I can't. Eddie and Amber will be here any minute. We will see if we can figure out who the killers were in my previous lives."

"I wish you could leave that in the past, honey. I fear for you," she said as she walked toward her daughter. "Besides, how can the three of you investigate something that happened to you in the past?"

"I have a few ideas I want to try out, so we are doing an experiment."

"Well, do nothing dangerous or stupid. And please don't leave the house unlocked," Thelma said. She bent over and kissed her daughter. "We'll be back in about three hours. It's amazing that we can be on time, but the doctor still makes us wait for two hours. Never fails."

Clarence stepped out of the restroom and said goodbye to Tianna. As he opened the front door, Eddie had his hand ready to press the doorbell. Clarence laughed and said, "Come on in, Eddie. Oh, and here comes Amber. You kids have fun and don't eat all my cookies. I'm hoping the Doctor will let me eat the rest of them tonight."

"Bye," said Amber as she held the door open. "We'll stay out of trouble.."

The two walked into the living room. Amber sat next to Tianna on the couch, and Eddie sat in the large wooden rocking chair. Tianna had something on her mind, so Amber asked, "And what hell's troubling you?"

"Good one, Amber. Just jump right in there with the questions," laughed Eddie.

"That's OK. Your dad called, and they found Ricky in an abandoned drug house. He was trying to kill himself with a gun, and he confessed to shooting us," Tianna said, as her eyes filled with tears.

"Oh God, Tianna. He didn't kill himself, did he?" asked Amber.

"No, he's at the Central Precinct. They will question him and then decide what to do."

"I hope they throw the bastard in jail," said Eddie. "Christ, he shot the two of you and he needs to pay the price."

Eddie's attitude surprised Tianna. "Before we condemn him, we need to find out why he did it. I mean ... if he shot us. Lots of people confess to crimes they didn't do."

"Well, at least now you don't have to worry about him trying again. It should make you feel safer," said Amber.

"I'm sorry I spoke out like that, Tianna," said Eddie. "I hate that the two of you got shot last Friday, and you've suffered so many times in the past. Whoever did this to you deserves punishment."

"I agree," said Tianna. "What I want to suggest is an experiment I think I can pull off. I want us to travel back into my memory."

"Do what?" asked Amber.

"I'm getting stronger, and I think I can walk the two of you back in time. I know it sounds like science fiction, but I have to try. If you can come back with me, the two of you will look for the killer. I'll be me, getting ready to die again, but you two should be able to view the event."

"Holy crap. Are you serious?" asked Eddie.

"Very serious. Are you ready to join me in the past?" asked Tianna

With a nervous laugh, Amber said, "What do we have to do?"

"Eddie, push the chair closer so we can hold hands, in a circle."

Eddie got up and moved the chair. "Wouldn't it be better if we were sitting in the kitchen, at the table?" he asked.

"Great idea, Eddie," responded Tianna. "Everyone into the kitchen."

Tianna stood and walked toward the kitchen. Amber exclaimed, "Look at you! You're walking without the crutches, and without a limp. How did that happen?"

"I don't know, but I've been getting a lot stronger. I don't think I'd be able to run, but I almost feel normal again."

The three friends sat at the kitchen table. Tianna put her hand out and asked them to form a circle holding hands.

"I'm doing what my first grandfather taught me. He was our medicine man and the spiritual leader of our tribe. He was also instrumental in negotiations with the French and other tribes. Everyone trusted his wisdom and skills as a shaman. We will go into the spirit world of my ancestors to view my previous life."

"Should Amber and I do anything other than hold hands?" asked Eddie.

"No. If we get to the other side, don't become alarmed. I'll can talk to you, but because I was there, I'll be doing what I did in the past. I want the two of you to look around for any sign of the killer. Make mental notes and then give me the descriptions when we return. Understood?"

"Got it, Tianna," said Amber. "Sounds crazy, but I understand what to do."

* * *

As the three teenagers held hands around the table, Tianna spoke several words in native Algonquin and then she said, "We come to the spirit world as visitors, to do no harm. We come seeking knowledge and understanding. We come with hearts filled with peace and love."

Without warning, Amber and Eddie were standing in a misty forest on a dirt path. At the end of the path, Amber could see what looked like a wooden wall.

"Is that the fort in Detroit?" she asked.

Tianna was running, but she stopped. Everything was still, and Eddie and Amber heard her whisper, "Yes, I can talk to you. I wasn't sure I could. As Arianna, I ran toward the fort because there was an Indian fight going on and I feared my future husband, Louis Beringer, was in danger. Louis was a French soldier, and he was on guard duty at Fort Ponchartrain. The killer will follow me; watch for him."

"Look, Amber, there's Arianna. How are we going to identify the killer?" asked Eddie.

"How should I know? You're smart. You can figure it out," replied Amber as she ran toward the Fort, following Arianna.

Eddie reached into his pocket and noticed that he had his iPhone. He stopped in amazement when he realized he had Wi-Fi and a cell signal. "Why do I have my phone, and why does it still have a signal? We're in Detroit in the 1700s. I'm sure they didn't have a cell tower!"

Tianna laughed. "You're sitting at the kitchen table, dummy. Why wouldn't you have a signal?"

"Oh, I got it. I guess," he said. He saw Arianna had reached the fort, and he said, "Amber, stop here. We have to watch for anyone who might be our killer. They will have a gun pointed in this direction."

The two kept looking around. There was a light mist, but they could see a young man in a uniform walking out from behind a tree. He was carrying a long rifle and pointed it at Arianna. "Oh God! There he is," said Amber. She described the man but was having difficulty with her words.

Eddie took his iPhone and pointed it at the man. Snap, snap, snap. "Look, photographs of the killer. Let me see if a movie works." He continued taking pictures as the young man shot Arianna.

Amber screamed and fell to her knees. "I can't handle this. It's too much, Tianna. Oh, God. No!"

In a flash, they were back at the kitchen table. Tianna stood and hugged her friend, who was crying. "It's OK, Amber. That was then; this is now."

Amber caught her breath and relaxed. "I will be fine, but seeing that young Indian girl getting killed was too much to handle."

Eddie was holding his iPhone, watching the video. "Then you won't want to watch this, would you?" he asked.

Tianna put her hands out, and Eddie handed her the phone. She looked through the pictures, and her face reflected pain and anguish.

"What is it? Is the killer someone you knew?" asked Amber.

"Yes! It's Louis. Why would he want to kill me? We were getting married the next day. This is crazy," she said, handing the iPhone to Amber. "It makes little sense."

Amber looked at the first photograph. "Damn, he's hot, Tianna. No wonder you fell for him."

Tianna took the phone and handed it back to Eddie. "We have to get to the second killing. The iPhone works, so keep it safe. We will figure this out, damn it. Give me your hand and let's get going."

Tianna's new attitude surprised Amber, but she understood. *Being betrayed by someone you love is difficult to digest*, she thought.

With their hands joined around the table, Tianna again spoke several words in native Algonquin. The group stood in a clearing. It was early morning, and the sun was rising behind the massive trees. Tianna spoke, "I was Shawnna, and I had spent the night with my Indian family. Our brave young men were in battle, fighting with Pontiac against the British. The boy I was in love with, Achak, the brave warrior, told me not to follow him into battle, so I stayed behind. You will see me running out of the woods and into this clearing. The shots will come from over there." She pointed south, where there stood two massive trees. "Are you ready, Eddie? Because here I come."

Deadly Sixteen

Eddie lifted his iPhone and watched the screen. A loud scream of a young man echoed in the woods, and Shawnna came running out of the woods to the north of the opening. A handsome Indian warrior stood next to the trees with his long rifle pointed toward Shawnna. Eddie kept clicking photographs and then switched to movie mode.

The shot rang through the morning mist. Tears flooded Amber's eyes as she watched Shawnna die. There was a flood of Indian women and young children who rushed into the opening and cried at the sight of Shawnna's motionless body.

Tianna whispered, "I'm going to my third death. Amber, remember this is all in the past. We're all alive and sitting around the kitchen table."

"I understand, Tianna. It's just shocking to see how you die."

The three stood in the middle of a narrow road. There were woods on one side of the road, with a small creek running along the road. On the other side, there were fields and in the distance a two story wooden farmhouse and a barn.

"As Josephina, I'm coming from my father's general store. I fought with Father and planned to meet Travis, my boyfriend, to convince him to leave Detroit with me. Watch along the road for the killer, Eddie," Tianna said. "Here I come now."

A beautiful horse pulling a small carriage came racing down the rutted road. It was bouncing and was going much too fast, but then it stopped and Josephine stood.

Amber cried out, "Josephine is so beautiful, Tianna. You're white with high cheekbones and long black hair."

"Watch for the killer, don't watch me."

A handsome, thin teenager, wearing a cap, long pants and a long-sleeved work shirt, stood with a rifle. He had the saddest look on his face, and Amber couldn't help but wonder why. If he were the killer, why was he so sad? Amber didn't watch Josephina die. She kept her eyes on the young man as he fell to his knees, crying. Eddie continued to take photographs.

The three teens opened their eyes at the kitchen table. Their hands still clasped together. The phone was still in Eddie's pocket. He was almost afraid to look at it. The scene they witnessed on the phone was brutal.

"Well, I want to see the pictures, Eddie," said Tianna.

* * *

Eddie pulled the phone out and handed it to Tianna. She studied the images, and then said, "It's what I feared. The second killer was Achak. We intended to wed after I turned sixteen. Travis, the boy I would meet along the road, was my killer when I was Josephina."

"That's sick, Tianna," said Eddie. "Are you sure that's who the guys are?"

"Eddie, I was in love with them. Do you think I would forget what they looked like?"

"Sorry, Tianna, but I had to ask?"

"No, Eddie. I'm sorry. It makes me angry that the spirits are killing me, using my own lovers as their killers. That is sick. They are sick."

"Are we going to go back and watch you get killed again?" asked Amber.

"Yes, after I pee," answered Tianna.

"Me too," said Eddie.

Tianna told Eddie to use the upstairs bathroom, and she and Amber would use the one downstairs. When she returned, Amber checked out the kitchen and found Clarence's cookie jar. "Can I have one of these cookies?" she asked.

"Oh God, NO! Get the ones in the other jar; they're better anyway. And Eddie, get glasses from that cupboard. We can have milk with our cookies."

While they enjoyed their snack, Tianna and Eddie went through the photographs and transferred copies to Tianna's phone. She then sent several to her color printer. The images were remarkable in their clarity.

"Amazing, Tianna. We can go back in time and record events. Now that should be useful, somehow," said Eddie.

"OK, crew. Time to travel again," Tianna said as she reached across the table for Amber and Eddie's hands. A few Algonquin words, and they stood north of the Detroit River, at the intersection of Fort and Beaubien Streets. It was the dark of night, and the only light was from a few flickering lights coming through the windows of the old wooden homes crowded along the street. There were the sounds of steamships making their way up and down the river and freight trains coupling with each other to the south. The smells of the city were stringent, with a mix of smoke from nearby factories, horse droppings in the street and trash thrown alongside many homes.

"In this life, I'm Carol Ann Davis. My family and I are walking up Beaubien Street, toward our home. I died at this intersection. The killer must have been hiding behind one of those houses," she said, pointing north of the intersection.

Eddie took out his camera and snapped a picture. "It will be dark, but I'll try. Once we get the picture back home, we can adjust it to make it brighter."

"Listen, Tianna. I hear singing," said Amber.

"That's my group. I'm sorry you have to see this, Amber. I have to be with my family."

Amber watched as the group of people approached. They were singing the song that Tianna told her and Eddie about, *Steal Away To Jesus*. When she saw Carol, she smiled. *Again in a past life, Tianna was a beautiful Black girl, with long black hair and high cheekbones*, Amber thought.

"Amber, look! It's the killer, standing there," Eddie said, pointing to a building across the street. Eddie ran toward the tall, muscular, young Black man, trying to get as close as he could. He kept snapping photographs as he ran. Fire burst from the end of the long rifle, and the air filled with the smell of gunpowder. Amber screamed, as did Carol's family. Amber looked back and saw Carol lying in the road, her mother and father cradling her lifeless body in their arms.

"Oh God, here come the tears again, Eddie."

"Me too, Amber. Me too."

"We're out of here," whispered Tianna.

The three teens stood in a dark alley, next to a trash can overflowing with rotten food. Amber jumped when she felt something run across her foot.

"Oh no, it's alive, Tianna," she said.

"Just rats," said Eddie. "They are all over the place."

Even though the teens could smell rotting trash and the caustic factory smoke and auto exhaust, they could also smell amazing food cooking in nearby restaurants. The exciting sounds of 1930s music were coming from everywhere.

"We are standing in the alley behind the St. Antoine Cafe. Esther and her boyfriend Burton; my boyfriend, Joshuah Bernstein; and Sarah Weinberg are in the cafe eating. In a few minutes, a car with three men in dark suits will drive up there… at the end of the alley, and one of them will talk to Joshuah in the restaurant. They'll come out, and I will follow them. Then, someone kills me. I have an idea who the killer was, but I need proof," Tianna concluded.

"You're sure they can't see Amber and me?" asked Eddie.

"Positive! Remember, we are still in the kitchen, at home."

Amber shivered and brushed snow off her shoulder. "Yes, but I wish I would have known it was December here, because a coat would be nice. Damn, I'm freezing," she said.

"I have to go," Tianna whispered. "It will be over soon."

Eddie and Amber walked around the alley trying to get warm. A huge 1925 black Packard drove into the alley and stopped. Eddie snapped pictures as they all got out of the car, and the tallest man started toward the kitchen door of the St. Antoine Cafe.

"Do you recognize any of them from past lives?" Eddie asked

Tianna.

"No. Should I?"

Eddie answered, "I'm not sure, but I recognized the guy who went in there… I don't know why, but I remember him from somewhere. Perhaps…?"

Sarah's boyfriend, Joshuah, a handsome white teenager dressed in a beautiful suit, came out with the tall man. They walked over to the car, and the second man pulled a rifle out of the back seat and put it in Joshuah's hands. Joshuah seemed reluctant to take it, but the three men crowded around him and kept whispering in his ears. Joshuah looked like a stone statue with no emotion showing on his face.

Sarah stepped through the door, into the alley. She stopped and looked toward the men and the black auto. Joshuah lifted the gun and fired into Sarah's face. Amber collapsed to the ground, sobbing. But Eddie kept the camera going, snapping as many pictures as he could. The door burst open again as Sarah's friends came out and screamed at the sight of Sarah's lifeless body. Joshuah and the three men sped away, down the street.

The three teens were back, sitting around the kitchen table. Tears were streaming down Amber's face, and Eddie looked as if he had just seen a ghost. Then he became enraged. "Damn it! God damn it! Why the hell are all of your boyfriends killing you, Tianna?" he asked.

Tianna grabbed Eddie's iPhone and sent pictures to her phone and the printer. As she studied the images, she realized she knew the three men talking to Joshuah. "These men," she said, pointing them out in the print, "are the same men who came into the living room and threatened me. I think they are from the spirit world."

Amber, having gained her composure, said, "When they were talking to Joshuah, it looked like they were controlling him. I mean, his face went blank when they handed him the gun. At first, it looked like he was refusing to do what they wanted, then like a zombie when he took the gun and killed you. Could it be some kind of mind control?"

Eddie agreed, "I think Amber is on to something. What scares me is that I've seen these guys around here, and near my home. When I saw them today, I knew I had seen them before. After giving it more thought, I think they've been following me."

"Oh crap, Eddie. What if they try to turn you into a killer? They might want you to become a killer like Joshuah and Tianna's other boyfriends," said Amber.

Tianna chuckled. "Amber, Eddie isn't a killer. But we have to act fast to make sure they don't turn him into one."

"Come on, let's get the pictures from my last life," said Amber.

Holding hands again, Tianna spoke her magical words, asking for entrance to the spirit world.

In an instant, they were standing in a parking lot in downtown Detroit. The cars were all from the 1960s, and it appeared to be a quiet day.

"It's Sunday morning, July 27, 1967. The first day of the riot. I am walking north on Woodward Avenue, and then I'll turn here onto Winder Street. My home is over there, in those tall apartments."

"This is when Ronald Woods kills you?" asked Eddie.

"Yes, he'll be there, close to the street. I'll be across the street, walking. I always walked on that side of Winder and then crossed over to the apartments down there." Tianna pointed to the apartment buildings. "Let's walk across the street. I think it will be a better location to take pictures."

Amber and Eddie crossed the street, then Tianna said, "Get ready, I'm turning the corner."

"Eddie, look, a black car is driving into the parking lot," Amber said. They watched as the car found a spot to park, close to Winder Street. Three men dressed in black got out of the car. They pulled a tall, black boy from the back seat and talked to him. One man pointed toward the corner, and another took a rifle and tried to put it in the boy's hands. At first he refused the gun and tried to run, but he halted and turned toward the street.

"See, they're making him take the gun. I told you, it's mind control," said Amber.

Eddie watched on the screen of his iPhone. Amber yelled, "There's Amanda Carson. Look, she's being stopped by those white police officers. Did she tell us the police stopped her? What would happen if this time she didn't get killed? Is it possible for us to change the past?"

"Amber, enough with the questions. Ask them when we're back at the table," Eddie insisted.

"I thought we were still at the table. Sorry, I'm nervous. Here she comes. Have you got the pictures?" she asked.

Before Eddie could answer, the sound of the gunshot filled the air. Eddie continued to shoot pictures, and Amber again was on her knees crying. Tianna pulled them back to the kitchen and whispered, "It's OK, Amber, I'm still here with you two."

"I saw your mother running down the street. God, she saw you get killed. I wonder if she ever got over the pain?"

"I don't know, Amber. If she's still alive, I could find her, and ask. That sure would be an awkward conversation, wouldn't it?" Tianna said.

CHAPTER 29

When Tianna had all the pictures she wanted on her phone, she finished printing the best ones and laid the images on the kitchen table so she and Eddie could study them. Amber was on the couch, trying to get the images of the killings out of her mind.

The door opened, and Tianna's mom and grandfather walked in. "Hi, honey. Hope you three had an enjoyable Saturday afternoon because we didn't," Thelma said.

"Thelma, it's not that bad. At least we got to talk to a doctor," Clarence said.

Thelma responded, "We waited three hours to see his doctor, and then they tell us he doesn't come in on Saturdays. I ask, *why the hell did you give us a Saturday appointment if he would not be here?* And she said, *Oh, I'm sorry. Do you want to make another appointment?*"

"I liked the doctor I had today. She was young, beautiful and smart. I think she liked me, too," laughed Clarence. "Let's tell my regular doctor where to go, and I'll keep going to the young female doctor."

"Whatever," said Thelma as she approached the table. "What are these — still images from an old movie?"

"No, Mrs. Thornson, these are from Tianna's past lives," Eddie said. "Tianna took us with her on a spirit quest, and I could use my iPhone and take these photographs. I even recorded movies of when she died."

"Oh, God! Tianna? Why would you want to do that? This is disgusting!" Thelma said, sitting down, cupping her face in her hands.

"Mom, don't get upset. We needed to find out who the killers were.

I don't want to get killed again. I love my life with you and Grandpa, and I want to live this life into my old age. Please don't cry."

"It's so hard, Tianna. I almost lost you last Friday to that gunman, Ricky. Then I learned my daughter had died six times in the past. I want this over. I want to get back to a normal life."

Tianna's grandfather was looking over the images. "These are amazing. You could take photographs of the past? Tianna, do you think therefore someone is trying to stop you?"

"I don't understand the question, Grandpa."

"If you can do this, imagine what else you might do. Perhaps you can change history? Perhaps bring Dr. Martin Luther King back to life? Or Robert Kennedy? You might even erase the Vietnam and Iraq wars. You could bring your dad back to us. Perhaps this is the reason *they* are killing you every time you get to your sixteenth birthday. Perhaps you got this ability because you reached that magical age."

"You know, Tianna, that makes sense. If the spirit world always knew you would have this ability, they would want to stop you," Eddie said.

"Yes," said Tianna as she looked at the photograph of the three men talking to Ronald in the parking lot. "And it appears they like to use my boyfriends to do their killing."

Amber was standing in the doorway as everyone's gaze turned to Eddie.

"Hey, I already asked Tianna if I could be the next killer," he said.

"And?" asked Amber.

* * *

Tianna turned to Amber. "Where is your dad today? I need to talk to him."

"He's at police headquarters. He went in this morning, and he said he would work all day. Why?"

"I need to talk to Ricky. Will you call him and see if he can have us visit Ricky this afternoon? Please?" begged Tianna.

"You know I will, Tianna," Amber said as she took her phone out of her back pocket. She pressed the screen and put it to her ear. "Dad? Hi. I'm at Tianna's, and she needs to talk to Ricky. Is there any chance we could do that this afternoon?"

"But Dad, it is important. We have photographs from each time Tianna died, and..."

The entire room could hear Amber's dad respond to her statement. "You have what?"

"Dad, Tianna took us back in time, and Eddie took pictures of each time she got shot, and of the boys who killed her. Since the killers were all Tianna's boyfriends, I guess she wants to talk to Ricky. Please, Daddy?"

Amber listened for a moment. Then she asked, "Mrs. Gulliver, could you drive us to the Central Precinct Station?"

Thelma looked at Tianna and said, "No. I won't be any part of this insanity."

"Did you hear, Dad?" asked Amber. She listened for a few more minutes and then put her phone back into her pocket.

"Well?" asked Tianna. "What did he say?"

"There will be a patrol car around in about an hour to pick us up. He said he would make the arrangements for us to see Ricky. He wants you to bring the photographs too."

Tianna said, "Thanks, Amber. You're the best!"

"I know."

Tianna walked up to her mom and put her arms around her. "Mom, if everything goes well, this whole mess should be over soon. Then we can get back to normal, just like you want."

Mother and daughter hugged and then Thelma said, "Thank you, Tianna. You better get cleaned up. That car will be here before you know."

Amber ran down the street to her home. She wanted to change

clothes and tell her mom where they were going. She knew if she didn't explain, her mom would get upset when she saw them getting into a police car. "I'll be back in a minute, Eddie," Amber yelled as she walked out the door.

Eddie and Clarence stood at the table, looking at the photographs. Eddie asked if Clarence wanted to watch the video, and Clarence became as excited as a schoolboy being offered candy by the teacher. Together they studied the history they were seeing and became saddened by the violence. Clarence told Eddie to keep the images on a safe storage device so they don't get destroyed. He suggested his desktop hard drive, and together they transferred all the files to his computer.

When Tianna returned from her bedroom, Eddie beamed and said, "Wow! You sure look beautiful, Tianna."

"Thank you, Eddie. How long before the police get here?"

Eddie checked his iPhone and said, "We've been waiting almost half an hour."

Tianna watched as her grandfather studied the pictures on his large computer screen. "Grandpa, did you want to come with us?" she asked.

He turned. His eyes were sparkling, and there was a huge grin on his face. "Can I?" he asked.

"Yes, you can," she said.

* * *

Tianna saw the police car pull up to the curb before anyone else. She yelled, "Eddie, Grandpa Gulliver, they're here!"

She opened and front door and waved at the officer who was standing by the car door. "We're coming, Sir." Turning, she said, "Eddie, don't forget the envelope with the pictures."

Clarence stepped out, followed by Eddie, who had the envelope in his hands. As they walked down from the porch, Amber came running down the sidewalk. She was in high heels, so she couldn't run fast. "What's with the heels?" laughed Tianna.

"I wanted to look nice, and taller," she said. Eddie held the back door for her and Tianna. "Mr. Gulliver, you can sit in the front seat," he said, looking at the officer for approval. "If it's OK with you, Sir?"

"That's fine. Clarence can ride shotgun," the officer said.

Eddie seemed disappointed when he learned the officer would not turn on the siren. "Tianna, this is what it feels like when they take you downtown to jail."

"How do you know that?"

"I watch detective shows on TV."

Clarence turned to the officer and said, "Kids."

"Yes," said the officer. "They're good kids, so I don't mind giving them a ride downtown." He looked at Clarence and smiled. Then he turned the lights and siren on. The three teens laughed, but the officer turned the siren off after a few moments. "I can't keep it on unless it's an emergency," he explained.

"That's OK. It was fun while it lasted, Sir," said Eddie.

As the patrol car sped up I-75, Tianna pointed out where the Brewster-Douglass Projects used to be. "They tore all of them down," she said.

Clarence sighed, "I have a lot of wonderful memories there."

To reach East Grand Blvd., the officer exited at Clay. Clarence asked, "Could you go down Oakland Avenue?"

"Sure thing," the officer responded. "Any special reason?"

When the car reached Oakland, Clarence said, "Kids, we are just north of the end of Hastings Street. If we turned right on Oakland Ave. and drove a mile, we would be at the empty lot where the Sugar House stood. It was owned by the notorious Sugar Gang during prohibition, and this entire area had many Purple Gang hangouts and hotspots."

The police officer turned left and proceeded to E. Grand Blvd. While stopped at the intersection, the officer said, "If we had time,

I'd drive down to what's left of Hastings Street. Not much there, but it might bring old memories back, Clarence."

Tianna signed, "For me too," she said.

The officer wasn't sure what she meant. He turned right on E. Grand Blvd. and continued a half mile to the Central District Station. The huge white building was on the right, and the officer turned into the parking lot and drove to the back of the building. There were many police cars and a few people milling around. "We can go in this way," he said.

Amber noticed that her dad was standing next to his car, near a doorway. There were other people she knew with him. "There's Dad," she yelled.

The group walked up to Detective Thornson. He smiled at them and said, "It took a little arm twisting, but Ricky Carson is inside with his lawyer. His mother didn't want to be here, but this is Tora Eastman. She is the assistant prosecuting attorney in charge of Ricky's case, and you guys know Jason Arborsen, our Crime Scene Investigator."

Lester turned to Tora and introduced her to his daughter and the rest of the group. She shook each of their hands, and when she reached Clarence, she said. "Mr. Gulliver, you don't remember..."

Clarence cut her off before she could finish her sentence with, "You were in three of my History of Detroit classes at Wayne State University. Yes, I remember you. All A's as I recall. Good to see you're moving up in the city."

"I see you still have your charm, Sir."

Lester suggested they get in to see Ricky as they wouldn't have much time. He led the group into the building, and they worked their way to a large interrogation room. Through the window, Tianna saw a sullen Ricky sitting with his lawyer, an older man in a wrinkled suit. Ricky had a distant look on his face and was listening, but she didn't see him say anything.

Detective Thornson asked that the group go into the adjoining room. "I want to see what pictures you have. Amber tried to describe them, but I can't believe you think you have pictures from the past." He led them into the small room, and Eddie took the photographs from the envelope and spread them out on the conference table. "Here they are, sir. I can attest to the fact that I took these while Amber and I witnessed the murders of six young girls in the Detroit area. The murders started in 1706 at Fort Ponchartrain, and the last murder was that of Amanda Carson in 1967," Eddie said as he pointed to the photographs. These images show the shooter with the gun, and the second group shows Arianna and Amanda being struck by a bullet.

"Wow!" responded Jason. "Are these real, or did you do magic with Photoshop and create them?"

Tianna laughed. "They are real, Mr. Arborsen. If you want to go there to see for yourself, I can take you."

Jason looked perplexed, but said, "That's OK, I'll take your word for now." He picked up two pictures and looked at them closely.

Lester took Tianna aside. "Honey, why do you want to talk to Ricky? You know he's still messed up. His lawyer says he remembers nothing between the time he started his drive to school at Wayne State University and when he realized he shot you."

"Mr. Thornson, each of my past killers was my boyfriend. There were three men who used some kind of mind control on them. The images we found show the three men talking to my boyfriend. Then the men put the guns in their hands and made them shoot it. I think I can show Ricky that he was powerless to stop. It was not his fault."

"Well, his lawyer will love that. She's talking about pleading temporary insanity."

"Ricky was not insane. Someone else controlled him and acted without his knowledge, Sir," Tianna insisted.

Tora Eastman, the Assistant Prosecuting Attorney in charge of Ricky's case, was listening to the conversation. She walked up and asked, "Is this real, Detective Thornson?"

"Is what real, Tora?" Lester asked.

"The pictures that Jason's been looking at for the last fifteen minutes, and the story that this girl can go back in time and witness murders. That's what I want to know. Is it real? Because if it is, you better hire her for the police force."

"Well, Tora. I'm a believer in Tianna. I believe she lived before and has reincarnated. As for going back in time? That's up for debate," Lester said. "And if you tell anyone about this, you'll suffer now and in the afterlife." Lester stood and walked to the door. "Tianna will talk to Ricky. I am serious about not talking about the pictures and the possibility of Tianna being able to go back in time. We don't want to create a circus here. Understood?"

"I understand, Sir," said Tora. "That would be the last thing we need. Another circus in Detroit."

* * *

Detective Thornson opened the door and led Tianna and Tora Eastman into the room where Ricky was sitting with his lawyer.

Detective Thornson began, "Mr. Farver, this is Tianna Gulliver, the victim of the crime that Ricky is being charged with, and you know the Assistant Prosecuting Attorney, Tora Eastman. As you know, Tianna has asked to have a word with Ricky. She feels there were extenuating circumstances regarding this case and does not want to see Ricky suffer any more than he has."

Hearing the detective's words, Tora's face turned a bright shade of *angry red*. "Detective, where is this coming from? You mentioned nothing about trying to get Ricky's case dismissed."

"Tora. Ricky shot my daughter and Tianna. I know this young man, and I want what is best for everyone, not just what is best for the legal system. Let's let Tianna talk to him, and then we can discuss the case."

Mr. Farver smiled at Ricky and then said. "If you think it will help my client's case, I'll let anyone talk to him. But I want everything that's said here to be off the record and not used in court. Is that understood?"

Tora looked down at Ricky, then at Lester. She turned to Mr. Farver and said, "Agreed. It's off the record and not used against your client. This meeting never took place."

"Tianna, have a seat," said Lester.

Tianna sat across from Ricky. He didn't want to look her in the eye. He kept his head down and was silent. Tianna put her hand out and clasped Ricky's hand in hers. Ricky responded by holding her hands.

"Ricky, close your eyes and let me talk," she said. After uttering a few of her native Algonquin words, the two were in a misty field, holding hands as they faced each other. Tianna screamed, "Oh God… NO! Ricky… I'm so sorry. OH God! It was you all along. You have been following me throughout all my former lives. They trapped us both in the same vicious cycle."

Lester, Tora, and Mr. Farver didn't hear Tianna scream. They saw the two sitting while they held hands, but tears were streaming down Ricky's face. Neither of them spoke a word. It was as if they were in a trance.

Tianna had pulled Ricky deep into the world of the spirits so she could speak with him. "Ricky, I didn't know. And I'm sure you didn't understand what was happening. Let me show you your past. I want to take you to the time when you were my first love, Louis Beringer." Tianna led Ricky through all the lives he had lived in the past. She talked about the love and the dreams they had shared. With the new knowledge of each former life, Ricky became calmer. He talked to Tianna about the pain he felt when he realized he had killed his one and only love. Each time he shot that rifle, he awoke from a mist and saw her die. Killed by him. The tremendous pain and self loathing caused him to end his life through more violence.

Ricky. It wasn't your fault. Let me show you the men who have been forcing you to kill me. These men are the ones who are evil, not you. They have been killing me and must free both of us from this cycle of violence. She walked Ricky back so he could hear the three men as they forced him to do their bidding. The weight of three hundred years of guilt lifted from his heart, setting him free.

They hugged and then returned to the present. Both Tianna and Ricky opened their eyes, and they both smiled. Ricky turned to his lawyer and said, "Sir, I am innocent and I don't want to go to prison. I want to finish my education and make my life complete. For the first time, I must fulfill my dreams, and not let this stop me."

Lester turned to Tianna. "What did you do? You were just sitting there, and now he's a changed man?"

Tianna laughed. "Mr. Thornson, we discovered that Ricky and I have been having a three hundred year romance that always ended in both of us dying. Each time I died, Ricky held the gun. Like me, both of us had reincarnated six times."

Mr. Farver wasn't paying attention to the conversation, but Tora pushed her head closer and said, "Are you crazy, girl? You want me to believe the two of you have lived for the last three hundred years? Never!"

"Ms. Eastman, would you and Mr. Thornson sit down with us for a moment? I need to hold hands with Ricky and two of you. Please humor me."

Tora sat next to Ricky, and Lester next to Tianna. Mr. Farver excused himself, because he needed to have a drink. Tianna said, "Let's hold hands." She spoke Algonquin, and Tora said, "This is nuts."

Lester and Tora suddenly stood in the middle of a dusty road, next to a stream. Josephina Collingwood stopped her horse-drawn buggy and stood, looking for Travis Monroe, her boyfriend. Tianna whispered, "I'm the girl in the buggy, and Ricky is standing next to three men dressed in long black coats. Ricky's name is Travis Monroe, and those men are forcing him to kill me. If you want Ms. Eastman, you can use your phone and snap a photo. Use it for evidence of how they forced Travis to kill me."

Tora took her phone out of her suit pocket and snapped several images. She winced when she saw the bullet explode into Josephina's face. The young girl fell into the stream along the dusty road. Tora cried out, "Please, let's get out of here."

They still sat around the table. Mr. Farver opened the door and said. "Are we done? I have a dinner appointment."

Tora turned toward him and said, "Go, get the hell out of here. I will not charge your client with attempted murder or assault with a deadly weapon. I don't know what I will do, but you can go, Mr. Farver. If the judge needs to see he will call."

"OK, bye," Mr. Farver said as he closed the door.

"So, Tora. Are you serious about not charging Ricky?" asked Lester.

Tora was still shaking. She looked at her phone and slid her finger across the glass. "There are photographs on my cell phone from a murder in 1817, of the girl who Ricky shot a week ago, Friday. The accused is also the accused from that 1817 murder. I saw three men put the gun in his hand and force him to shoot. Yes, damn it. I saw that. And I even have another photo of that one. So? What do you think I should do?"

Lester thought for a moment. He turned to Tora and said, "I have an idea. We tell no one about today's events. You get a judge to declare that Ricky is a minor. I'll find him a new attorney, and you can charge Ricky with simple assault, with extenuating circumstances, those being a mental condition. After a few months in a nice cozy recovery home, we will have him declared cured. If Ricky behaves until he is twenty-one, he will have his records expunged."

Tianna, still holding Ricky's hands, said, "Can you live with that, Ricky?"

"Sure. Since I know what happened; I have hope for the future. The only request I have is that I can get back to college. Perhaps I can get my professors to help me make up the classes I've missed. I could do that from a recovery home, using my computer."

"I'll visit you," Tianna offered.

"Perhaps when I get out, you can visit. I loved you, Tianna, but with your help today, I no longer have those obsessive feelings about you. You will always be my friend forever, but we both have to go forward on our own."

"Yes, I agree," Tianna said. She walked around the table and hugged him. She turned to Lester and asked, "Can I go now? I want to talk to my new boyfriend, Eddie."

"Sure, we have paperwork to do."

Tora began making phone calls to judges, and Lester asked Ricky if he was hungry. Together they walked to the vending machines for a snack. He peeked into the next room where Tianna was talking to Eddie and Amber, and Jason was still talking to Clarence about the history behind each photograph on the table. Lester smiled and announced, "Sorry, it's time for everyone to go home. I will finish my paperwork here, and you guys need to get home for dinner. Amber, tell Mom I love her, but I'll be late again."

Amber gave her dad a huge hug. "I love you, Dad. Are we going to church in the morning?"

"Yes, Honey. We have a lot to be thankful for."

* * *

After dinner, Tianna was ready for a little television and a lot of relaxation. Her grandfather was out with some old friends. It was a Saturday night ritual known as poker night, which he never missed. The night out was more about visiting with his friends than about the game of chance.

Thelma came down the stairs dressed to kill. She was going out to a movie with Mr. Ewald. "Tianna, are you sure you don't mind spending the evening alone?"

Tianna reached for her iPhone and said, "I won't be alone, Mom. I plan on talking to Amber and Eddie this evening."

The doorbell rang, and Thelma let Carson Ewald in. He spoke for a few minutes and then asked, "Tianna, will I see you in school on Monday?"

"Yes, Mr. Ewald. I'm almost recovered. I still walk with a slight limp, but I think it's getting better."

"A miracle. Absolute miracle," he said. "Well, Thelma, if we want to see the movie from the beginning, we better get going. Good night, Tianna."

Thelma gave Tianna a hug. "Good night, Honey. I'll be home around one. You have my number, so if you have a problem, call."

"I will. Take good care of my mom, Mr. Ewald."

After talking to Amber for an hour, she went into the kitchen for a soft drink. It surprised her when the doorbell rang. She went to the door, turned the outside light on, and opened the door part ways. The man standing there was a tall, thin American Indian dressed in blue jeans and a plaid shirt. He looked familiar to Tianna, but she was leery and only opened the door a crack.

"Can I help you?" she asked.

"Tianna, I'm a shaman from the Wyandot tribe. I live in the Monroe area, and while I was on a quest last night, three spirits who said they knew you visited me. They asked that I come and negotiate a peace treaty with you."

Tianna had a strong feeling she knew the man from her past. "What is your name?" she asked.

"My name is Eluwilussit, but my name here is Seth Rodgers," he said. "I was your first grandfather when you were Arianna."

"Yes, Eluwilussit, I felt that's who you are. Come in," Tianna said.

Eluwilussit held out his hands to Tianna, and she placed hers into them. She could feel the warmth of his spirit and knew he was her former grandfather. "Please come in, Grandfather. We can sit here at the table. Now, what did the spirits want to negotiate?"

"Peace. They believe I can arrange a treaty with you. They say they do not want to harm you, but they need assurances from you. It seems you have attained your power. When you were a young girl, I warned you about these powers. I told you that when you reached sixteen, you would have to be very careful not to let your human heart overrule your spirit. That is why the spirit leaders decided they had to stop you."

"So what changed this time?"

"You were not to live, but when you did, they watched and saw what you did. You proved you are worthy of the opportunity to continue your life here. They will let you live your life into old age if you agree to some restrictions," Eluwilussit said.

"Why? I don't understand why they kept killing me. And I don't understand what restrictions they would want to place on me. To be honest, Grandfather, I'm getting quite upset with them. It's taken over three hundred years for me to reach sixteen, and now they expect more from me?"

"Tianna, you know you can walk back in time. You can travel throughout the spirit world. What they fear is that you may also get the ability to change the past. If you can do that, you could end all time. That is why they stopped you. You could be the most dangerous person ever to walk the earth, or you could end up using your ability to help humanity. The spirit leaders will give you the opportunity to live this life, and you will not reincarnate again. At the end of this life will join your family in heaven for eternity. You must vow never to seek the ability to change the past. The Guardians will allow you to go into the spirit world; you can take others on a quest, and you can show them their past, but do not change the past. Do you agree to their terms?"

"What will happen if I don't agree?"

"You will die before the night is over, and those you love will also perish with you. Tianna, they are serious. They do not want to harm you, but God trusts them to guard the spirit world. If you agree to their peace terms, you must heed this warning: If you ever attempt to seek the power to change the past, you will die."

Tianna took a deep breath. "Grandfather Eluwilussit, your name means *holy one*. I have always loved you, and I would do nothing to harm my family or my people. I pledge I will never alter the past. For three hundred years, it has been my dream to live to be a wife, mother, and grandmother. I want to pass my heritage to my children, die an old woman, and be with Jesus. Yes, I want peace."

A mist formed around the shaman, and the three men were standing there. They grinned with joy. Tianna thanked them, and they disappeared into the mist. Eluwilussit turned toward the door, looked back and said, "I have to get ready for church tomorrow. I'm a Sunday school teacher, and I need to prepare my lesson. Tianna, I am proud of you." He opened the door and walked down the steps.

Tianna wanted to tell her friends what had happened, but waited. All she wanted to do was sleep because she, too, had to prepare for Sunday.

CHAPTER 30

After sleeping through the entire night, Tianna knew her long nightmare was over. A few hours after breakfast, she went upstairs to dress for church. She looked through her entire closet until she found the beautiful sleeveless and form-fitting dress in dark aqua, which she combined with a short white jacket. She put her cell phone and lip gloss in a small white leather handbag, slipped a pair of white high heels on, and started down the stairs. The heels slowed her down, but she was still graceful.

"Don't you look beautiful, and all grown up," Clarence said. "Your mother is getting dressed now."

"Grandpa, you're looking handsome, as usual. Did you win any big money last night?"

"No, I'm sorry. I'll be selling the house next week to cover my losses," he said laughing. "Just kidding. As usual, I broke even. We never play for high stakes. Just for fun."

"Good, because I would hate to see you spend all of my inheritance on a game of chance."

"Your inheritance? The only thing you'll inherit is my wisdom and good looks."

"That's even more valuable than the house. Thank you."

Tianna sat down with a glass of Coke to listen to the soft gospel music playing on the radio. The two smiled when Thelma entered the room dressed in a beautiful red dress. Her white pearls hung around her slender neck. "Wow, mom. You sure look beautiful, and happy," Tianna said.

Thelma had a glow about her. Tianna knew her mother was in love, and she felt nothing but happiness for her. For the first time since her husband died, she had opened her heart to a man. "Mom, I'm so glad we both survived my birthday."

Thelma laughed and said, "It's time to get to church. We can be thankful there."

As Tianna walked up the steps of the Bethel New Harmony Baptist Church, the Rev. James stood, greeting the parishioners. Tianna whispered in his ear and handed him a piece of paper. He smiled and gave her a hug. The usher escorted the Thornson and Gulliver families to a pew at the front of the church. Lester questioned why, and the usher smiled and said, "At the request of Rev. James, Sir."

The organist was playing soft music and the choir members, dressed in long red gowns, organized their sheet music. The music grew louder and Rev. James came walking down the aisle. He was singing *Praise To The Lord* and when he reached the altar, the choir joined him. Soon the entire congregation was standing. The music came to a dramatic end, and Rev. James said, "Praise to the Lord. Amen. Yes! Praise to the Lord. Last week we asked Jesus to save the lives of our children, Tianna and Amber. We asked the Lord for his help and did he help?"

"Yes! Praise to the Lord," exclaimed the congregation.

Rev. James continued. "Jesus blessed us and saved both of our children from the evil inflicted upon them. Jesus heard our prayers, and Jesus spoke. Tianna came close to death last Friday, but today she will speak to us. Tianna Gulliver, show your brothers and sisters how the Lord has blessed you."

Tianna stood and walked up to the podium. The Rev. James, put a microphone on her dress, saying, "Honey, these are your friends and family. You have nothing to fear."

"Rev. James, I'm not afraid. I am thankful," responded Tianna.

The congregation heard her response and said, "Amen."

Tianna smiled at the congregation and said, "A week ago Friday, I could have been another entry in The Free Press' obituary. One more youngster killed. A life lost to crime. Another statistic to used by the media to denigrate our great city. Because of your prayers the Lord performed a miracle. Doctors told my mother I would die and the only hope they offered was prayer, and an experimental medical treatment. The Lord told my mother to follow her heart and then He guided the doctors through their experiment and blessed me with the opportunity to pass into my sixteenth year on Earth."

"With all my heart, I thank the Lord, my family, and each of you for your prayers. In my short life I have seen the history of Detroit, and our people. I have seen the struggles we have all endured. I have seen African, Indian, French, German, Irish, British, Latino, Oriental, Eastern European, Arab and many more immigrants come to Detroit looking for a better life. Many of them came with their prejudices and fears of those whom they did not know or understand."

"Rev. James, Jesus told us to love our neighbors and do for them, as we would for ourselves. Jesus told us to help those who are in need. Jesus taught us how to live our life in joyous harmony with God. We have lost the true meaning of His teachings. We embrace him as our Savior, but do we embrace the homeless man looking for a way out of poverty? We accept the comfort that Jesus gives us, but why do we give comfort to those poor souls who need our comforting?"

"The Lord has given me the opportunity for a full life. My *Praise to the Lord* will be to live my life as Jesus taught me. I will love my neighbor, give unto others, help the poor, comfort the weak, and care for the sick. Following his teachings I can change myself, my neighborhood, my country, and my world. Thank you, and Amen."

"Amen," sang the voices of Amber, Thelma, Lester, Alice, and Clarence.

"Amen," sang the voices of the congregation.

As the congregation came forward to hug Tianna and Amber, the choir burst into a lively rendition of the old gospel song:

Do All The Good You Can.
Marching on together, Thro' this fleeting world below,

DUANE WURST

Helping one another, Onward as we go;
Think of what a blessing, God the Father gave to man,
Try and do for others, All the good you can;
Let your smile be cheerful, Ever warm and bright,
Make the hearts around you, Happy with its light.
Amen

EPILOGUE

School became a blessing for Tianna as it allowed her to immerse herself in studies and put the past behind her. She still had thoughts of her previous lives, but she kept thinking about the warning given to her. "If you ever attempt to seek the power to change the past, you will die."

As long as she could keep her mind on her homework, friends and school events, she was fine. However, there was a hidden sadness deep within her soul. She felt something was missing., but tonight wasn't a time for worry. Tonight was the big dance, and she was ready for her fifth date with Eddie. They had become good friends. During this life, Tianna decided she would control the unbound passion she had in her previous lives, and avoid becoming tied down to one relationship. She can see a future filled with new opportunities, and her goal is to avoid anything that will slow her down — not that a good man could do that, but at her young age she must keep problems from getting in her way.

Eddie's father agreed to drive the teens to the dance, and Tianna's mom would pick them up after the dance. Thelma had a date planned, but she could drive the two teenagers home. As Tianna put the finishing touches on her outfit, she saw her grandfather reading another history book.

"Grandpa, someday we must go back and see the history for ourselves," she suggested.

"Sounds interesting, but for now, I'll read about it."

The doorbell rang, and she grabbed her overcoat. "Mom, I'll see you after the dance," she yelled.

"OK, Honey. Have fun."

Eddie took Tianna's advice and dressed in a black suit. He threatened to wear blue jeans, but Tianna said she would stay home unless he dressed up. The Thanksgiving dance, also known as the Coming Home Dance, would attract former students returning from college for the holidays.

After Eddie's father drove off, the couple showed their tickets, had their hands stamped and proceeded into the gym. The band was playing soft dance music, with multicolor lights creating a techno feeling on the dance floor. The King High Music Group, who were a favorite of the students, played a variety of styles. When a slow ballad started, Eddie asked Tianna to dance.

They stepped onto the floor, and he pulled her close to him, and they danced. Tianna felt a tap on her shoulder. It was Mr. Ewald, dancing with her mother.

"Mom? Why are you at my dance?"

"Carson asked me. We're chaperones tonight."

"Why didn't you tell me?" Tianna asked.

"I didn't want to ruin your dance. So, I figured I would wait and tell you when it was too late for you to complain."

Mr. Ewald took Thelma in his arms and danced her away from her daughter. Tianna told Eddie that her mom would cramp their date. Eddie was watching the two adults and said, "No! Look at them! They're so into each other they won't have a clue what we're up to."

"So what do you plan on being up to, Eddie?"

The two laughed and continued to dance.

***

At Christmastime, Tianna gave her grandfather an unusual gift. She told him to set three hours aside on Christmas Day. After opening the presents, eating dinner, and doing the dishes, Tianna and Clarence sat at the table, alone. Thelma was in the living room listening to music.

"Mom, are you sure you don't want to join us?" Tianna asked.

"No, Honey. You two go have fun doing your history project. I will write letters to my relatives down south," Thelma said.

"Are you ready, Grandpa?"

"Yes, but I still don't know where we're going," he said.

"It's a surprise."

Tianna said a few Algonquin words, and the two of them stood in what appeared to be an old dusty bookstore. Clarence looked around, ran to the front door, stepped outside, and exclaimed, "Oh my God, Tianna! How did you know?"

"You told me when I was a little girl about a bookstore on Hastings Street where you read your first Detroit history book."

"Yes. It was Silas Farmer's book, _The History of Detroit and Michigan_. I found the 1884 copy in the store and read it. I couldn't afford the book. So, the owner said I could read it in the store if I helped him sweep floors. It was a wonderful two weeks. That's how long it took to read the enormous book."

Clarence walked around the store. He put his hand out to pick up a rare book, but he wasn't able to. "Why can't I pick up the book?"

"Sorry, you can look, but you can't touch. It's the rule I must follow if I want to stay alive."

"Oh yes. But how can touching a book cause the end of time?"

"Let's say you touch the book. The book falls and breaks a rare vase. The vase was the same one that should have ended up at the White House. But now it's broken and never got placed there. Time has changed. A big change could rip time apart, causing the end of all time. At least that's what the spirits told me," exclaimed Tianna. "But you can use the camera on your cell phone and take pictures. Those are fun!"

Clarence laughed and took his phone out of his pocket. "Let's walk down Hastings Street and recapture old memories.

***

Tianna talked to Lester Thornson after the Good Friday church service. Lester told her that Ricky had got released from the hospital. He completed his treatment plan and one semester of university coursework. Lester asked the court if Ricky could call her since they had ordered him to stay away from her. The judge said they could talk if Tianna rescinded the order.

"Tell Ricky that I would love to talk to him. But make sure he knows I am not interested in starting a relationship. I understand that we both need closure, and perhaps I can help him," she said.

Lester smiled and pulled a folded piece of paper from his suit pocket. "This form needs your signature. I figured you would want to talk, so I had it drafted, and I'll fax it to the judge this afternoon."

On Easter Sunday, Tianna received a call from Ricky. After an extensive conversation, Tianna arranged for Ricky, Eddie, Tianna, and Amber to meet. Ricky was picking them up at Amber's for a ride around Detroit. "Remember, Ricky, we need to find closure and learn how to go our separate ways."

"I understand," Ricky said. "I have a plan I think you will like."

On Monday, the day after Easter, Ricky arrived in a brand new black Mustang. It impressed Eddie, surprised Amber, and Tianna feared he might have stolen it.

"Relax, Tianna. If you check out the paperwork in the glove box, you'll see it's mine. I won the lottery. Not a big win, just enough to pay off my college loans and buy this car," Ricky explained.

"OK. Congratulations, Ricky," Tianna said. "Now, where are we going in your nice new car?"

Amber jumped in the front seat, and Eddie and Tianna sat in the back. Ricky turned to the back seat and asked, "Eddie, do you have the directions?"

"Yes, I sent you a link to the coordinates of our first stop," Eddie said.

Ricky took his iPhone out of his pocket and swiped the screen.

"We are on our way, and now we will find closure to the past."

Tianna grew curious about something other than where they were headed. "So," she asked, "Ricky, how much of your previous lives do you remember?"

"Everything. It all came back after we met in jail. Then, for a while, I couldn't stop remembering. It's getting easier now. I've been working on school and having fun."

Ricky announced, "First stop is ahead." Driving west on the Jefferson Service Drive, Ricky turned into the UAW-Ford National Programs Center's drive. Tianna laughed, because she knew where they were. "We're at the spot where Fort Ponchartrain was located."

Ricky stopped the car and told Amber to go to the trunk and get one. She walked around the car, opened the trunk and took out one white rose. Everyone got out and walked to the approximate spot where Tianna had died in 1706.

"Tianna, would you like to do the honors?"

"Yes, Amber, I'll take the rose."

Tianna took the rose and placed it on the grass. "Arianna, I will always be yours. You gave me my Indian heritage, and my place in the spirit world. May you rest in peace," she said. Everyone exclaimed, "Amen."

The group jumped back into the Mustang, and Ricky said, "Eddie, send me the next location."

"I get it," laughed Tianna. "We're going to every spot where I died, to place a rose. I like it. I like it a lot."

Amber smiled. She wanted to tell everyone it was her idea, but she let Ricky have the glory.

Ricky looked at Tianna and said, "It was Amber who suggested doing this. I wanted to drive around in my new car to show it off."

"Ricky, you haven't changed one bit," Tianna said.

Ricky drove back on Jefferson and turned left on Mt. Elliott Street, past the huge Elmwood Cemetery. He then turned west on Vernor Highway. Eddie yelled, "Ricky, turn into the condos on the left. You can park there."

The Mustang pulled into the parking space, and they all got out of the car. Amber picked out another white rose, and the group walked up to the fence of the Elmwood Cemetery while Eddie checked his iPhone. "This is the spot. Pontiac's warriors were back along the creek attacking the British troops. Shawnna was running toward the fighting and died here." Tianna took the rose from Amber and laid it on the grass.

"Shawnna, you may you rest in peace, because I found the love we needed," said Tianna. "Can I walk to where Josephina died?"

"Sure. How far is it?" asked Amber.

Tianna walked across the parking lot, and fifty feet west along Vernor Highway, she stopped. "The river ran north beside the old road. Daddy's farm was about a quarter mile further north, but this is where I died."

Amber handed her another white rose. Tianna kneeled down and placed the rose on the side of the road. "Josephina, even though you felt unloved by your father, you know everyone loved you and you had so much potential. May you rest in peace."

Eddie showed Ricky where the next location was. "We have to get going," Ricky said.

The group returned to the Mustang, and Ricky drove back to E. Lafayette St. He drove into downtown Detroit and turned left at Beaubien Street. Amber pointed out the people mover, and Tianna said, "When I lived here, there were a few factories and warehouses along the river and north of the river, a lot of businesses along Beaubien Street, and there were lots of homes everywhere else. In the 1840s, it was becoming the neighborhood of our Black community."

Ricky found a parking spot near Fort Street. He said, "To do this, we would have to go stand in the middle of Beaubien Street. So, I suggest we place the rose here."

Amber handed Tianna the rose, and she said, "Carol Ann Davis, you were a beautiful Black girl. Your heart was so pure and open. Just the thought of people being hurt by others upsets you. I am proud that you became part of the solution. Your work on the Underground Railroad helped many of our brothers and sisters reach freedom. God bless you, and may you rest in peace." Tianna placed the rose on the sidewalk, and the group jumped back into the car. There were horns honking behind them because Ricky had parked in a no-parking zone.

Ricky took Lafayette Ave. to I-75 and headed north.

"You could say we are driving up Hastings Street. They removed the entire community to make room for this freeway. Another thriving Black community replaced with cement," Tianna lamented.

Ricky turned onto Mack Ave. and headed west to St. Antoine. The Detroit Medical Center replaced the entire old business area. Eddie yelled, "Pull over, Ricky."

Ricky pulled to the side of St. Antoine St. and parked. Tianna got out of the car, put a coin in the meter and stood, staring at the hospital. "I have several reasons to be here. Closure and to thank DMC for saving my life."

Eddie said, "We need to walk over to the median."

The group walked across the road and stood on the grassy median. Amber handed Tianna the rose. Tianna placed the rose on the grass and said, "It's hard to believe an alley once ran along here, and a great restaurant's back door was at this spot. Sarah Weinberg, you had spunk. Of all the lives I've led, you were the most energetic and fun loving. I will carry that energy and spirit with me always. Thank you, and may you rest in peace."

"One more," said Ricky. The group got back into the Mustang. Ricky turned around and headed south. They crossed Mack Ave., but the street changed to Beaubien Street. Tianna explained that when the hospital expanded, they moved St. Antoine and made a curve. Ricky pointed out the empty lot where the Brewster-Douglass Projects once stood. He jogged right, then left, and turned down Winder Street. Tianna recognized two older buildings. But after they passed

John R. Street, there was new construction. Ricky checked the location on his phone and pulled into a parking space in front of a row of townhouses.

"There was a parking lot on this side of Winder Street, and Amanda was across the street." Everyone got out for the last time, and Amber handed Tianna the last rose. She walked across the street and placed it on the sidewalk. "Amanda, I'm sorry you didn't get to be the woman you always wanted to be. I will reach the goals set by you and all the other girls I've had the honor to be these past three hundred years. May you rest in peace."

Tianna had tears in her eyes, and the four teenagers formed a group hug. Ricky suggested heading back to Amber's home, but Tianna asked if they could go to Elmwood Cemetery. After finding the graves of Josephina, Sarah, and Amanda, they sat for an hour at Amanda's gravesite. They talked not about the past, but about the future. Tianna and Amber discussed their dreams of college and good-paying jobs. Ricky said he would be a better father to his future children because he had missed getting the support of a good father. And Eddie said, "I'm just glad I'm from Detroit. I love this damn city, and I love my friends and family."

Tianna smiled and took Eddie's hand. "Amen."

DETROIT HISTORY BOOKS AND WEB SITES:

The following books and Internet sites provided the author with a historical background. .

If you would like more information regarding Detroit's history, you can use these sources, as well as your public library.

Book References:

Atlas of the City of Detroit and Suburbs, E. Robinson Publisher

Detroit: A Biography by Scott Martelle

All about Detroit : an illustrated guide, map and historical souvenir, with local stories. Silas Farmer Co.

Detroit in History and Commerce: A Careful Compilation of the History, Mercantile and Manufacturing Interests of Detroit by James J. Mitchell, 1891 Rogers & Thorpe Publishers

The History of Detroit and Michigan, Silas Farmer, 1884

The Michigan Book: A State Cyclopedia, Silas Farmer, 1901

Legend of Le Detroit by Marie Caroline Watson Hamlin, Second Edition, 1884

The Early History of Michigan, By A.S. Barnes & Company 1856

Million Dollars Worth of Nerve, By Ken Coleman

Web Sites of Interest:

https://www.facebook.com/pages/Million-Dollars-Worth-of-Nerve/403667606449664pnref=story

http://detroithistorical.org

http://www.legendsofamerica.com/20th-purplegang.html

http://www.freep.com/article/20130811/NEWS06/308110066/Michigan-History-President-James-Monroe-1817

http://www.davidrumsey.com/luna/servlet/view/earch?q=detroit&sort=Pub_List_No_InitialSort%2CPub_Date%2CPub_List_No%2CSeries_No&search=Search

http://www.thejewishnews.com/2013/09/26/digging-for-purple/

http://www.wyandotte-nation.org/

http://www.accessgenealogy.com/native/michigan-indian-tribes.htm

http://rosecity-mi.us/purple-gang/

http://corktownhistory.blogspot.com/2013/04/corktown-pre-history-rom-farmland-to.html

http://www.modeldmedia.com/features/DPL-digital-collections-112414.aspx

http://onedayindetroit.com/tours/20

http://www.detroityes.com/mb/showthread.php?16259-1888-Detroit-Map-with-Hastings/page3

http://ohiohistorycentral.org/w/Wyandot_Indians?rec=646

http://www.nanations.com/wyandot/history.htm

http://nanations.com/jesuits/huron.htm

http://faculty.marianopolis.edu/c.belanger/quebechistory/encyclopedia/HuronIndiansEC.htm

http://www.daahp.wayne.edu/1800_1849.html

http://www.metrotimes.com/detroit/hastings-street-breakdown/Content?oid=2168732

http://pushnevahda.com/detroit-black-bottom/

http://olddetroit.tumblr.com/page/5

https://www.flickr.com/photos/southofbloor/sets/72157622694919380/with/4144352395/

http://turtle-island.com/native/the-ojibway-story.html

http://www.historicdetroit.org/building/graystone-ballroom/

http://www.rootsweb.ancestry.com/~miafamer/directory.html

http://www.detroits-great-rebellion.com/12th-Street---Requim.html

http://www.onthisday.com/events/date/1916?p=2

http://ilovedetroitmichigan.com/detroit-architecture/albert-kahn-400-buildings-in-metro-detroit/

http://reuther.wayne.edu/taxonomy/term/1720

http://www.med.umich.edu/haahc/Hospitals/hospital1.htm

http://departmentstoremuseum.blogspot.com/2010/05/j-l-hudson-co-detroit-michigan.html

http://historydetroit.com

Deadly Dance

THE SPIRIT WALKER SERIES

BOOK 3

The big bands are playing your favorite tunes,
but a killer is on the loose. Can Tianna and Charlie help
stop a killer from Detroit's 1930s?

www.duanewurst.com
duanewurst.com@gmail.com

The author's other novels.

In Search Of Elysium

Kevin Carpenter is learning disabled. In a touching adventure he leads his friends on a search for God, taking them deep into space, in search of a planet called Elysium.

Death on the Point

The Blackwell Series - 1

Colton Blackwell, a football star and teenage detective, stars in this fast moving mystery series; a humorous and romantic novel filled with action and adventure

Blood Bath

The Blackwell Series - 2

Colton Blackwell is faced with another murder. The humor, romance, and adventure continues.

Deadly Sixteen & A Killer With

The Spirit Walker Series - 1 & 2

Psychological thrillers with emotional weight. They feel like a blend of Shutter Island, The Sixth Sense, and small-town Americana horror. The pacing and character dynamics are powerful.

Doyle Mysteries

No. 1 - The Scent Of Murder

Doyle, a retired police detective and master chef, and his Bloodhound (Copper) face a life filled with luxury and murder. A cozy mystery for all ages.

www.duanewurst.com

duanewurst.com@gmail.com

Share your opinion and do a review.

DUANE WURST

www.ingramcontent.com/pod-product-compliance
Lightning Source LLC
Chambersburg PA
CBHW060305260626
47160CB00007B/2508